HAWK'S FLIGHT

CAROLE - Thanks for your help - all the best to you
Ron Holtman

Ronald E. Holtman

This is a work of fiction. Names, characters, places, and incidents either are products of the author's imagination or are used fictitiously. Any resemblance to actual events, locales, or persons, living or dead, is entirely coincidental.

ISBN: 1533661669
ISBN 13: 9781533661661

THE AUTHOR

The author holds a Bachelor of Science degree in mathematics from Denison University and a Juris Doctor degree from Case Western Reserve University. Following graduation from law school, he served in the Judge Advocate Corps of the US Air Force from January 1968 through December 1971. He and his wife, Prudence, live in Wooster, Ohio. This is his first full length work of fiction.

OTHER WORK

Limit Theory
A collection of poems, published by the Wooster Book Company in 2013

For Prue,
for more than fifty years - my best critic

GLOSSARY

AFB: air force base
arty: artillery
CIB: combat infantry badge awarded only to troops who have been in combat
claymore: refers to a claymore mine, an antipersonnel weapon used by troops in Vietnam
CO: commanding officer
C rats or C rations: military-issue food packs used by soldiers in the field
dustoff: a four-man unarmed rescue helicopter used to extract wounded soldiers from the front lines. The name derives from the radio call sign used in 1963 by Major Lloyd E. Spencer, commander of the US Army 57th Medical Detachment (helicopter ambulance), the first aeromedical evacuation unit in Vietnam
FNG: fucking new guy, a derogatory term for the green recruit arriving in Vietnam for the first time (used often with *cherry*, another derogatory term for a new recruit)
LZ: helicopter landing zone.
LRRP: long-range reconnaissance patrol
medevac: a hospital flight, usually by helicopter from a battle zone (the term was also used for long-range evacuations by plane from Vietnam to other hospitals at bases outside Vietnam)

MUST unit: mobile unit self-contained transportable (typically, a MUST unit consisted of a surgery shelter, an inflatable patient ward, and a power supply; other expandable areas could be added for administrative purposes or to serve other patient needs)

National League of Families of American Prisoners and Missing in Southeast Asia: Founded on the West Coast in the late sixties, the league was determined to call attention to the plight of prisoners of war and soldiers missing in action. It was incorporated in Washington, DC, in May 1970. In 1971, the organization formally adopted the POW*MIA flag. The background of the flag is black. White letters across the top read "POW*MIA." A white circle in the middle shows a silhouette of a serviceman with a prison guard tower behind him. Below the circle are the words "You Are Not Forgotten."

NVA: North Vietnamese Army

REMFs: rear echelon motherfuckers, a derogatory term for the administrative soldiers and command staff who made combat decisions from behind the lines

R&R: rest and recreation—a few days awarded to combat soldiers during their Vietnam tour (soldiers often went to Bangkok for their R&R because of its proximity to Vietnam)

short: the period before a soldier's scheduled date of return from Vietnam, usually thirty days or less.

slick, chopper, or bird: references to a helicopter

surge: army surgical hospital, typically located near a battle zone to provide triage and emergency surgery to stabilize a wounded soldier before transport to a more permanent medical facility

VA: Veterans Administration

VC: Viet Cong

waxed: a term indicating death or severe injury by enemy fire

the world: a reference to the United States or civilization, compared to Vietnam

PROLOGUE

This is the story of Sergeant George Wheeler, First Lieutenant Joseph Walking Horse Manawa, and Charles Soaring Hawk Manawa. All three served their country during wartime.

George and Horse, members of an elite army Ranger unit, fought together in Vietnam. Hawk, the fourteen-year-old brother of Horse, aided his country in the way that all family members endure when a loved one leaves home for military service.

War injures all combatants and inflicts collateral damage on their families. Restoration takes courage, patience, and loyalty.

CHAPTER ONE

Fire Base Zebra—Quang Tri Province—South Vietnam
16 March 1969

In the early morning, Horse gathered the squad leaders to describe their mission. George knelt beside Horse, looking over Horse's shoulder at the map spread out on the ground. The heat was already rising to what the men knew would be another oppressive tropical day.

"Intel puts a large NVA force in this general area," Horse said, pointing to the map. "We'll land here, then probe from there."

"That's some bad Indian country," one of the men said.

Horse glared back at the soldier. "Excuse me?"

"Sorry, Lieutenant. I meant VC territory."

Horse turned back to his map and continued the briefing. "We're not expecting contact, but we'll have artillery support if we need it. Our job is to get in, scout it, and get out."

As the LRRP team leader, Horse was respected for his soldiering skills. A full-blooded Cherokee from eastern Oklahoma, he was tall and rangy, with black hair and a bronze complexion darkened by the Asian sun. He wasted no energy around the base, walking and talking in slow mode, but in the field he morphed into a swift and tireless warrior.

George had arrived on Horse's team a few months earlier, bringing with him a good knowledge of weapons. Only a few years removed from playing a smashmouth nose tackle in high school football, George was solidly built and had a quick temper. Horse looked to him for strength and reliability.

After the briefing, the men rested against their battle gear at the edge of the landing zone, killing time while they waited for helicopter transport.

"So, Lieutenant," George said. "What're you gonna be when you grow up?"

"A stockbroker," Horse said.

"My old man owns the biggest stock brokerage in Tulsa," George said. "I've got a job there if I want it. But I'm thinking a wilderness life. Screw the stock market."

"My old man's a drunk on the reservation," Horse said. "I could do that, but I'd rather be a stockbroker."

"Tell you what," George said. "I'll get my dad to hire you, and then I'll be your first account. I'll give you twenty-four dollars to invest."

Horse didn't get it.

"You dumb Cherokee, that's what we palefaces paid for Manhattan the first time. This is your second chance."

"Talk about dumb, white man," Horse said. "We didn't even own it, but we sold it to you anyway."

"Still, I'll get you the job."

"I'll give you my tomahawk."

George pulled two Cuban cigars from his pocket, part of the stash his dad had sent, and offered one to Horse, who declined. George lit one and blew a couple of smoke rings. "Why the army?"

"I wanted it for my résumé," Horse said. "In your world, military service has more cred than a Cherokee bloodline." He paused to look out over the landing zone. "What about you? You had the perfect out—a rich dad with connections. You could be sitting on the beach in a Florida reserve unit."

"Yeah, well, I hated college. I watched my high school friends get drafted and decided I should go, too."

"What'd your parents think?"

"It freaked 'em out. I didn't tell them until I got to Fort Benning. Of course, they didn't tell me they were getting a divorce, either. When my orders came, Dad was away on business, and Mom was on a cruise with her new husband. So I said good-bye to the maid."

"My dad was zonked on the couch," Horse said. "I left my kid brother standing on the front porch, waving. A buddy drove me to the airport."

Horse pored over his maps. "This terrain around the DMZ is ugly."

"Neutral territory, my ass," George said. "The place is honeycombed with VC tunnels and supply routes. We're the only ones who think it's demilitarized."

They both knew that the American bombing runs were making no impact on the flow of men and material from the north through the DMZ and, as a result, American commanders had shifted their attention to that area.

"You're short," George said. "How many days you got left?"

"Twenty and a wake-up."

"You getting out?"

"Yeah, I'm done with war. Time to move on."

"You don't need this mission. Just call in sick. Tell them you've got a pounding headache and a runny nose."

Horse laughed. "Uh, Captain, sir, I'm not feeling up to par today, so I think I'll just stay in bed until I feel better. George will handle everything for me."

"Your time's up," George said. "Jump a slick and go south for a few days, make it home safe."

"Yeah, I know how it works, but I'm going anyway. You guys couldn't find your way to the shitter on your own." Horse extracted some white papers folded up behind the maps. "Check these out," he said to George. They were pencil sketches.

"These are good," George said. "Who did them?"

"My kid brother, Hawk. He's got talent. Unfortunately, he spends more time drawing than studying. But I'm glad he sends them to me."

"Never had a sibling," George said. "Probably a good thing—I would have corrupted the kid."

"Naw. I don't parent my brother. We just do stuff together, fishing, camping, things we both like. He's a good kid. Loves the outdoors, like you. I can't wait to see him again."

Within the hour, they heard the rotors of the approaching helicopters. George cut off the burning end of his cigar and ground it out. He put the unburned stub back in a plastic bag for later. They hustled to saddle up as soon as the birds settled onto the landing zone.

"We've got a short flight," Horse said, "and then it's party time."

"Rock and roll, pardner," George said.

CHAPTER TWO

As their helicopter approached a barren hilltop at the edge of the jungle, Horse elbowed George and shouted above the roar of the chopper's engines, "There's no cover. Get on the ground as soon as possible and over to that tree line." Using hand signals, George relayed the message to the team. As they touched down and jumped out of their chopper, the Rangers spread out to organize the other troops as they landed and began moving them toward the trees.

By the time they reached the edge of the jungle, the helicopters were gone. The squads moved forward into an area where the underbrush had been partially cleared. Horse immediately signaled for everyone to get down. The ground was well trodden and dotted with the black remnants of cooking fires.

"The NVA's been here recently," Horse said. "Watch for booby traps."

George passed the word along. Horse and George worked their way slowly across the clearing and then signaled the others to move in behind them. Spread out and wary, they were still exposed when the jungle erupted with withering enemy fire. Horse yanked George to the ground just as the NVA opened up.

"Call arty," Horse said. "We're in deep shit." He pointed off to the side. "There's a squad pinned down. I'm going over there to get them."

"I'll go with you," George said.

"No, stay here and guide in the shelling. That's our only chance."

George got on the radio then, yelling the map coordinates into the artillery unit. Wounded men were calling for medics. Pinned down by the intense fire, George watched Horse work his way through the smoke and confusion toward the isolated squad. As he moved them back into some cover, the initial artillery rounds began to drop. George continued calling in instructions, adjusting arty's aim until the shells were exploding danger close, but on top of the enemy's position. When he had their aim pinpointed, George called, "Fire for effect" into the radio. As the barrage began, Horse appeared again, an apparition running through the smoke toward George's position, carrying a wounded soldier on his shoulders. Machine gun bullets sprayed the ground behind him, chasing him as he ran. George yelled for covering fire as he shot at the jungle location of the machine gun, but about ten yards from George's position, the bullets caught up with Horse, cutting him down. George left his position then and crawled toward Horse, another soldier following him. George dragged Horse out of the line of fire, and the soldier behind him recovered the man Horse had saved.

George yelled for a medic. He kept talking to Horse to keep him conscious. "Stay with me, man. We'll get you out of here."

"I can't feel my legs," Horse said.

The artillery shells, called in by George, were now pounding the enemy. The NVA's intense fire waned as they withdrew from the fight. George got on the radio again, calling for air rescue. "We need a dustoff. We've got a lot of men down." He left Horse with a medic and organized the survivors to move the wounded back toward the open area where the choppers could land. They marked the area with smoke canisters to guide in the birds.

Lying in a poncho, Horse was the first soldier lifted onto a helicopter and handed up to the medevac crew. George grabbed his hand. "Hang in there. I'll see you soon." Others were loaded after Horse; then a crewman yelled, "Clear!" George stepped away from the skids, and the dustoff lifted away. George and the rest of the survivors worked frantically to move the remaining wounded onto the birds. When they were all loaded, the survivors began cleaning up, recovering weapons and filling body bags with the dead soldiers.

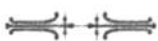

Back at the fire base, an orderly collared George as he dismounted from his helicopter. "CO wants to see you."

"Not as much as I want to see him."

George, filthy and exhausted, piled his gear outside the captain's hootch, ducked in, and threw his helmet on the floor. It clattered against a propped-up M-16, knocking it over.

"Some entrance, Sergeant."

"Well, sir, that was a fiasco," George said. "We're running a lightly armed recon, and they drop us in the middle of the entire friggin' NVA. We lost a lot of good men because of that."

"Blame the rear echelon geniuses."

"So no one here checks the orders against our own intel?"

"We do what we're told."

"Yeah, well, sir, maybe you should take the point next time out."

"Get off your high horse, Sergeant. You were running a recon, and you found the enemy. You weren't sent for a walk in the park."

"Horse got waxed, saving another soldier."

"Heard that. I'm sorry. He's special."

"Do you know where they sent the wounded?"

"The dustoffs flew the serious ones to the Twenty-Second Surge at Phu Bai."

"Can I get over there to see him?"

"Not now. Anyway, as soon as they're stabilized, they'll be medevac'd to Camp Zama, Japan. He'd be gone by the time you got over there."

George picked up his helmet. "Dammit. I wanted to check on him."

"Did you get an enemy body count?"

"They left three behind."

"I'll make that thirty."

"So the REMFs will think it was worth it?"

"Give it a break, Wheeler," the captain said, "and get your head together. You'll be going back out again as soon as I can get replacements for your team."

George stared the captain back to his typewriter. "Yes, sir," he said. He stepped outside, picked up his gear, and went to the MUST area. The unit was busy with soldiers being treated for their wounds.

George found a nurse applying a bandage on a soldier.

The nurse looked frazzled, her smock splattered with blood. She wiped a wisp of hair away from her face with her forearm to avoid touching herself with her bloodstained glove. The hair fell back across her face.

George wiped his hands on his fatigues and then tucked the hair under her surgical hat.

She managed a cracked smile. "Thanks. What happened out there?"

"Ambush."

"Well, they made a mess of things."

"CO says the others went to Phu Bai. Do you have any way to contact them? I'd like to check on my lieutenant."

"I'll see what I can find out," she said, "but it'll be a few days before we can get an answer."

CHAPTER THREE

20 March 1969
Crooked River Community
Cherokee Territory—Oklahoma

When Hawk got home from school, his dad, Albert, was asleep in his La-Z-Boy chair, their dog Sooner lying beside him. On the end table by the chair, next to a half-empty bottle of whiskey, a glass of melting ice sweated condensation into a puddle. The dog raised his head as Hawk came through the door, got up slowly, and approached, wagging his tail.

Hawk knelt down and petted him. "Want to go outside?" Hawk opened the screen door and watched the old dog go gingerly down the steps over to a disabled pickup truck, lift his leg, and relieve himself on the flat tire. Hawk checked the dog's dishes, filled one with fresh water, and let the dog back in the house.

There was a yellow envelope on the kitchen table from Western Union. The envelope had been ripped open in a ragged tear, but the telegram was missing. Hawk found the letter on his dad's lap. The message was short.

This is to advise you that First Lieutenant Joseph Manawa was severely wounded during combat operations in Quang Tri Province, Vietnam, on 16 March 1969. Current location, Camp Zama Military Hospital, Japan. Est return to the US by medevac 15 Apr 1969. Destination Tulsa VA Hospital.

There was contact information included below the body of the telegram. Hawk prodded his father but got no response. He took the telegram and sat outside on the front steps and read it again, trying to make sense of it. Horse was due home soon, but now this. Other young men had come back to the tribe with war injuries and had struggled. He wondered what this meant for Horse.

Hawk took the telegram to his neighbor, Three Songs, a tribe medicine elder. "Do you know what to do?" Hawk asked. "My dad's asleep. I can't get him awake."

They sat at the kitchen table while Three Songs called the number in the telegram and spoke to the officer in charge.

"They don't have much information yet," Three Songs said after the phone call. "We'll just have to wait and see until he gets home." Three Songs stood up and handed the telegram back to Hawk. "Let's go for a walk."

Outside, they strolled across the fields toward a rise overlooking the river. It was a sunny day, but the March wind still had a bite. They sat on a couple of large rocks at the edge of the high ground, looking out over the river below. "You know," Three Songs said, "Joseph will be changed when he comes home."

"What do you mean?"

"We won't know the extent of his injuries for a while. But depending on the severity, your brother could be disabled for life. That will change everything for him and you."

"Won't he get better?"

"I hope so, if the injuries aren't permanent. Regardless, it will be a long process of recovery. Some of the burden will fall on you."

"I'll help him."

"Yes, you will. But most of it will fall on Joseph himself. Getting better might mean learning to live with his condition. It could be the hardest thing he'll ever have to do."

"I can't wait to see him, even if he's injured."

"We both know your dad's situation, so you should come see me anytime you need help."

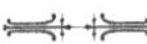

In April, Albert was notified of Horse's arrival date. Three Songs drove Hawk and Albert to the VA hospital in Tulsa. They found Horse in a large ward full of seriously injured soldiers, lying in bed below a trapeze that extended down from the ceiling.

When Horse saw Hawk running down the aisle toward him, he reached for the trapeze and pulled himself into an upright sitting position. Hawk dropped a manila envelope on the bed, then gave Horse a big hug. Albert followed, shaking Horse's hand. Hawk was surprised that Horse looked so good. His upper body appeared strong, he had no visible injuries. A sheet covered him from the waist down. Hawk helped arrange some pillows behind Horse to prop him up. Horse explained about the medevac and the travel from Japan. Eventually, the ward nurse came by.

"This is my family," Horse said as he introduced them to the nurse.

"It's pretty crowded in here," she said, "and you're stretching the visitor rules. Perhaps one of you could wait in the lobby. Take turns visiting."

"I'll wait outside," Three Songs said. "Is there a doctor we can talk to?"

"The doctor should be making his rounds soon. He'll be able to give you specifics about Joseph's situation."

Three Songs left the ward for the waiting room.

"How did it happen?" Albert asked.

"We stepped into an ambush," Horse said. "I was carrying a wounded guy back to safety when I got hit."

Horse spoke to Hawk. "You've grown a lot. You look good."

Hawk handed him the envelope. "I drew these for you," he said. Horse looked at the pencil sketches inside. "Man, these are really good. I love this one of the cabin. I can't wait to see it again." They saw the doctor enter the ward, going bed to bed, checking the charts, talking to the patients. When he reached Horse, Albert introduced himself. Hawk went out and brought Three Songs back. The doctor stood among them, describing the situation.

"Joseph has a number of problems," he said. "His upper body is strong, but he has lost the use of his legs. He'll need to stay here for a while longer, until his mobility improves to the point where he can manage at home. When he does go home, he'll need a hospital bed and a ramp into his house for wheelchair access. He is still experiencing loss of bladder control and problems with his bowels. He has a catheter in place now, but we may be able to take that out by the time he leaves here. We have braces for his legs. He'll learn to stand for short periods using the leg braces and his crutches. With some work, he can get himself to the bathroom. He can't sit or lie down for long periods in one position, or pressure sores will cause more problems. The sooner he learns to get himself up and around, the better off he'll be."

"Should we get some nursing help at home?" Three Songs asked.

"He'll need help for a while, especially with the toilet and bathing." He looked at Horse. "You're a big guy, so you'll have to use your upper body strength to help folks move you." Then he added, "By the way, be alert for depression. You're going to be frustrated, angry, and depressed. Unfortunately, one of the side effects of your pain medicine is that it will worsen your depression." The doctor looked at Albert. "And no alcohol."

When the house was ready, Horse insisted on moving back home. The doctor consented as long as Horse came back for therapy. "There's not much we can do here in terms of daily care that can't be done at home, so yes, you can go."

Three Songs found a woman on the reservation with some practical nursing experience, and she agreed to work part-time.

Each day, when Hawk came home from school, Horse would be sitting on the porch, waiting. Then, with Hawk's help, Horse practiced walking up and down the ramp using his crutches and leg braces. As Horse walked, Hawk would describe his day at school.

One day as Hawk was complaining about his teachers, Horse stopped midway up the ramp and looked at him. "Suck it up," he said. "You should be glad you're in school instead of home watching daytime television."

"I don't know why Dad leaves the TV on all day," Hawk said. "He's asleep half the time."

"It's mostly habit and lack of energy to do anything else, but it's depressing, hearing that crap all day."

CHAPTER FOUR

At Horse's request, Three Songs agreed to take him and Hawk for the day to the cabin their dad had built near the river. "We'll take my forty-five," Horse told Hawk. "That'll give us something to do."

The cabin sat in a clearing at the edge of a wooded area. In that spot, the river narrowed into a short run of rapids that poured into a deep pool at a bend beyond the trees. The rough structure had a couple of bunk beds, a small woodstove for cooking, a table, and a few chairs. A porch overlooking the river stretched across the front of the cabin. Near the cabin, Albert had built a fire pit encircled by large stones with a cast-iron grate on legs at one side. Some logs made low benches around it.

Three Songs parked close to the porch and helped Horse get down to his wheelchair. They rolled Horse up a sheet of plywood onto the porch.

Horse took a deep breath. "Being out here sure beats the hell out of staying in that house. Between Dad's cigarette smoke and the smell of his booze, it's about all I can take."

"Once you get more mobile," Three Songs said, "maybe we can find another living arrangement."

"Anything would be better than where I am."

Three Songs helped Hawk gather firewood and then had him start a fire. He brought a cast-iron dutch oven from his truck. "Build up a good fire," he said. "Then bury this in the coals and let it cook all afternoon for your dinner." He set a thermos of ice water on the porch beside a bag with a few dishes, utensils, and some sandwiches for lunch. "I'll be back this evening to pick you both up," he said.

After Three Songs left, Hawk sat on the edge of the porch next to Horse as they ate the sandwiches. "Do your legs hurt?" Hawk asked.

"Not the legs, there's no feeling there, but there's a lot of phantom pain below the injury. My brain thinks the legs are there but can't get any response, so it registers the pain. So yeah, it hurts."

"What was the war like?"

"War is weird. One minute it's quiet with nothing happening, and then in the next instant, it becomes total chaos."

"How did you know what to do?"

"When you're in a messy situation, your training takes over, and you go into automatic mode. Then as fast as things happen, it seems like slow motion."

"What do you mean?"

"During a battle, your focus changes. You're acting quickly, but you have a more heightened sense of what's happening around you. You're in the middle of it but also detached, in a way. Before I got hit, I could see myself running in advance of the bullets, like I was there, but I was also above, watching. I knew the bullets would catch up to me, that I was going to be hit, but I was in a zone where I couldn't hear any noise. I just watched the scene from above as I was running through, like watching a silent movie of myself. Then, after I was hit, everything was noise and smoke. It all became a blur, and I lost all sense of time until I got to the hospital. It all seems futile now—stupid, really."

"It must have been bad."

"There's nothing good about war."

When they finished lunch, Horse asked Hawk to get his pack. "You ever shoot a forty-five?"

Hawk shook his head no.

Horse pulled the gun out, ejected the clip, and cleared the weapon. "Time for a lesson."

Hawk set some short logs up on end and balanced some tin cans on the tops. "Stand facing the target, legs spread slightly," Horse said. "Hold your arms out and point toward the target."

He showed Hawk the aiming posture from his sitting position. "You'll need both hands on the gun—it's got some kick when it's fired." He handed Hawk the gun without the clip in it and showed him how to rack the slide to verify that it was clear. They practiced the posture. "When you're ready to shoot, take a breath, let it out, and squeeze the trigger. You'll get some recoil, so you'll have to get used to that."

Horse took the gun and loaded the clip, racked the slide to chamber a round, and then handed the gun back to Hawk. "When you're ready, squeeze the trigger. Don't jerk it."

Hawk aimed and pulled the trigger. The gun lurched back from the recoil. "I see what you mean," he said.

"Because you know there will be recoil, there's a tendency to jerk the trigger in anticipation. Resist that urge. Just squeeze the shot off."

Hawk fired several times in succession. His last shot hit a log.

Horse reloaded the clip, took the gun from Hawk, and from his wheelchair, drilled one of the tin cans.

"Yeah," Hawk said. "Good shot."

Horse handed the gun back. "Keep practicing."

After a couple more clips, Horse showed Hawk again how to clear the weapon. "Anytime you pick up a gun, assume it's loaded. You should always clear it first thing to prevent any accidents." He had Hawk practice the procedure. Then he stuck the gun and clip in the pack and hung it over the back of his wheelchair. "Enough for today," he said.

When their dinner was ready, Horse asked to be rolled down by the fire. Hawk got behind the chair. He started to push him toward the plywood, but Horse stopped him. "You'll have to take me backward, or you'll lose control."

Hawk backed him to the edge of the plywood.

"Keep my weight over the wheels," Horse said. "Otherwise, I'll be too heavy for you."

Hawk rocked him back while Horse held the wheels to keep them from rolling. Together they moved down the ramp, Horse slowing the chair to help Hawk keep control. At the bottom of the ramp, they turned the chair, and Hawk began to push him across the ground. The smaller front wheels immediately got stuck in some ruts.

"It's not easy getting over this ground," Hawk said. They turned the chair around and backed Horse toward the fire while Horse helped turn the large wheels. After Horse was settled in front of the fire, Hawk went back to the porch for plates and utensils. He pulled the pot from the fire and lifted the top and stirred the beef stew Three Songs had prepared. Hawk served it together with some bread and poured water for them. They ate silently.

"This is really good," Horse said. "Sometime I'll have to get some C rations—let you try the crap we ate when we were in the bush."

After dinner, they sat watching the sun set. Hawk cleared the plates and then sat next to Horse, playing with a stick in the fire. He let it flame up and waved the end to make smoke patterns in the air.

"I'm sorry you got hurt," he said to Horse, "but I'm glad you're home."

"How did you do in school this year?" Horse asked.

"Lousy," Hawk said. "I hate school."

"Yeah, I know, but do you want to end up like the other young guys around here, out of work, on welfare? If you don't, then you've got to get an education."

"Three Songs wants me to work with him to learn the medicine ways."

"I agree with that. You should learn those things, but you need an education if you want to get a decent job."

"I'll stay and help take care of you."

"No," Horse said. "I'm screwed. I'm an anchor around your neck. I'll have to find my own way and take care of myself. You have to plan for your own future. You can't build it around caring for me."

"I don't know."

"Hawk, listen to me. Pay attention to Three Songs, but remember what I'm saying. I won't always be around."

"What do you mean?"

"Things happen. That's the way life is."

Three Songs arrived, and together they sat watching the sky turn dark. They took turns pointing out constellations.

"I love this place," Horse said. "I hope you always remember it like this."

"We'll come here as often as you want."

"By the way," Horse said. "Your art has really improved. You should keep working on that."

"It's the only thing I like about school," Hawk said.

"I understand, but you've got to get the rest of your schoolwork done as well. You need to promise me that you'll try harder.

"All right," Hawk said, "but I don't have to like it."

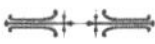

A few weeks later, on another Saturday afternoon at the cabin, Hawk was out gathering some firewood. When he returned, Horse was on the ground, crawling toward the river. "I'm sorry," he said, "but I just messed my pants again. I was trying to get to the river, but I tripped and fell."

"What do you want me to do?"

"Let's see if you can get me down to the water so I can get washed off."

Hawk helped him back up on his crutches and walked him across the ground toward the river. At the water's edge, Horse said, "this is the tricky part." With Hawk holding the crutches, Horse started lowering himself down to sit in the water, but lost his balance. They both fell into the river.

Hawk laughed. "You big klutz," he said. He splashed his brother, who splashed back, the two of them soaking each other in a water fight. Finally, Hawk retrieved the crutches. "You okay?"

Horse nodded. "So much for my ballet career." Hawk helped Horse out of his pants and took off the leg braces. While Horse washed himself, Hawk rinsed out the clothes.

"I'm sorry you have to do this," Horse said.

"Don't worry about it."

When they got back to the cabin, Hawk built a fire. Once it was blazing, he and Horse held their clothes up in front of the fire to dry.

"This is no way to live," Horse said.

When Three Songs came to pick them up, they sat for a while by the fire talking.

"I need to get my head together," Horse said. "I'm going to stop taking those meds. They're not doing any good—just making things worse."

"I think you're making progress," Three Songs said.

"Some progress. I'm still in diapers, sitting in a house full of cigarette smoke with a drunk and an old dog."

"There's also me," Hawk said.

Horse leaned over the arm of his chair and gave Hawk a punch in the arm. "Yeah," he said. "I'm sorry. I didn't mean to insult you. You've really been helpful. I couldn't ask for a better brother; but there's nothing anyone can do about where I'm headed."

"One day at a time," Three Songs said.

CHAPTER FIVE

A week later, Horse asked Three Songs to take him back to the cabin.

"What about me?" Hawk said. "I'd like to come along."

"I know," Horse said, "but I've got to try this on my own. See if I can manage."

"We'll take you there for a short period," Three Songs said, "as long as we can check on you periodically."

"That's not necessary," Horse said. "You can just leave me there for a while."

"You can't expect miracles. You have to take this gradually so you can learn how to care of yourself."

"Let's give it a try," Horse said. "I'm tired of taking it slow."

Later in the day, Hawk and Three Songs drove Horse to the cabin and got him set up with bedding, some food, and water. Hawk took Horse's pack into the cabin and set it up on the table where Horse could reach it. He filled the wood box by the stove, then put wood in the stove so that it was ready to light. He looked into the matchbox on the shelf but found it empty. He opened

Horse's pack, looking for a lighter or matches. The pain pills were on top of some clothes. Hidden below was the gun and a loaded clip. He closed the pack back up.

He went outside. "Three Songs, do you have any matches? The box in there is empty."

"I've got a lighter in the glove box." While Three Songs was at the truck, Hawk asked Horse about the pills.

"I thought you stopped taking them," Hawk said.

"I tried, but I can't get rid of the pain. I'm afraid I'm getting addicted to them."

"What about the gun?"

"What about it?"

"Why did you bring it?"

"I just wanted to practice. At least my trigger finger's not paralyzed."

"Do you want me to set up some targets for you?"

"No, thanks. I'll just plink at the stumps you set up before."

"There's no other reason for the gun?"

"I'm good, Hawk. Don't worry about it."

Hawk went over to the truck and got the lighter from Three Songs. He thought of mentioning the gun, but he took Horse at his word, that he had brought it just for target practice. Hawk didn't want to contradict his brother and decided not to tell Three Songs.

After everything was ready for Horse, Three Songs shook Horse's hand. "We'll be back in the morning." He headed for the truck.

"Hawk," Horse said. "Thanks for bringing me here. I appreciate everything you've done for me."

For an instant, Hawk thought Horse looked different somehow, maybe sad; he wasn't sure. Hawk shook it off and gave Horse a hug. "See you tomorrow," Hawk said.

On the way back home, Hawk asked Three Songs if they should leave Horse alone.

"I'm not sure," Three Songs said, "but sooner or later, he's got to discover what he can do to get past his injuries."

"He's getting more mobile."

"Yes, but I don't think that's the issue. Your brother has to believe that he can find a future for himself."

"He hates living in the house. I don't really blame him. In a way, Dad's more crippled than Horse. Neither is much help to the other."

"I've been thinking about that," Three Songs said. "I'm wondering if he should go back to the hospital where he could get more regular rehab and some counseling for his depression."

"I don't know if he'd do that. He's pretty independent. I just wish I could do more."

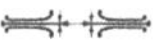

When Three Songs and Hawk returned the next morning, they saw the wheel chair on the porch, an empty food can beside it with a spoon still in it. The door to the cabin was swinging open in the wind.

"Stay out here," Three Songs said.

He went into the cabin. After a few minutes, he came back out, looking distraught.

"What is it?" Hawk asked.

"You were right, Hawk. We should never have left him alone."

"What do you mean?"

Three Songs put his arm around Hawk. "I guess we didn't know how bad he was feeling."

"He seemed to be getting better. He told me yesterday he was okay."

"Well, he's not okay."

"What's the matter?"

"He's gone."

"What do you mean 'he's gone'?"

"He's dead."

"What? Is he inside?"

Three Songs nodded, his lips tight in a grimace.

"That can't be." Hawk tried to break away. "I want to see him."

Three Songs held him back. "Not like this," he said. "I don't want you to remember him the way he is in there."

Hawk twisted free and entered the cabin. He found Horse lying on the floor in a smear of dried blood, the pistol still in his hand. Hawk knelt beside Horse and felt his cold stiff arm. He couldn't believe it. Just the day before, Horse looked healthy from the waist up. Only the legs were the problem. They could have fixed that. Made Horse more mobile. Now everything was mangled, his strong face blown apart, the scene a mess. Hawk was in the zone Horse had described. There was no sound. Nothing appeared real except that he was above the scene, watching himself kneeling beside Horse, crying. He pried the gun from Horse's hand and came back outside carrying it, still dazed, his face and eyes red.

"Let me have that," Three Songs said. "It's probably still loaded."

Hawk backed away, looking at the gun, turning it over in his hands. Three Songs walked slowly toward him, his hand out. "Hawk," he said. "Please."

Hawk raised the gun in front of his face, examining it. He looked at Three Songs, then back at the gun. As Three Songs neared, Hawk ejected the clip and racked the slide to clear the chamber. The sound seemed to snap him out of his trance. He ran to the river and heaved the gun into the rapids. He watched the gun hit the water and then sat down on the bank with his head in his hands.

Three Songs came over and sat beside him. Hawk began picking up stones, throwing them hard into the water.

"What do I do now?" Hawk said.

"You're free to do anything you want. That's what your brother hoped for."

"I just wanted to be his brother."

"You still are."

"I knew he had the gun. I saw it in his pack. I could have taken it and stopped him."

"Maybe then, but if he was going to do it, no one could have prevented it."

"Shit," Hawk said. "It's just shit."

"Yes, it is. That's exactly what it is."

After a long silence, Three Songs said, "Come on, Hawk. We need to go see your dad."

CHAPTER SIX

Fire Base Zebra, Quang Tri Province—South Vietnam
15 July 1969

George was sitting on a pile of sandbags cleaning his weapon when Lieutenant Brad Coaker approached. A West Point graduate, Coaker had been in-country for several months when he was assigned as team leader to replace Horse. He was experienced and knowledgeable.

"Wheeler," he said. "Pack your trash. There's a slick on the way to pick you up."

George gave the officer a puzzled look. "Your dad's real sick," the lieutenant said. "You're headed home. You'll pick up your orders at battalion headquarters and fly out of Tan Son Nhut."

George finished cleaning his weapon and reassembled it.

"What about the rest of my tour?"

"In another ten days, you're officially short, so you've got an early out."

"Are you serious?"

"I'm not sure who your dad knows, but there's a senator somewhere who thinks you need to be back in the world, so get saddled up."

George felt a momentary pang of guilt about leaving, but that feeling faded once he'd thrown his gear on the floor of the chopper and they were lifting off. Now he was filled with the exhilaration of escape, mixed with dread about his father's condition.

As they cleared the tree line, they left the dust and fumes of the LZ and entered into the moist air over the jungle canopy. From up there, the scenery was mostly varied shades of green with occasional markings of smoke from peasant cooking fires or military engagement. He began to relax. Clearing an LZ could be dicey, but once they were underway, there was little danger of taking ground fire.

Sweeping over the jungle canopy, feeling the wind in his face, his hearing deafened by the roar of the chopper, he thought about how screwed up the war had become. Combat soldiers were no longer in charge. Instead the conflict was being run by politicos who didn't know a claymore from a cow pie. Clearly Congress wanted out and had taken control away from the military. Special ops advisers were expected to bring the South Vietnamese along to bear the brunt of the fighting, but the scheme wasn't working. Combat strategies designed over Washington luncheons and sent to rear echelon commanders didn't fit the battlefield. The grunts got the worst of it. They were dispatched on inane missions with nothing to look forward to but some first-class weed and a blue-ribbon wound that earned a one-way ticket back home.

Coaker said it best. "This war is turning into a pile of dog shit. Let's keep our heads together and do our jobs, but pay attention."

George was fed up with that politicians' war, and he was happy to leave it behind. His only regret was for his comrades in arms.

He knew they would have to soldier on through the morass without him.

⸻

Aboard the government charter headed back to the States, George wondered how his dad would receive him. To the frustration of his parents, John and Nancy, George had cruised his way through high school, skipping academics to concentrate on sports, spending his free time hunting, fishing, and generally carousing with his buddies. He was slow to apply to college, but under pressure from his folks, got admission to an Ivy League school thanks to their large financial donation to compensate for his poor grades. The eastern atmosphere didn't sit well with George. He longed for the wide-open skies of Oklahoma and the locker-room mentality of his friends. He was underwhelmed by his privileged classmates, who spent their time stalking long-haired, doe-eyed coeds protesting the war. The guys joined the antiwar groups to meet the freewheeling girls, a sure ticket to getting laid, but to George, they were all phonies who didn't seem to mind spending the old man's money while protesting the Establishment.

After a mediocre freshman year, George enlisted. With boot camp orders in hand, he left the campus on a bright October day and drove his Harley straight to Fort Benning, camping roadside along the way. His parents' first knowledge that he'd left school came when he called them from a barracks phone.

"Dammit, George," was all his dad could say before he handed the phone to his mom. "Nancy, you talk to him."

George wondered now if his parents still resented his abrupt decision to join the army.

When he arrived at Travis AFB, George walked through the base operations portion of the terminal headed for personnel to process out. He passed by a ragged line of GIs in fatigues, looking as if they had just come off the battlefield. Back home from Nam, they were undisciplined and raucous, obviously penned up for one last military procedure while they waited to be discharged. Across from them was a second line, made up of newbies, spit shined and polished, carrying their new duffels full of gear. They walked by the veterans to board their flight for Southeast Asia. The vets catcalled and whistled, shouting insults.

"Yeah, cherries, FNGs, you're screwed. Take a good look around, suckers, this is the last time you'll see home. Ever. So long, chumps. You're walking dead."

George approached the fresh troops, who were now gathered at a departing gate, waiting for their boarding instructions. The officer in charge stopped George. "Can I help you with something, Sergeant?"

"Yes, sir," George said, saluting. "I just got back, getting my discharge this morning. I thought maybe I could talk to some of these guys and let them know what they're in for, besides the catcalls."

"Sorry," the major said. "They're getting ready to board. Anyway, they'll find out soon enough."

"Knowing the army, they'll be standing here for another hour," George said. "You know the drill—hurry up and wait."

"Either way, you're free of it now, so butt out."

"Yes, sir." George turned on his heel and started walking down the line of soldiers. "Hey, you grunts," he said in a loud voice. "When you get over there, pay attention and keep your heads down. Get back safe." He fist-bumped a few of the troops as he went by them, heading toward the personnel office.

As George left Travis for the San Francisco airport, his cab ran a gauntlet of war protesters, lining the entrance to the base. Carrying signs, yelling, they were strident now, not like the protesters of George's college days. A couple of eggs hit his window, and George watched the yellow yolks run down the glass. At the airport, he tipped the driver an extra ten dollars. "Sorry, man," George said. "Here's some money to get your cab cleaned."

The driver refused it. "Don't worry about it," he said. "I been there, too. Them freaks got no right." He pulled George's duffel from the trunk. "Use that ten bucks to buy yourself a couple of drinks. No one else will." He shook George's hand. "Good luck."

After checking in for his flight, George found a pay phone and called his mom.

She was not expecting his call.

"It's George," he said.

"Where are you? Is everything okay?"

"I'm fine, Mom. I'm in San Francisco. I got an early discharge, and I'm on my way to see Dad. He's in the hospital."

"I'm so glad you're home."

"Do you know anything about Dad's condition?"

"Not much. He called to tell me he was bringing you home and said that he had cancer, but he wouldn't give me any details. When can I see you?"

"I need to go to the hospital first. Then I'll call again. I'll see you soon."

George then called his buddy Earl Schlemmer, who was already back from his tour in Nam. George got Earl's answering machine and began to leave a message. Part way through the message, Earl picked up.

"Wheeler! Are you back?"

"I'm sitting in the San Francisco airport. Got an early out. My dad's in the hospital."

"I'm sorry to hear that. How's he doing?"

"I don't know much yet, but I'll call you after I see him and find out the situation."

"Welcome back to the world."

"We need some Budweiser time."

"Roger that. Call me when you get home."

George hung up and went to the airport bar. He had two hours before his flight was called, sufficient time to get in a good drunk before boarding the red-eye.

⟜⟝

George got a cab at the Tulsa airport and went straight to the hospital. At the reception area, he talked with the volunteer at the visitor's desk. "I'm looking for John Wheeler," he said.

She checked the admissions board. "Room 312. Go through that door and then take the elevator on the left."

From his bed, John shook George's hand, then pointed to his CIB and the airborne wings above it. "Quite a chest full," he said. They exchanged small talk, interspersed with silence. Occasionally, John slipped in and out of consciousness with each surge of painkiller.

"Tell me about the war," John said, finally. George gave him the condensed version.

"It's pretty much a quagmire," George said. "Most of the time, I was assigned to a small unit of Rangers operating out of the Central Highlands. My team leader was another Oklahoman, a Cherokee Indian, Lieutenant Manawa. He grew up in Broken River, near Eldon in the territory. A great soldier. Somehow, he survived his home life with a drunken father and got himself an ROTC scholarship to Oklahoma State. He saved my life more than once. He's out now and wants to be a stockbroker."

"Is he back in Oklahoma?" John asked.

"Yeah, and sitting in a VA hospital. He was wounded on his last mission."

"Talk to my partner, Sam Lieberman. We could get him into our training program."

"He's a brilliant guy," George said. "He'd be a great addition to your firm." George leaned back in his chair, letting his dad rest.

A nurse entered. "How's he doing?"

"He seems okay," George said. "He's been awake mostly."

John raised his hand at her. "I'm all right," he said. "It's the drugs, they really knock you out." The nurse puttered around the room, checking charts, reading instruments.

"I'm dying, George," John said when she'd left. "That's why I had the senator bring you home. I wanted to see you again, get you the hell out of there. You've done your time; now you can get on with your life."

George winced. He had worn his uniform thinking that the medals and badges would tell his dad the story of George Wheeler, the soldier, someone who amounted to something. But it was clear that John still considered George's military service a dead end.

"Dad," he said. "I'm glad you brought me home, but I would have stayed and finished out my tour. The war's all screwed up, but there's still honor among the soldiers who were sent there to serve."

John sighed. "There's no honor left in that war." He reached for an envelope on the bedside table, handed it to George. "I've written some instructions for you detailing my final arrangements. It's all been planned. Sam also has a copy, and he'll help handle the details. There's a house key in the envelope. The cars and your motorcycle have all been serviced, ready for you." He lay back on his pillow and closed his eyes.

As they sat together in silence, John's face turned ashen. George had seen that look—he knew death was approaching. A nurse brought a Styrofoam cup of coffee.

"I thought you might need this," she said. "Can I get you anything to go with it? Cream or sugar?"

George shook his head. He sipped the coffee while she checked John's pulse.

"It's thready," she said. "Weak, irregular."

"He seemed pretty good when I arrived."

"It's not unusual for patients to rally, knowing that they're going to see their family. I know he was worried about you and wanted to be sure you got home."

"His breathing is a bit ragged," George said. "He doesn't sound good."

"You're right. It won't be long." She put a hand on George's shoulder and bent down close to him. "I'm sorry," she said.

George set the cup on the bedside tray. He leaned over, put his arms around his dad, and kissed his forehead. "Thanks for bringing me home, Dad. Don't worry about me. I'll be okay."

An hour passed. George took his kit into the bathroom and washed and shaved. In the early evening, George's mother, Nancy, knocked quietly on the door. She walked into the room and burst into tears as she embraced George.

"I'm so glad you're home," she said. "I was worried sick." She looked over at John. "How's he doing?"

"He's been unconscious for a few hours now. The nurse says it won't be long."

"Well, I thought you could use some company. I hope you don't mind."

"Thanks, Mom. I'm glad you came."

"You look great. Fit. Handsome," Nancy said. She went over to John's bedside and took his hand in hers. "John, it's Nancy. You're a good man. Thanks for bringing George home." She bent down and kissed his forehead.

"Have you had anything to eat?" Nancy asked.

George shook his head. "It's okay. I'm not really hungry."

"Why don't we go down to the cafeteria and get something? You could be in for a long night."

"I think I should stay here," he said.

Nancy got up. "I'll go get some food. I'll be back in a few minutes."

She came back with some sandwiches, chips, and coffee for both of them. "Sorry, there wasn't a lot of choice at this time of night."

"It's okay," he said. "Now that I see the food, I am hungry."

"Did you get any of my letters?" Nancy asked. "I wasn't sure because you never wrote back."

George nodded. "I was in-country most of the time, but eventually they'd catch up to me when we were resupplied. I'm sorry I never wrote. I tried a couple of times, but I didn't know what to say. All I had to talk about was the war, and I wasn't sure you'd want to hear about that."

"You know I'm remarried?" she said.

"I found out before I left. He sounds like a good guy."

She nodded. "I think you'll like him. He's different from your dad, not as hard-driving, but genuine and solid."

"I never really knew why you left Dad, but I assumed it was partly because of me. I made your lives hell back then."

"George, it had nothing to do with you. John was totally immersed in his business and was gone all of the time. I just needed some personal attention."

By late evening, John's breathing became labored. The evening-shift nurse came in to check his pulse again. "He's still hanging on," she said.

"Mom," George said. "I'm going to stay here all night. Why don't you go home and get some rest. I'll call you if anything changes." He showed her the envelope. "Dad said he's made all the arrangements and given the instructions to Sam. I'll also give him a call."

"That's your dad," she said. "Planned to the last detail."

"Seriously, Mom, go get some rest. Thanks for coming and getting the food. I can take it from here."

Nancy got up and hugged George. "Okay, but call me," she said.

George settled into a vigil in one of the chairs, dozing off occasionally. By early morning, he awoke to the sound of his dad's breathing, which had become a distinct rattle. George went to his bed and took his dad's hand. "Time to go, Dad," he said as he squeezed the hand. A few minutes later, in one final exertion, John took his last breath and relaxed. George sat down again and bent forward, his head and forearms on the mattress. After a few minutes, he summoned the nurse who confirmed that John had no pulse. She listened to his heart through a stethoscope, disconnected all of the equipment, and covered John with a sheet.

"Your dad listed a funeral home on his intake forms. I'll call them and have them come."

George picked up the envelope and looked through the papers again. By the time the funeral home staff arrived and removed the body, it was past eight. George called Sam. "This is George Wheeler. I called to tell you that my dad passed away this morning."

"I'm very sorry," Sam said. "John was a fine man. It's a big loss for all of us. I'll get started right away on the arrangements. We can schedule the memorial service sometime next week." They agreed to meet the following day.

After he left the hospital, George called his mom again. "Would you come to the funeral?" George asked.

She seemed hesitant. "I don't know, George. I'm not sure how others will react."

"Mom, you're still part of the family. I'd like you to be there with me. You're all I've got now."

"All right, then. I just didn't want to be out of place."

"Stick with me," George said. "It'll be okay."

"Honey, do you want to stay with us while the arrangements are being made?"

"Thanks, Mom, but I need to get myself organized and check Dad's house. Let's meet for dinner the night before the funeral."

CHAPTER SEVEN

John's funeral was held in the chapel at the state college where he had served as trustee. George remembered the building. He had accompanied his parents to a graduation ceremony there when John gave the commencement address and received an honorary degree.

Before the service, George met Nancy and her new husband, Stan, in a small room near the chapel. They were escorted to seats near the podium. The eulogies were extensive. They painted a picture of generosity and business acumen that both surprised and impressed George. He wished then that he had paid more attention. He even wondered how his life might have been different if he had stayed in school and joined his dad's firm.

George thought he was tough enough to get through the chapel service without a display of emotion. After all, he'd seen plenty of misery already, even burying some of his comrades, but when the crowd stood to sing "Amazing Grace," George lost it. He found himself sobbing uncontrollably with Nancy wrapped around him, her head on his shoulder. Once the hymn concluded and they sat back down, George regained his composure and steeled himself for the reception following the service.

George stood with Sam to greet friends and his dad's business associates. Nancy and Stan stayed off to one side, talking with her friends and acquaintances and eventually slipping away, leaving George with his friends.

CHAPTER EIGHT

The day after John's funeral service, George met Sam at his office, where Sam explained George's inheritance. The trust left for George by his dad was substantial, a fact that was momentarily beyond George's comprehension.

"This is really unexpected," he said. "It's funny, but I've been such a screwup, I figured he'd just cut me out."

"You're his only heir, George. He was a closed, private man and didn't express his feelings much. I know he didn't like the fact that you left school, but a part of him was proud of you for serving your country. I never heard him say anything bad about you. He was mad at the government for getting us into that war in the first place, and that's part of why he wanted you back home in one piece. As you heard, he's already given a lot to charity. This inheritance is rightfully yours to use wisely."

George talked about his wounded friend Horse. "He graduated from Oklahoma State with a degree in finance," George said, "and as soon as he's discharged from the VA hospital, he'll be looking for a job. Dad said maybe he could go through the firm's training program. I owe my life to him."

"We have a training program for vets," Sam said. "It would be good to have a Native American be part of that." Sam agreed to interview Horse and discuss a plan to train him for his securities licenses.

"I don't know the extent of his injuries yet," George said. "He was severely wounded in the legs. He may have mobility issues."

"That's not a problem at the office. Everything is wheelchair accessible. And there are decent apartments nearby. Arrangements can be worked out."

"That's great," George said. "I'm going to visit him tomorrow at the hospital. He'll be excited to hear the good news."

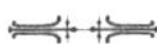

The next morning, George rode his Harley to the hospital. Inside, he stopped at the second-floor reception desk. The nearby waiting area was jammed with families waiting to see their sons.

The desk clerk was busy working on a medical chart. She spoke without looking up. "Can I help you?"

"I'm looking for Lieutenant Joseph Manawa."

"The Indian?"

"No, the lieutenant."

She looked at a clipboard, paging backward.

"He checked out two months ago," she said. "His people came and took him home. It would have been better for him to stay here to get regular care, but he insisted on leaving."

"Can you tell me where I could find him?"

"Do I look like a travel service?" She shuffled some papers on her desk. Her desk phone rang, and she answered it. "Anyway," she said after the call, "it's private patient information."

"He was my friend," George said. "We served in Nam together. I put him on the helicopter after he'd been shot. I'd like to find him."

"I'm sorry," she said. "It's hospital policy. We can't give out that information."

She got up, busying herself with tasks related to other patient files. When she turned back, George was still standing in front of her desk.

"Is there something else?"

"Yes, there is," George said, this time speaking louder. "I've come halfway across the world to see my commanding officer who was severely injured in the service of his country and, if you'll excuse my French, I'm pissed off that an agency of the government that sent him into battle won't give up his address to a fellow soldier." The waiting room suddenly got quiet, all eyes on the nurse.

"There's nothing I can do."

"There is something you can do," George said. "You can hand me the file jacket with his medical record so that I can copy down the address. That's not medical information. That's personal information." The nurse studied him for a minute, looked out over the waiting room, and brushed a strand of gray hair from her eyes.

"I'm sorry," she said quietly. "It's been a rough week." She took a pad of paper and wrote down a room number. She picked up the phone and punched an extension. "Eddie, I'm sending a young man to see you. He needs an address from a file. Thanks, hon." She hung up the phone and turned back to George. "The file has already been sent downstairs to the records department. When you get there, look for Eddie, a tall black man. He's a World War Two vet and doesn't care much about policy. He'll help you out."

"Thank you," George said.

CHAPTER NINE

Two hours later, George turned off the Broken Arrow Expressway and headed east on Route 51 toward Eldon. There, he stopped and got directions to the Broken River community. As he progressed deeper into the back roads, he began to get a sense of Horse's world. The houses were mostly gray boxes with wood siding and tin roofs. While a few seemed to be maintained, most were disheveled and weatherworn, with vehicles abandoned in the tall weeds and junk equipment scattered about. Some kids carrying buckets were gathering water at a hand pump near one of the houses. George stopped to talk to an old man who was picking up his mail.

"Could you point me to Broken River?"

The man gestured up the road. "About a mile thataway. Turn right on the dirt road by the barn."

After George made the turn, he came to an old school building. The sign out front read BROKEN RIVER ELEMENTARY SCHOOL. Some boys were playing basketball at one end of the school parking lot. The pavement was in disrepair, with weeds growing up through the cracked asphalt. A few strands of net hung from the basketball rim. George pulled up onto the pavement and sat on the idling Harley, watching the game. The boys ignored him until an errant pass sent the ball bouncing toward him. He fielded it one-handed and held it ready to toss back. The boys approached.

"I'm looking for Walking Horse's house," he said as he flipped the ball back.

The boys came closer to look at the Harley. "Were you in the army with him?"

"Yeah," George said. "We were Rangers together."

The boys looked at one another, not sure what to say. One of them, George guessed he was probably fourteen, pointed up the street. "Turn left out of the parking lot, then right at the next corner. It's about a quarter mile up that road, on the left," he said. "Cool bike."

George revved the engine a couple of times for them.

The boy spoke again. "If you give me a ride, I'll show you the house."

George reached behind himself and patted the seat. "Deal. Hop on."

The boy settled onto the seat.

George looked back. "You good? Hanging on tight?"

"Yep."

"Here we go." George jumped the bike with a quick wheelie. As they ran the length of the parking lot, George accelerated to keep the front wheel off the ground. The boy had a fistful of George's jacket and was laughing. At the road, George turned left and then right at the next intersection onto another dirt road. He slowed to reduce their trail of dust. They passed another clutch of houses, lining both sides of the road. An elderly woman waved at them from her porch rocker. The boy tugged George's sleeve, then pointed off to the left. "That one up there," he said speaking loudly over the engine noise.

They rode up to a log cabin set off by itself. The cabin had a porch across the front and appeared to have been remodeled, years ago, by adding a metal roof and a room to one side. A new-looking ramp had been attached to one end of the porch. There was no lawn around the cabin, only packed dirt. A battered pickup with a flat tire and the remains of a decapitated snowmobile sat in front. Miscellaneous boxes of junk were piled beside the porch and throughout the yard. A hand water pump stood to one side of the house. As George leaned the bike on its stand, the boy spoke again.

"My dad's probably drunk," he said. "He usually is, by this time of day."

"You're Horse's brother?"

"My name's Charles."

"Charles Soaring Hawk?"

The boy nodded.

George gave him a high five. "Why didn't you tell me in the first place?"

Hawk shrugged. "I wasn't sure what you wanted."

Hawk called into the house for his dad, then opened the screen door into the kitchen. A white-haired man staggered to the door. He leaned on the door frame with one hand, the other combing back his long white hair.

George extended his hand. "I'm George Wheeler," he said. The old man stood a minute, swaying, his eyes adjusting to the sunlight. A cigarette dangled from his mouth. He looked at Hawk, then at George.

"Joseph said you would come." He shook George's hand. "Name's Albert." He stepped back to let George in.

The cabin was sparsely furnished. In the small kitchen, there was only a sink, small stove, refrigerator, and cupboards. A Formica-topped kitchen table with four aluminum-and-plastic chairs took up the center of the floor. Looking into the living room, George could see a rag rug in the center and a La-Z-Boy lounger. A black-and-white television flickered in the corner. An old dog, lying in the middle of the rug, raised its head, wagged its tail briefly, and settled its head back on its front paws. The place smelled of cigarette smoke and spoiled food. A half-empty bottle of cheap whiskey sat on the kitchen table.

"Sit down," Albert said, pointing to a chair. On the table, in front of George, was an old chipped butter dish. The stick of butter had melted into a blob and looked rancid around the edges. A cockroach crawled across the table toward the butter. Albert slapped his hand onto the bug and brushed the squashed carcass off the table onto the floor. In the corner, a cardboard box overflowed with beer cans and food containers. The counter was stacked with dirty dishes encrusted with leftover food.

Albert took two old jelly jars from the cupboard, and poured them each half full of whiskey. He set one on the table in front of George and sat down across from him. Albert studied the glass in his own hand and then drained it in one swallow. He looked at Hawk, who was standing by the sink.

"Didn't the boy tell you?"

George shook his head. "Tell me what?"

"Joseph is dead," he said. "After we brought him home, he asked us to take him to our cabin down by the river. He said he wanted to be there alone for a while, get his head straight. When Charles returned for him, he was gone."

"How did he die?" George said.

Albert coughed a deep smoker's hack. "Gunshot."

A wave of nausea flooded over George, but he caught himself, swallowing the bitter bile in his throat. He took a deep breath and then a sip of the whiskey. Hawk stood silently, looking at the floor.

The old man left the room and came back with a deer-hide pouch and laid it on the table in front of George.

"He wrote a note. It said that when you came to visit, I was to give you this."

George opened the pouch. It was Horse's tomahawk.

"I want you to tell me about my son," Albert said. They sat quietly. George swirled the whiskey in his glass, trying to regain his composure. He took another sip and felt it bite. He leaned forward toward the old man.

"Your son was a warrior." George took another sip. "It's not all pretty."

The old man wiped his eyes with the back of his hand. "I want to hear everything," he said. He looked at Hawk and spoke to him in Cherokee.

"No," Hawk said in English. "I want to stay."

Hawk pulled a chair away from the table and sat down, his eyes fixed on George.

CHAPTER TEN

It was late afternoon when they finished talking. George said his good-byes to the old man and walked outside with Hawk.

"Where's the cabin?"

Hawk pointed off to the west.

"Can you take me there?"

Hawk nodded and climbed on the Harley behind George. They followed a farm lane that ran from the cabin across the field behind and continued on a rough trail toward the river. They dismounted beside the cabin and stood for a minute in the silence left after George killed the engine.

"Where did you find him?"

Hawk walked to the front of the cabin, across a low porch to the door. Two old wicker rocking chairs were on the porch. A few empty beer cans were scattered where they had been dropped. Hawk lifted the latch and creaked the door open. George followed him in.

The inside was in disarray. Cobwebs hung in the corners. A table and chair had been pushed to one side, another chair tipped over. George stood inside the doorway, trying to orient himself, looking for signs of Horse's death. Hawk walked to the middle of the room and pulled back an old rug, revealing a dark stain in the unfinished wood. George took a couple of steps in, knelt by the stain, and put his hand on it. *What a waste,* he thought. Hawk stood silently beside him, his hand on George's shoulder.

Finally, George stood. "Was he given military honors at his funeral?"

Hawk turned away and went outside and sat on the edge of the porch. George followed and sat down beside him. George asked again.

Hawk's voice cracked. "They treated him like shit," he said. "Dad was embarrassed that Joseph shot himself. He thought Joseph had dishonored the family in front of the tribe. He insisted that there be no ceremonies, only a plain burial with just family."

"I can fix that," George said.

Hawk shook his head and wiped his face with the sleeve of his T-shirt. "The elders will do nothing without Dad's approval. He's screwed now."

"What do you mean?"

"According to our customs, a warrior who has fought bravely can be honored with a new name. It frees him from his past life and helps him go on his journey to the afterlife. Dad didn't feel he was worthy because he shot himself." Hawk picked up a stone and threw it hard toward the river. "Without the new name," he said, "no one will respect him."

"I'll talk to your dad and the elders," George said. "There's a national cemetery nearby. I'll see that he gets military honors, even if it has to happen off the reservation."

"I don't get why he shot himself."

"Sometimes suicide just happens."

"He didn't have to do it."

"Horse was the best soldier I've ever known. He was good at everything. His dream was to come home in one piece, get a good job, and be successful. He didn't want to return handicapped. When he got wounded, his only complaint was that I should have let him die there on the battlefield."

"He was making some progress. I was helping him."

"He probably thought he was just a burden, holding you back."

Hawk got up from the porch and started to walk toward the motorcycle. "He was not a burden," he said.

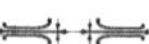

Back at the house, Hawk dismounted from the bike but stayed, holding on to the handlebars.

"Could you take me with you?" he asked.

George placed his hand on the boy's shoulder. "Where's your mom?"

"She left," he said. "I haven't seen her for a while. I think she's in Tulsa somewhere, living with an oil-well rigger. He doesn't like kids much."

"I can't just pull you out of your home. I've only been back a few days myself. I need to get some things organized, but I'll stay in touch. See what we can do."

"Yeah, whatever," Hawk said. He turned to walk back in the house.

"Hawk," George said. Hawk turned back to face him.

"Do you mind if I call you Hawk?"

"No, I don't mind. Thanks for telling me about my brother."

"Hawk, I will come back for you."

"That's what Mom said a year ago when she left." Hawk turned toward the house. George dismounted the bike, leaned it on its stand, and reached in the saddlebag.

"Hawk," George said.

George held up the deer-hide pouch. "Horse's tomahawk is the most valuable thing I own. Would you keep it for me until I get back?"

Hawk's face changed into a smile. "Yeah, sure," he said. "I'll keep it for you. It'll be safe."

"I won't be back right away, but then I'll fix things for your brother. I'll talk to the elders and to your dad. In the meantime, you have to do some things for me," George said.

"Okay."

"Respect your dad, and clean up that god-awful mess in your house."

Hawk lunged at George, gave him a hug, grabbed the pouch, and disappeared into the house.

CHAPTER ELEVEN

As he took the tomahawk back to his room, Hawk could hear George's motorcycle leaving the reservation.

"Why didn't he take it?" Albert asked.

"He'll be back for it. He just got home and has to get some things done first. He asked me to keep it safe until he comes back for it."

"Don't get your hopes up."

In his room, Hawk opened the pouch again and lifted the tomahawk, hefting it in his hand, then swinging it, getting its feel. He ran his finger across the blade edge. *Still sharp,* he thought. He remembered Horse showing him how to throw it, and he wanted to try it again—but it was George's now, and he did not want anything to happen to it. He put it back in the pouch and laid it on a bookshelf on the wall beside his bed. When he came back out of his room, his father was stretched out in his chair, watching television, the only visible sign of life a spiral of cigarette smoke trailing from his lips. A half-full glass of whiskey sat on the end table within reach.

At the kitchen, Hawk stood for a moment, surveying the wreckage. Then he looked under the cupboard and found a box of black plastic bags. He began clearing the food containers, cans, and bottles into two bags, which he tied and put outside next to the house. He put the dishes into a dishpan and filled it with soap and hot water to soak them. He found a can of Bon Ami cleanser and an old sponge and cleaned the sink, wiped down the countertop, swept the kitchen floor with the remnant of a broom from the closet, stuffed another plastic bag in his pocket, and went outside.

Hawk walked back to the river and cleaned up the trash scattered around the cabin. When he was finished, he found a stick, took out his pocket knife, and sat on the porch, whittling a sharp point, making some markings on the shaft, occupying his hands while he thought about what George had said. He knew his dad was right, that he should not get his hopes up, but there was a chance that George would come back and fix things for Horse. He wouldn't say anything to his dad until George returned, fearing his dad's reaction. He remembered then that he had left a pencil and a pad in the cabin that he used when he was with Horse. They were still in the cupboard. He picked them up and went back out onto the porch and began sketching, drawing parts of the cabin, working on his perspective. He was getting hungry and realized it was past dinnertime. He picked up the bag of trash and went back home.

The kitchen was a mess again. A hamburger lay in its cooking grease in an iron skillet. A can of Campbell's pork and beans had been opened, and some of its contents were still in a saucepan on the stove. His dad's plate was on the table, the cold grease congealed there, next to the butter dish and an open bread wrapper. Albert was back in his chair. Hawk tested the temperature of the hamburger, then relit the stove to heat it up. After his dinner, he washed the dishes and wiped down the stove.

CHAPTER TWELVE

After George left the reservation, he rode back to Tulsa. It was early evening when he stopped at the Cowboy Roadside Inn to get some dinner. He sat down at the end of the bar up against the wall and ordered a beer while he looked over the menu. The evening crowd was arriving, noisy and raucous. While George was eating, some young guys and their dates began to crowd the stools beside him. The guys were wearing jeans, fatigue jackets with the sleeves cut off, and headbands around their long hair. The women were in cowboy boots, short skirts, and vests embroidered with peace signs over their blouses. The band was playing a version of Glen Campbell's "Wichita Lineman."

A news broadcast came on the television over the bar. A picture of some special ops soldiers appeared as the newscaster talked about developments around the alleged execution of a Viet Cong double agent. The media was calling it the Green Beret affair. George recalled Coaker bringing rumors of other investigations of atrocities. He thought about all the times his team was angry and frustrated. It would have been easy to take revenge, but

Horse would have none of it. He often reminded his team of the Geneva Convention. "Our job is to take prisoners, not kill them," he said.

One of the young men standing near George pointed to the screen. "There's the trouble with that war," he said. "They's a bunch of psychos runnin' wild over there."

Another looked over at George and noticed his short haircut. "Y'all a vet?"

George nodded.

The man pointed to the television. "What do you think a that?"

George had his mouth full, so he finished chewing. "I don't believe everything I see on TV." George took a sip of his beer. "Were you in Nam?"

"No."

"In the service anywhere?"

"No."

"Then you're clueless, so shut up about it." George began to eat again.

"You're pretty touchy. You like shootin' gooks?"

George set his fork and knife down, took the napkin from his lap, wiped his mouth, and laid the napkin on the bar.

"Here's the deal, dickhead. I spent this afternoon with the family of my Ranger team leader. He was gunned down while saving the life of another soldier. I just found out he committed suicide when he got home. So right now, I'm pretty pissed off."

As color rose in the guy's neck, George continued. "So I come in here, hoping to eat my dinner in peace, and you show up in your army dress-up clothes playing big-shot know-it-all. I don't need your shit right now, so buzz off before I kick your ass into next week."

The man stood up and started over toward George, pushing his friends aside. "You guys all come back, talking tough, chips on your shoulders," he said. "Well, y'all are in my corral now, and this ain't my first rodeo."

George eased off his stool to face the man. His leather jacket fell open to reveal his khaki army-issue T-shirt. "All right, numb nuts. Let's go outside, and you can try me out. I've been to a couple of rodeos myself."

The man's girlfriend looked George over. She stepped between them, wrapping her arms around her boyfriend. "Come on, Tommie," she said. "Let's go dance while you cool off." She tugged him out to the dance floor, looking back to see if George was following them.

"I coulda taken him," he said to her.

"Yeah, honey, I know, but you're with me tonight." The others drifted away from George, talking among themselves. George sat back down and started to eat. He pushed his plate away. The barmaid came over, turned her back on the other patrons, and spoke quietly.

"Sorry about that," she said. "Can I get you anything else? Warm up your food?"

"Just a check, please," George said. When the check came, George left cash on the bar. Then he rode on to Tulsa and spent the night at his dad's home.

The next morning, he called Sam again. He explained about Horse's suicide and the younger brother left behind. "I promised the kid I'd come back for him. If he doesn't get out of that hovel, he'll end up like his old man. I owe that much to Horse."

"You have any idea what you're in for?"

"Probably not, but it doesn't matter."

"George, honestly, that's a lot to take on. Maybe there are some things you can do short of assuming a parental role."

"What else could there be? He's either forced to stay on the reservation, or he finds another place to live. If it was just for school, maybe his father would consent. His mother's long gone."

"I'll speak with the company attorneys," Sam said. "They'd have to do some investigation, and the court would no doubt require that we find the mother, but it's probably workable." George authorized the expenditures from his funds. "If things can get started right away, then maybe we could get it done before school starts in the fall."

"One other thing, Sam. Horse is due a Purple Heart. Our commander also put him in for a Silver Star. Contact the senator and have him get those medals to us. I'll arrange for a ceremony to present them to his family."

CHAPTER THIRTEEN

George packed some clothes in his duffel, and by mid-afternoon, he found his mother's house in a Tulsa suburb. Entering through a gate framed by brick pillars, he rode up a winding driveway that ended in a half circle in front of a large Tudor-style house. Leaning the Harley on its stand, he walked past a VW microbus painted over in huge psychedelic flowers. On one side of the rear bumper there was a sticker: SAVE WATER. SHOWER WITH A FRIEND. The rear window showed a decal of a marijuana leaf. Inside, the windows were decorated with beaded curtains. An aluminum peace sign was mounted above the front bumper.

His mom greeted him at the door, throwing her arms around his neck. "George, honey," she said. She held him in a tight hug for a long time. "Thanks for coming."

She tugged at his arm to bring him inside the house. As they entered the foyer, Stan emerged from the living room. Away from the formalities and grief of the funeral and the trauma surrounding Horse's death, George relaxed and noticed his mother's beauty. Her dark hair, with a few streaks of gray, was pulled back into a tight bun. She was dressed simply in a cotton top and modest skirt, casual but still elegant. George guessed that Stan was a bit older. He had a thick shock of white hair but was erect and fit. He could see why his mother had chosen him.

"Good to see you again," Stan said. "I'm glad you could visit for a while." They shook hands. "I bet you could use a beer."

They walked through the living room into the den, a room elegantly paneled in walnut. Hanging on one wall behind the bar was a picture frame containing an army insignia and various badges and medals mounted on red felt. In the center was an army 119th Regiment patch surrounded by captain's bars, three unit citations, a European Theater medal, a Bronze Star, and a Purple Heart.

Stan pulled two bottles of Budweiser from the refrigerator. He held them up to George as if to ask if the brand was okay and popped the tops. He saw George looking at the medals.

"Ardennes, 1944, field promotion," Stan said.

"Battle of the Bulge?"

Stan nodded. George raised his beer, and their bottles clinked in a quick toast. Stan poured a glass of wine for Nancy, and they walked back into the living room past a white sofa. Two matching leather chairs flanked a glass coffee table over an oriental rug. George swept his arm in a gesture of silent compliment.

"Living well is the best revenge," Stan said.

Nancy led them toward double glass doors that separated the house from a swimming pool and patio. "George, come and meet Stan's son, Todd, and his friend," she said, sliding a door open.

They stepped onto the patio in front of a large rectangular pool. A young man and woman were stretched out on deck chairs, sunning. A James Brown song wailed on a portable radio at their feet.

"This is Todd and his friend Carolyn," Nancy said.

"How's it going?" Todd said as he straddled his deck chair, rising to shake George's hand.

"Peace," Carolyn said, raising her fingers in a V without getting up.

"George is home from Vietnam," Stan said. "His father just passed away. That was the funeral Nancy and I attended."

"Sorry," Carolyn said. "Had he been sick long?"

"No, not long. By the time they got word to me, he was nearly gone." George looked toward the music. "James Brown—I haven't heard him in a while."

Nancy explained that Todd and Carolyn had just graduated from college and were passing through on their way to the West Coast.

"I'm taking an MBA at Stanford this fall," Todd said. He tossed his head, flipping the long hair away from his eyes.

"Keeping the deferment alive," Stan said. There was a note of sarcasm in his voice.

"I'll go when I'm done," Todd said. Carolyn pulled her sunglasses down, shot a sharp look at Todd, and settled back into her chair.

"You're safe," George said. He looked back at Carolyn but couldn't see her eyes through her sunglasses. "It's all politics now. It'll be over by then."

Over the next few days, George and Stan talked about the war and Horse's death. Nancy hovered in the background, prodding quietly, talking future plans, finally politely asking about the black panther tattoo on George's bicep.

"It seemed like a good idea at the time," George said. "Horse and I were on R&R in Bangkok. We each got one, encouraged by a bit of alcohol."

"What does it mean?"

"We were thinking stealth," George said, "and a nasty bite." He chuckled. "It looks weird now back in civilization, but at least it's something to remember Horse by."

CHAPTER FOURTEEN

Carolyn and Todd were cordial but gave him a wide berth. George spent his mornings working out, running miles, doing rounds of push-ups and sit-ups, trying to stay fit. As he ran through the neighborhood, he could smell the fresh-cut grass, reminding him of the early summer two-a-day high school football practices when they were preparing for the season. But in the afternoon sun by the pool, the Oklahoma heat took over, and he could feel his head slipping. He began to notice Carolyn, her long straight hair, her sexy body that she flaunted casually while lounging by the pool in her bikini or just hanging out around the house, braless in a T-shirt and shorts. George couldn't imagine what she saw in the skinny, goateed Todd, but he resigned himself to the old high school credo that the dorks always got the best-looking women.

"Join us in the sauna," Carolyn chirped on the last afternoon. When George opened the sauna door, he was met by Carolyn's bare breasts. Todd was shaking his beer can, squirting her with fizz, and she was gyrating in a slow dance in front of him. As

George entered, she feigned surprise, then wrapped a towel around herself and sat on the bench. She took Todd's beer, leaned against him, and sipped from the can.

The sauna was like the midday jungle heat, intense, stifling. In Carolyn's scent, George flashed back to the steambaths in Nam. Returning from the jungle, when the men were allowed time back at the main bases, they went to the saunas expecting the steam to soak away the smell and rot of jungle warfare. "Steam 'n' creams," they called them, for the Vietnamese prostitutes who worked there. George stepped back outside to clear his head, showered, then joined Stan at the barbecue grill.

"What was the Ardennes like?" George asked.

Stan turned the tenderloins. He closed the grill again. "When the sun was out, the forest was beautiful even in the icy weather; but most of the time, we froze our butts off. We didn't have winter gear, and we couldn't build fires without attracting German fire. Most of our casualties came from frostbite and trench foot."

"The jungle was like that," George said. "It was everything all at once. Beautiful, terrifying, friend, enemy."

"What was it like," Stan asked, "to fight without any battle lines?"

"It got totally screwed up. We'd set up a firebase in the middle of nowhere. As soon as we arrived, the local Vietnamese would trade with us, selling food, that kind of thing. We were never sure if they were on our side and glad to have us there, or if they were reconning for the Viet Cong. Most nights, our perimeters would be tested by the VC. So we'd trade by day, fight by night.

"We'd be sent off on a mission to take some patch of ground at a huge cost of lives. Then we'd be ordered to give it up and chase after the enemy somewhere else. The VC always knew where we were, but they never stayed in one place."

"The media here never liked the war," Stan said. "They've had nothing good to say about it."

"They're right about part of it—the politics, anyway. We never had a clear mission because the bureaucrats couldn't decide why we were there."

Nancy came out onto the patio, carrying a tray with some snacks. "We're eating light tonight," she said, "so everything is ready when the meat is done."

"It's got a few minutes yet to cook," Stan said. "We've been exchanging war stories."

"Well, for now, let's put the war aside and enjoy the evening."

CHAPTER FIFTEEN

Three Songs, the tribe's medicine elder, was sipping coffee on his front steps when Hawk arrived the morning after George's visit. "You're late," he said.

Hawk nodded. "George Wheeler, my brother's friend, came yesterday. They were in Special Forces together."

"I heard that someone came. What did he tell you?"

"My brother was a hero in the war. That's how he got shot." Three Songs put his cup away and picked up a knapsack. He helped Hawk into the straps and then picked up his own pack. "Come on," he said. "We have things to do. We'll talk on the way."

They walked together toward the river while Three Songs listened to Hawk recount George's visit, retelling the stories about Horse. When they came to the cabin, Three Songs ushered him inside. "We'll stop here first," he said. "Close the door." Three Songs closed the damper on the stovepipe and then built a small fire, adding some sweet grass, dried mullein blossoms, and tobacco, allowing the smoke to leave the stove and fill the room. Together they sat on the rug over the bloodstains. "Close your eyes." As the smoke enveloped them, Three Songs sang in Cherokee and offered a prayer for Horse. When the fire had died out, Three Songs stood up. "It's good that George Wheeler came," he said.

They walked through the woods, following the river, gathering plants. Three Songs explained their uses. "When you gather a plant, always leave some untouched so that they will be there again when you need them."

When they finished the morning's lessons, they walked back to Three Songs' home. He looked at the sky. "Come back tonight," he said. "We'll study the stars."

That afternoon, the other boys gathered, as always, looking for things to do. As they hung out together, they asked about the guy on the motorcycle. "He was in my brother's unit," Hawk said. "He was with Horse when he got wounded." They began walking toward the river while Hawk talked. An older one was skeptical.

"If Horse was a hero, why'd he shoot himself?"

Hawk tackled him and shoved him to the ground, ready to punch the kid. The others pulled him off.

"Jeez," the kid said as he got up off the ground, brushing himself off. "I didn't mean nothing."

Hawk reached out to shake his hand. "I'm sorry," he said. "I think he felt he would be worthless after his wounds."

Another boy spoke up. "Maybe that's the way it should go. Who wants to be a cripple his entire life?"

The boys shuffled down the dusty road in silence. Finally, Hawk spoke again. "If I had been there with him, I could have stopped him."

When they reached the far edge of the field, they took the trail down toward the river. As they approached the water, one of the boys took off running, and the others followed. Next to the pool, they stripped and splashed into the water.

After cooling off, they sat on the bank skipping stones while the sun dried them.

The boys dressed and walked the river's edge, turning over rocks, playing into the late afternoon. They threw sticks as if they were spears, war whooped, and messed around until it was time to head home for dinner.

As Hawk got to his house, he sat on the front steps for a while before going inside. It had been a day since George had been there, and Hawk wondered when he would come back. His dad had said not to get his hopes up, but Hawk was sure that George would return.

CHAPTER SIXTEEN

After dinner on their last evening together, George, Todd, and Carolyn sat together on the back patio, drinking beer and watching the sun go down.

"We're leaving tomorrow," Carolyn said, tilting her head toward George.

"Where are you going?"

"We have an apartment in Berkeley. I've got a job waiting. Todd starts grad school."

"Well, good luck to you both."

"Would you mind telling me about the war?"

"Uh, Carolyn?" Todd said, "Maybe it's not a good time for George to talk about it."

"What do you want to know?" George said.

"Were you in combat?"

"Yes."

"What was it like?"

"You don't really want to know."

"I would."

"Carolyn, let's not talk about this now." Todd put his hand on her shoulder, but she brushed it away.

"It's all right," George said. He looked over at Carolyn. "I was part of a team."

"Which means?" Carolyn asked.

"We did what had to be done."

"Sorry, I still don't get it."

George explained the army's counterinsurgency tactics in broad brushstrokes—how they mixed with the Vietnamese villagers, trying to win them over and get information. He talked about the Viet Cong and his team's long-range reconnaissance, the night ambushes, and the air strikes called in on VC compounds. He described their efforts to disrupt enemy supply depots and command centers and the fierce firefights with the tenacious NVA fighters. He talked with pride, partly from strength, partly thinking that his warrior skills would impress Carolyn. Finally, she interrupted him.

"How could you tell the enemy from the civilians?" Carolyn asked.

"They were usually trying to kill us."

"What about the peasants, the women, their children?"

"Sometimes they were combatants, and sometimes they were civilians caught in the middle."

"So the pictures we've seen of the burned villages, the dead women, the homeless children, those are all true?"

"Every day a GI dies because a kid hands him a live hand grenade or because a Viet Cong, dressed as a peasant, sets a land mine. Some villages were set up to be VC ambush sites. Our rules were simple. If we received fire, we returned fire. If we faced a threat, we trashed it. It was life or death, kill or be killed."

They sat again in silence.

"War was black and white for you, wasn't it?" Carolyn said.

"That's how I stayed alive," George said. "There are no shades of gray. Gray is a good way to die." They were quiet for a while. George crushed the beer can in his hand, and then spoke again.

"Gray is guys on drugs, guys who trust that things will work out all right, guys who fall in love and get homesick, guys who take too long to act and don't rely on their own instincts. Soldiers who want to stay alive stick with black and white. You choose instantly. Yes or no. Shoot or don't shoot. Live or die."

"My God," she said under her breath.

Darkness settled in, enveloping the patio lights. The summer air was still hot and humid. A june bug, attracted to the lights, crashed into Todd's chair and landed upside down on the patio. It buzzed frantically trying to right itself. George thought of Horse lying on his back on the ground as they waited for the dustoff. George was furious, yelling at the medics to work faster while he held Horse's hand. "Stay awake," he kept saying. "Stay with me." He could still smell the dirt and exhaust that sprayed over him when the choppers finally lifted off with the wounded.

George blinked away the scene at the landing zone, drained his beer, and retrieved another one. He looked directly at Carolyn. "Why do you care, anyway?" he said. "It's nothing to you."

"Don't be so self-righteous. I do care."

"Carolyn has volunteered at a VA hospital," Todd said.

"And?" George said.

"And," she said, "I can see in black and white, too."

"You two risk nothing, but you question everything."

"Peace is black and white," she said. "Gray is young men maimed or dying for no good reason, homes destroyed, families disrupted, countries overrun for political or economic reasons."

"You have no idea," George said. A cooler breeze filtered past them. Carolyn pulled a cigarette pack from Todd's pocket, lit one, and took a long drag. Her hands were shaking.

"I do have an idea," she said. "I know about the French rubber plantations, the offshore oil in the South China Sea. Black and white may have kept you alive, but war is waged in shades of gray." Her voice cracked as she laid her head on Todd's shoulder.

George silently recalled his commanders' briefings describing the early British explorations for oil in the region, how certain French plantations were declared off limits and, as a result, became VC sanctuaries. In a burst of sarcasm, to piss off the French, he and Horse had blown up a fountain in the middle of a circular drive in front of a French villa. "No pain, no gain," Horse had said, laughing. For good measure, they had called in napalm over the villa's fields of rubber trees. George pulled himself out of his chair.

"Don't believe everything the media tells you," he said. He raised his shoe over the june bug as if to squash it, hesitated, then flipped it over with his toe. The buzzing stopped.

Carolyn lifted her head from Todd's shoulder. "What are you living for now, George?" she asked. "What are your hopes and dreams?"

George stared down at his hands. He hadn't expected the question and realized he didn't have an answer. He finished his beer and crushed the can in one hand. He dropped it into the trash container at the edge of the patio. "For now, I'm going to bed."

George woke early, struggling out of a dream. He was in Nam again, alone, entangled in the dense foliage. He was trying to escape. He could hear voices all around him speaking in Vietnamese. The jungle rustled with their presence. Firefights flashed in the background. His compass face was blank, the radio dead. Capture was imminent. When he woke, he was twisted in his bedcovers.

Untangling himself, he rolled out of bed. Still in shorts and T-shirt, he went to the kitchen looking for coffee. Carolyn was there, in a nightgown, looking into the refrigerator. She jumped when George walked in. "Sorry," he said. "I didn't mean to startle you. Just wanted to make some coffee."

"That's okay. I couldn't sleep."

"That's my line," George said.

Carolyn closed the refrigerator. "I'm going up to get dressed. Then maybe I'll come back for that coffee." She pressed against him, wrapping her arms around him, holding on to him until he finally embraced her. She let him rub her back through the thin nightgown, kissed his neck, and slowly pulled away, feeling the strength in his arms and shoulders. George realized it was the first time he'd held a woman since he'd gone in-country. He'd forgotten the warmth and excitement it generated.

Carolyn's eyes were misty. "I can't imagine what it must have been like over there," she said softly, "but I'm glad you're home."

CHAPTER SEVENTEEN

Back at his dad's place, George called Earl again. "We need some R&R," he said. "I'll fire up the grill. How about tomorrow night?"

"I'll be there."

"Any of the rest of our team around?"

"A few. I'll get them."

About six o'clock the next day, a covey of motorcycles and pickups arrived. "I found these homeless guys on the street," Earl said. "Figured we'd feed them, put them up for the night."

They were the remnants of their high school football team, those still living around Tulsa. George had played nose tackle beside Earl, the center. The others played various positions on their team. Earl carried in a couple of bags of groceries. "C rats," he said. He put the steaks in the refrigerator, set a bottle of Jack Daniels on the counter. Some others brought in coolers of iced beer. George had already wrapped some potatoes in foil and turned on the oven. He cut up the start of a salad. Earl poured generous shots of the Jack around. He handed one to George. They all clinked glasses.

"State champs," someone said, and they drained their shots in one swallow. Earl poured another round. "Come outside," he said. "Got something to show you."

Earl climbed up into the bed of his pickup and pulled a tarp back to reveal a black Harley strapped into the bed.

"Your coming-home present," he said. "I know you already own one, but this is a newer model. Try it out for a couple of weeks. If you like it, you can pay me for it—you being a rich GI back from the war and all."

"Man, this is great," George said. "Where'd you get this?"

"I own a shop now. I restore and customize bikes. Rescued this wreck and rebuilt it."

They wheeled it off the truck bed. George straddled it, kick-started it, and revved it up. He rode it down the end of the drive and back a couple of times and parked it by the garage. "It's good," he said. "You've got a deal."

After dinner, they all sat on the patio, the coolers of beer at their feet, talking Oklahoma football and women.

"I can't wait for the season to start," George said. "I haven't seen a live game for a while."

Eventually, the discussion turned to the war. "It's totally screwed up, thanks to McNamara and his lapdogs," George said.

"Ever notice," Earl said, "that no one seems to care that we're back?"

George looked at Earl. "No kidding. I've already had my fill of it."

"Right after I got home," Earl said, "I went to an Am Vets meeting. You'd a thought I was the enemy. Them World War Two guys wouldn't have nothin' to do with me—like the war was my fault. To hear them tell it, they was the only ones ever in a war. I decided I'd never go back. Do my own thing."

"Just one more insult," George said. "The gates outside Travis were lined with protesters when I came home. I wore my uniform to the airport to get the discounted fares. I could feel the tension—thought maybe I had leprosy."

"So some of us are into POWs and MIAs. There's some guys who got the short end of the stick. A vet from my unit told me about a group in California that was started by the wife of a downed pilot. They're starting to get some traction."

"You heard of Admiral McCain?" Someone said. "His son's a navy pilot, shot down over Nam. They put him in the Hanoi Hilton. All of a sudden, Congress is beginning to pay attention."

"The problem," George said, "is the government just wants to be done with the war, whatever the cost."

"The guys left behind will be lost forever unless something happens."

"My dad had some connections," George said. "His partner, Sam, would know them. When I get settled, maybe we could rattle some cages. Help out."

By early morning, the beer was gone, the venting finished. "You guys better crash here for the night," George said. "You're all too drunk to drive home."

CHAPTER EIGHTEEN

While he was awaiting the results of the legal investigation, George called Albert and arranged a few days of camping on the reservation with Hawk and Three Songs. By then, George had purchased a used pickup. He loaded it with some camping gear and food and drove to the reservation. Hawk was sitting on his front steps, holding the tomahawk pouch. He jumped off the porch as George pulled in. "Here it is," he said, handing George the pouch. They walked around, looking at the truck. Albert shuffled to the door.

"You're welcome to join us," George said.

"Naw, you boys go on," Albert said. "Have a good time."

George and Hawk drove to the river and found Three Songs already there, waiting.

"I don't want to stay in the cabin," Hawk said.

"No worries," George said. "We'll sleep in the tent. I like it better outdoors, anyway."

George assembled his fly rod and tied a leader and a small weight to the line. He handed the rod to Hawk along with a pair of sunglasses. "These are mostly for eye protection," he said. "When you're casting a fly, the wind can easily take it, and you don't want to get snagged in the eye by a returning fly. The polarization will help you see through the water, too." George showed Hawk the casting motion and let him get the hang of it.

"The idea is to let the line ahead of the leader hit the water first," George said, "so that the fly makes a natural-looking landing." He took Hawk to the river's edge. "Practice casting out into the river. Then we'll move over to the pool."

After some practice casts, George replaced the weight with a fly he tied to the line.

Hawk moved over into the shallow water and began to cast into the fast water of the rapids, gradually working out into the deeper pool. George went back and sat on the ground next to Three Songs and watched. "The kid's a natural," George said.

Hawk made a series of casts, working back and forth across the pool. "Got one," he finally said and began to play the line in.

"Keep your rod tip up," George said, "and work him over into the shallow water where I can reach him. Don't rush it—let him tire out." Hawk played the fish carefully into the shallows, and George retrieved it and removed the fly. He held it up for Hawk to see before putting it in a large pot he'd filled with water. "A couple more like that, and we've got dinner."

They fished all afternoon. Hawk lost some but managed to catch enough for their meal. George found a flat piece of wood and asked Hawk to get another pot of water. Before the fish were cleaned, Three Songs placed his hand on the fish and said a prayer. He spoke to Hawk. "It's important to remember that the fish gave its life to feed us." George then laid a trout on the wood and demonstrated how to gut it, leaving the head on. Then he put the gutted fish into the bucket, rinsing it off.

"We don't have to skin these," he said. "Trout are tender and cook more easily with the skin on." He turned the knife over to Hawk. "Your turn."

When the fish were cleaned, George washed them again. He dumped the water, and Hawk refilled the pot for the fish. "The cold water will keep them fresh until we're ready to cook," George said.

Three Songs had already started potatoes and onions frying and had some canned vegetables sitting in the coals warming. George found a small tree, and Hawk helped him cut some saplings, then trimmed the branches to make spits. George inserted the saplings up through the throats of the fish, and then tied the fish over the trimmed branches. He held one over the coals, showing Hawk how to cook them. "These won't take long," he said, giving the others to Hawk to cook.

After dinner, they sat around the fire pit. "There's a lot of land here. Is it owned by the tribe?"

Hawk replied. "My grandfather Manawa received this farm when the Cherokee were resettled in Oklahoma. It was a hundred and sixty acres then, but Dad sold some of it for the other homes you see near us. There's about one hundred acres left."

"Over the years," Three Songs said, "the government has tried to get it back, and others have tried to buy it, but Manawa wouldn't sell. Albert inherited it, and he's holding it for Hawk."

"It's a nice property," George said. "It's good that the family has kept it."

Three Songs stood up and pointed to the western sky, where a huge anvil was forming in the distance. Lightning was shooting from the anvil to the ground, and they watched the rain march across the prairie. "That will pass away from us," Three Songs said, "but we should get the gear under cover just in case we get some rain from the edge of that storm."

Hawk and George cut up the rest of the wood. Sitting on a stump, George showed Hawk how to split a log using the ax and another piece of wood to drive the head of the ax. "Saves on toes," he said. "That's not the kind of accident you want when you're out away from civilization."

As Hawk fished the next morning, George and Three Songs talked together.

"You know Hawk's situation," George said. "That's no way for a kid to live. I'd be willing to work out an arrangement to let him live with me and go to school in Tulsa."

"It's not a simple request," Three Songs said. "It will be a burden on you. Hawk also needs to spend time here. I know that his dad is an alcoholic, but Hawk needs to understand how much his dad has meant to the community. All the houses around their cabin are there because Albert sold people land at very modest prices. It was the old way of *gadugi*, one Cherokee helping another. Albert has the only house with running water, so he lets the neighbors come to draw from his well. When Horse died, the neighbors tried to convince Albert to let him be honored by the tribe, but Albert just couldn't get over the suicide or the feeling that his family was somehow disgraced by it."

"It's made a big impact on Hawk," George said. "He and his brother were very close."

"While Charles is unhappy with his dad's decision, he also has a lot of his dad's native pride. He's headstrong, but one of the few kids who's fluent in our language, all because his dad insisted that he speak Cherokee first, before ever learning English. And Charles is the only one who's expressed interest in learning about Cherokee lore. I want to teach him all I can before he gets out of high school."

"He's a good kid. I'm sure we could work out a schedule for that."

"Albert would also have to cooperate, and I'm not sure he would think that it would be good for Charles to attend a school away from here."

"Has Albert ever tried to shake the booze?"

"Many times. He's given up because it's very difficult. And treatment is expensive."

"Would he be willing to try again?"

"Honestly, I can't say for sure."

"I don't know what's involved," George said, "but you have my word that I'll look after Hawk, and I'll do whatever I can to help his dad as well."

They sat in silence for a while enjoying the morning sun, watching Hawk. "One other thing," George said. "Horse was a hero in the war. I'm getting his medals delivered. I'd like to present them to the family, but I also would like the tribe to consider honoring him for his service according to your customs."

"That would take the approval of the elders," Three Songs said.

"If you would allow it, I will come and tell Horse's story. I owe my life to him, and he deserves to be honored as a warrior."

"I will consult the elders."

CHAPTER NINETEEN

After the senator's office delivered Horse's medals, George called Three Songs to arrange the meeting with the elders. They met in the community lodge, a round log structure located near the school. Initially, Albert did not want the meeting, but Three Songs convinced him to let George talk with the elders. George dressed for the meeting in his combat fatigues. At the elders' invitation, George sat cross-legged on the dirt floor. Hawk and Albert were also there, allowed to attend the session on the strict instruction that they were only visitors and would not have a say in the proceedings.

The ceremony began with a rite of purification. Three Songs began chanting in his native tongue as he placed cedar boughs, sweetgrass, sage, and tobacco on a low fire in the center, causing a fine pungent smoke to fill the room. George had been told that he would be given permission to speak, but only after the elders had considered the matter and the purification rites had been completed.

In a small pine box, Hawk carried the ribbons and insignias from Horse's uniform along with the Purple Heart and Silver Star.

After Three Songs' rites, there was a long pause as the chief elder, with a head motion, silently questioned the other elders. Each nodded in affirmation.

A ceremonial pipe was passed among the elders and then offered to George.

"Smoke that you may tell the truth," said the elder who passed him the pipe.

George took a long drag to fill his lungs, held it in with his eyes closed, then slowly exhaled. "Walking Horse was a great warrior," George said. "While he died by his own hand, his death occurred because of the severe injuries he sustained in battle. He was my brother in war. He was courageous. He saved my life at great risk to his own. I have come to ask you to open your hearts to him, to offer him the rites given to all great Cherokee warriors. If you will listen, I will tell his story and ask that you honor him with a new name."

George sat silently and looked into the face of each elder in turn. After a long pause, the chief elder spoke. "You may tell us the story of Joseph Walking Horse."

George began when he first met Horse on his arrival at a remote firebase in Nam. Horse had preceded him there by several months and was already experienced. "I'll teach you the ropes," Horse had told him.

"Horse was an extraordinary soldier," George continued. "He could move quickly through the jungle in complete silence. He always knew his position and where his men were. He was ferocious and fearless in battle, often taking risks others wouldn't dare." George paused.

"Albert Manawa has always spoken to his sons in Cherokee. As a result, Horse was fluent in his native tongue. When he was in Vietnam, Joseph also learned to speak Vietnamese. He was able to converse with the peasants. He understood their customs. He was proud of his Cherokee heritage, but he was also respectful of the Vietnamese culture and fought hard for them."

George took the box of medals from Hawk. "On the day he earned these medals, he saved my life. We were dropped into an ambush, and Horse was the first to recognize it. He pulled me to the ground even before the enemy fire began. Without his action, I would have been killed."

George concluded his story by reading the citation written by Horse's commanding officer commending Horse for the Silver Star.

> **First Lieutenant Joseph Walking Horse Manawa is hereby awarded the Silver Star for conspicuous gallantry and intrepid actions on 16 March 1969, while assigned to a Special Forces Long Range Reconnaissance Platoon attached to the First Brigade, 101st Airborne Division. During its operation, the reconnaissance platoon came under heavy fire from a numerically superior enemy force. Recognizing that a squad of his platoon was pinned down by intense enemy fire from crew-served weapons and grenades, Lieutenant Manawa, without covering fire, was able to reach the endangered squad and lead them to safety. Lieutenant Manawa then returned twice to recover two severely wounded squad point soldiers. On his second return, Lieutenant Manawa carried a wounded comrade through heavy fire back to safety. As he reached his unit's perimeter, Lieutenant Manawa himself was severely wounded in the hips and legs by enemy machine-gun fire and grenade fragments. Disregarding his own life, Lieutenant Manawa saved the lives of several of his comrades under the most extreme combat conditions. His extraordinary heroism in rescuing the wounded, while**

repeatedly risking his own life for his fellow soldiers, is in keeping with the highest traditions of military service and reflects great credit upon himself, his unit, and the US Army.

George paused, letting the citation sink in. "With your permission," he said finally, "we will now leave you to consider this matter. Thank you. We will abide by your wisdom." The elders near the door moved aside to allow Hawk, Albert, and George to exit.

It was night then, and the huge Oklahoma sky was clear, filled with brilliant stars. The three stood in silence in the cool night air. Albert stood beside Hawk, one hand on his shoulder. A lone shooting star made an arc across the sky.

Within the hour, the elders emerged from the lodge. The chief approached Albert. "We have heard the words of your son's friend, George Wheeler, and we believe he speaks the truth. We ask your permission to hold the ceremony honoring your son."

Albert nodded. "I consent."

The chief continued, "In keeping with our custom, we have given your son a new name because of his great strength and courage. From this day forward, he will be known as Stalking Bear." Each of the elders then passed by and shook their hands. To George, each said, "The friend of Stalking Bear." To Hawk, each said "Stalking Bear's brother." And finally to Albert, they said, "Stalking Bear's father."

CHAPTER TWENTY

The weekend celebrating Stalking Bear's life as a warrior began with a day of fellowship, the tribal members providing a potluck banquet followed by traditional dancing. The day concluded with an evening rite of purification in the lodge. George dressed in his class-A uniform. On a table in the lodge, Hawk and George had arranged Stalking Bear's uniform dress jacket and some framed photos of Stalking Bear taken in Nam. A solitary eagle feather lay across his jacket. The box of medals and the flag were placed beside Horse's uniform.

After the purification rites, George read Stalking Bear's commendation. Then the elders told stories of other tribal heroes.

The next day at dawn, a procession assembled at the edge of the community. Men, dressed in their traditional native dress, lined the road, some on horseback. Those who were veterans also wore some remnant of their uniforms, including their battle ribbons and medals. Each veteran had an eagle feather attached to his headdress. Behind a solitary drummer, the elders walked at the front of the procession followed by Hawk, leading a riderless horse.

George, again in full dress uniform, walked with Albert. Two of Hawk's friends carried a small pine box with Stalking Bear's medals pinned to black velvet and a folded American flag that George's senator had flown over the Capitol building and then sent to George for the ceremony. As the procession wound through the crowd-lined street, women sang their high-pitched ululations, and the men yelled war cries. Otherwise, the only sound was the slow beat of the drum. As the procession passed by, spectators fell in behind and walked with the group.

At Horse's grave site in the community cemetery, the chief elder spoke the eulogy in his native tongue, concluding by saying the name "Stalking Bear," which was then spoken in unison by the gathering.

George had installed a new monument inscribed with Stalking Bear's name, rank, and the earned medals. Three Songs offered more prayers, and then a bugler, arranged by George with the permission of the elders, played taps.

As the ceremony concluded, each of the tribe members came forward and shook George's hand and then warmly embraced Hawk and his dad. As they left, Albert thanked George. "You have brought honor to my family," he said. "I will not forget that."

CHAPTER TWENTY-ONE

In a telephone call, Sam described the attorney he had hired on George's behalf. "I've retained Christine O'Donnell," he said. "She'll be a good match to assist you. Part Cherokee, part Irish, she's dealt with a number of cases involving abuse and neglect of Indian children. Before she joined the firm, she was an assistant prosecutor, did some felony prosecutions, and then worked for the Oklahoma Children's Services Bureau. She's agreed to take on your case. You'll be hearing from her when she completes her investigation."

While George was awaiting Christine's report, he rode out to visit Earl at his place of business, Earl's Choppers, located in an old warehouse at the fringe of Tulsa's downtown. The outside of the warehouse looked shabby, but as George walked through the sliding metal doors, he was surprised at the sight inside. It was a huge, neatly kept garage full of motorcycles in various states of repair or modification. The place was buzzing with men working on the bikes.

A voice called from the back, "Yo, Wheeler." Earl emerged from a fenced-in stock area. He was in coveralls, sporting a red headband that had a white peace symbol on it. Earl had added the words *is for pussies* in black ink.

"I been working on something," Earl said. "It's over here." Earl directed George to an object covered by a large tarp. Earl pulled the cover back to reveal a three-wheeled motorcycle.

"Another salvage job?"

Earl smiled. "Look at the modifications. I put all the controls on the handlebars. This would have worked for your friend Horse."

"How'd you know how to do this?"

"I started a few years ago when one of my friends came back injured like Horse. In his case, he lost both legs just above the knees. Once we get all the controls worked out, I'll start making these on special orders. We can do the same with regular motorcycles as well. By the way, we're taking a ride this weekend. You're welcome to join us."

"Angels?"

"Some, but it's not exclusive. You just have to be able to drink, ride, and sometimes fight."

"I'll be there."

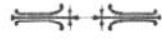

Saturday morning, George arrived to find the group already gathering. They were milling around, puttering with engines, and shouting insults at one another. A man in leathers approached Earl and George. He was smaller than Earl but wiry, head shaved clean except for his Fu Manchu. A tattoo collar of barbed wire wound around his neck.

"This here's Foster," Earl said. "He's a vet, too. Marines."

Foster and George shook hands. "Call me Fuzzy," Foster said.

"Fuzzy will ride beside you," Earl said. "Get you used to the group travel plan."

Earl went back into his garage and came out carrying a bunch of flags.

George unfurled one, held it up between them. It was an American flag, with a black pennant mounted below the flag. "I contacted the organization in California to ask about a flag, but they don't have one designed yet. So I figured we'd just use black and start flying these off our bikes."

Earl handed them out for mounting on the cycles. After the flags were secured, Earl mounted up. Darlene, a handsome woman with long bleached-blond hair, dressed in leathers with the Angels' chapter colors on the back, climbed up behind Earl. By then all of the cycles were idling. A burly man named Lead Dog roared out of the parking lot, followed by the group, riding in pairs.

In the late afternoon, they stopped at a roadside bar across from a cheap motel.

"In the old days," Earl said, "we would've camped on the ground. We're past that now."

They pulled tables together, brought the waitress over, and got her started bringing boilermakers. After the first round, Earl clinked a knife on his glass and stood up. "This here's George Wheeler. I invited him along today as my guest. He's very shy and quiet, so I thought maybe he needed to meet some new friends—polite ones like you."

"He could be our song leader," someone said. "We like hymns, mostly, like 'Kumbaya' or 'Peace Like a River.'"

"What's with the hair?"

"It's how they wear it in Nam," Earl said.

"Where'd you serve?"

"Northern provinces, mostly. DMZ," George said.

"You ever go in the tunnels?"

"Hell, no. We blew 'em—nothing there but snakes and booby traps."

"What was your unit?"

"Rangers. Before I left, we were doing recon for the 101st Air Cav."

They all banged their bottles on the tables in recognition.

Lead Dog stood up. "A toast to Wheeler. Welcome back to the world, soldier. You can ride with us anytime."

They spent the evening occupying half the bar, raucous, daring anyone to complain. No one took them on, and the bartender looked relieved when they closed up for the night without incident.

CHAPTER TWENTY-TWO

September 1969

Back home in Tulsa, a few days later, the mail brought Christine's legal memorandum. It was helpful but not encouraging. After reviewing the document, George called and set an appointment to meet with her personally.

The lobby of the law firm, plush and formal, was exactly the kind of place where George imagined his dad would have sought his legal advice. As he came off the elevator, an older woman dressed in a neat suit with stylishly short gray hair came around the desk to greet him.

"You probably don't remember me," she said. "I'm Alice Knowlton. Your dad brought you here years ago for a tour of the offices."

"Pleased to meet you," he said. "Honestly, I don't remember—I was probably awestruck."

"Have a seat. I'll let Ms. O'Donnell know you're here."

George settled into a chair and picked up a magazine from the nearby end table. It made a useful screen allowing him to survey the waiting room. As young attorneys bustled through the lobby, he tried to guess which one was Christine. A voice from behind startled him.

A woman approached and extended her hand. "Mr. Wheeler," she said. "I'm Christine O'Donnell."

In his mind, he had visualized an older-looking woman, conservatively dressed, but was greeted by tall elegance, a full head of red curly hair, green eyes, and a copper complexion reminiscent of the young Cherokee women he had seen at the reservation. She was svelte and athletic-looking, dressed in a dark suit over a simple white blouse. The only sign of adornment was a pair of dangling silver earrings, which George guessed were made by an Indian silversmith. She was carrying a client folder and a yellow legal pad.

Inside the conference room, she pulled out a leather chair at one side of the walnut table. A coffeepot and monogrammed mugs sat on a tray in the middle of the table. She motioned to the coffee, and when George nodded, she poured a cup first for him, then for herself.

She opened the folder labeled "Charles Soaring Hawk Manawa."

"I want to do whatever it takes to assist Charles," he said. "Cost is no barrier."

"Of course, we will pull out all of the stops if that's what you insist on. However, I think you would agree that our main task is to help Charles succeed without having to dislodge him from the tribe."

"So far, they haven't done much for him."

"The elders may be reluctant to interfere, but if they were asked, they might be willing to assist. If we stir up a hornet's nest around his mother, Charles could be placed in jeopardy. The courts would have no problem giving her custody if she appears to be a better alternative."

"She's ignored him for over a year. How could some judge make that decision?"

"With all due respect for the courts," she said, "most judges will opt for the easy decision, which means biological parents. It's simpler, it's legally sustainable, and they won't get their dockets tangled up with long proceedings. In all likelihood, a magistrate would hear the case, then make the usual recommendations necessary to move it along. Any private deal we could make would be better than that." She walked across the room and looked out the window. Then she returned and leaned on the back of her chair.

"One more thing," she said. "Don't take offense, but you're young, unmarried, and a veteran, and you have no parental qualifications. The court might not seriously consider you as a suitable custodian for Charles."

George slammed his hand on the table. "If I was good enough to fight for this country, I should be good enough to be a parent."

Unfazed by George's outburst, she motioned for him to relax. "You passed my first test," she said. "I wanted to be sure that you felt strongly about your position. Even though you have no parenting skills, your youth might be an asset, not a problem."

George slumped back in his chair and laughed, mostly at himself. "I guess you got me. Tell me what we should do."

She opened a folder and brought out some legal papers. "These are samples of temporary guardianship papers required by the Tulsa schools," she said. "We can't get Charles registered at a school off the reservation without these. We'll need his dad's signature. Do you think he'll agree?"

"Clearly Charles wants to do this. I think if he's there, he can help get his dad to go along with it. He can always go home on the weekends. I've also talked to Three Songs, the medicine elder who's close to the family. Charles has been working with him to learn Cherokee heritage ways. Three Songs seems willing to assist so long as Charles can spend time with him as well."

"Transportation back and forth could be a bit of an issue."

"I can take care of that," George said.

"For starters, we could go out to see Mr. Manawa and Three Songs together, but we need to do it soon to get Charles properly registered. School's already started. They'll have to accommodate him a bit as a new enrollee."

"Do you need to go with me?"

"The documents have to be notarized, which I can take care of. It might also be handy to have me there to answer any technical questions. I haven't met Mr. Manawa, but I've had some contact with Three Songs in past cases."

"Anytime you say."

"I'll go ahead and prepare these papers. We'll set a time for you to come in next week to review everything. Then we'll go to the reservation."

CHAPTER TWENTY-THREE

George rode out to the reservation on Friday afternoon and found Hawk hanging out with his friend Zeke. Hawk introduced Zeke. George walked over to the old pickup sitting in the yard.

"I been thinkin' about this truck," George said. He rubbed his hand along the hood. "It looks to be in pretty good shape."

"Hasn't been run for a while," Hawk said. "Not since Dad lost his license."

"Ever try to start it?"

"Yeah, Dad tried, but the battery's dead."

"Pretty soon, you'll be eligible to get a learner's permit. It wouldn't hurt to have something to drive around the farm, to practice on."

"You know anything about fixing trucks?" Zeke asked.

"A little. But it'd be a piece of cake for my friend Earl."

"I'll get Dad," Hawk said. "See what he says."

Hawk ran in the house and came out with Albert.

"What do you think, Dad? Can we fix it?"

"Okay with me," Albert said. "It's not doing any good a-sittin' there like that."

George pulled his truck up and retrieved a set of jumper cables from behind his driver's seat. He opened the hood of both trucks and connected the cables. "Albert, you got a key?"

Albert went back inside the cabin and came out again with a key ring.

George started up his truck. Then Albert cranked his truck's starter. The engine groaned and fired on a couple of cylinders, then kicked over and idled roughly. George turned his truck off and disconnected the cables. After Albert's truck had run a bit, he turned it off. George checked the oil level.

"Oil's a bit low," he said, "and we'll want to change it, get a new battery, and tune it up. But it seems to be all there."

"I've got a jack," Albert said. "We can pull the wheel and get a new tire put on."

"While we're in town getting the tire fixed," George said, "we'll get the registration updated so that it's legal to drive. Then we'll get Earl out here and get this jitney back up and running."

While they were pulling the tire, Hawk said, "I saw Stalking Bear in a dream last night. We were down at the cabin. He looked good. He was wearing a necklace of bear claws. I tried to apologize for not taking the gun, but he held his hand up and smiled. Then he crossed the river. I tried to follow, but he turned into a bear and ran off."

"It's a good sign," Albert said. "He's on his way, but you'll see him again."

They got the wheel off and put it into the back of George's truck. Albert pulled George aside.

"I don't have no money to pay for this," Albert said.

"Don't worry," George said. "Earl and I will handle it."

The following week, Earl came out with one of his mechanics. They put in a new battery. By then, the tire had been replaced and new license plates put on.

"It'd be best if I could take it into the shop," Earl said. "I've got the tools there to fix it right." With Earl following, the mechanic drove the truck back to Tulsa to finish the tune-up. Hawk rode in with George and got a tour of Earl's shop.

CHAPTER TWENTY-FOUR

At his next appointment, Christine took George to her office. "The conference rooms are all booked with larger meetings," she said. They walked through a maze of hallways until they reached a sign that read CHRISTINE O'DONNELL on the wall next to an office.

"Sorry, it's a bit of a mess," she said.

"Guess you've never seen the inside of a hootch in Nam. This looks pretty good to me."

He looked around the room. There were stacks of files on the credenza behind the desk. Framed photos of southwestern landscapes were mounted on the walls. A Pentax 35-mm camera with a telephoto lens sat on the corner of the desk. George looked at the photos and then picked up the camera.

"This yours?"

She nodded. "A hobby of mine. I keep a camera around in case something pops up."

He nodded to the photos on the wall. "So you took these?"

"Last year, when I was backpacking in Yosemite."

"They're beautiful."

He aimed the camera at her; adjusted the zoom. "Blam."

Christina took the camera and pointed it at him. "Soldiers say *blam*. Photographers say *click*."

"Let me try that again."

She set the camera down on her desk. "Tell you what," she said. "Your meter's running, so let's skip the horseplay and get to work."

She spread out the papers in front of them. "We could go to see Albert tomorrow morning. I had a trial cancel, so the day's free."

"Maybe when we get back," George said, "I could take you to dinner."

"You mean on a date?"

George laughed. "Yeah, I guess you could call it that."

"That's nice of you to ask," she said. "But I don't date my clients and"—she paused—"I'm in a relationship."

George held up his hands in a half surrender. "Got it," he said.

Christine swiveled in her chair and moved the camera to her credenza next to a framed photo showing her and another woman, taken in a southwestern landscape.

"I'd like to learn photography," George said.

"There are lots of technical programs around. You could use the GI Bill for the tuition. If you really want to become good at it, you should start there."

After they reviewed the papers, she walked him back to the lobby. "Be here by about eight tomorrow."

CHAPTER TWENTY-FIVE

At their meeting on the reservation, Albert seemed okay about Hawk living with George.

Three Songs was less enthusiastic. "I'm worried about him losing his connection with the tribe here. I've seen it happen when kids leave. They get used to life off the reservation and never come back."

They discussed Hawk visiting on weekends to continue his training with Three Songs. In the end, Albert signed the papers, but on the condition that Hawk would come back if he didn't follow through in his training with Three Songs. Christine took the documents back to her office. "These will be filed with the court tomorrow," she said. "We should have them back in about a week to ten days. Then we can go to the school and make the final arrangements."

George was up early the next day, resolved to explore the University of Tulsa and see about fall admission for himself.

As he approached the campus, he passed a coffee shop that looked like it was opening. He made a U-turn and parked his motorcycle at the curb.

A young woman, George guessed a student, was setting up the outdoor tables, getting ready for the day.

"Are you open?" he asked.

"In a few minutes," she said. "Have a seat, and I'll bring you some coffee as soon as it finishes brewing."

"Nice morning," George said.

"My favorite shift," she said. "I like watching the day arrive."

She disappeared into the pastry shop.

As George sat down at a table up against the building, he pulled a small book from his jacket pocket. She brought a coffee mug and a carafe and poured the coffee. She set a menu card on the table with silverware.

"Sugar or cream?"

"No, thanks, just black."

"So, Mr. Wheeler, would you like anything to eat?"

"A glazed doughnut would work." He handed her back the menu. "How'd you know my name?"

She pointed to the patch on his fatigue jacket. "A lot of kids are wearing those jackets with someone else's name on them. In your case, you looked like the true owner."

He smiled. "You pay attention."

"When'd you get back?"

"A couple of months ago."

"Vietnam?"

George nodded, looked at her apron. "So, you must be Ms. Bakery. Campus Bakery. Campus is an unusual name for a woman, but I like it."

"My name's Melanie, actually. You can call me Mel."

"I'm George."

"I'll get your doughnut."

Other customers began drifting in. They seemed to be regulars the way they bantered with her. Some made conversation. As she made her rounds, she dropped off the doughnut and refilled his mug.

"What are you reading?" She nodded at his book.

George pointed the cover at her so that she could read the title. "*A Coney Island of the Mind*," he said. "Lawrence Ferlinghetti."

"I've heard the name. Any good?"

"I just started it. I found it in a bookstore. Liked the cover."

"I think he was on campus last year," she said. "A beat poet."

"Does reading the book make me look like an intellectual?"

She laughed. "Let the hair grow a bit longer," she said. "Maybe add a beard."

She refilled George's cup again and circulated, not too close, but not so far away that he couldn't talk if he wanted to. Other customers came and went. By the end of her shift, he was still there. She approached his table again.

"Can I get you anything else?"

George pointed to his cup and made a two-fingers sign. "Just a bit."

Melanie filled his cup again and laid his check on the table. "Whenever you're ready," she said. She went back to her station, untied her apron, and went inside. When she returned, she had retied her red hair ribbon, dabbed on an unpretentious swipe of fresh lipstick. George was waiting by the cash register.

He handed her the check and some cash. "Mel, are you a student?"

"Yes."

He started to back away. "You took off your apron. Are you done for the day?"

"Here, but I've got classes," she said.

"Could I give you a lift somewhere?" George looked toward the Harley.

"Sure," she said. "If you can wait a few minutes, I'll close my register and get my books and jacket."

When she came back out, he was standing by the motorcycle.

"Where we headed?"

"The Art Center. Up two blocks that way and then two blocks to the right."

She got on behind George, put her arm around his waist, and leaned into him. He turned back into the street, and they rode to the Arts Building. He pulled up in front, letting the engine idle while she got off.

"Mel, you have any lunch plans?"

"My classes end about twelve thirty. I could meet you at the student union." She pointed up the street. "It's in that building. There are some parking spots behind."

George sat on the bike and watched her walk away. As she reached the steps of her building, she turned, gave him a little wave, and went inside.

He was waiting for her in front of the union when she came out of class. They went inside to a cafeteria, where she picked out a salad and ice tea. He grabbed a sandwich, some chips, and a Coke.

"So what's your story, Mr. George Wheeler?"

"College dropout. Fought in Vietnam. According to the media, I specialized in napalming women and children. Now, I'm worrying about someone's kid brother. How about you?"

"War protester, feminist, art student. Working my way through school, an inch at a time, burning bras as I go. It's a long process because I can't take a full schedule while I'm working."

"What kind of art?"

"Painting, mostly. Some sculpture. I like working with nude models."

George laughed. "Can I visit your classes?"

"To see the models?"

"Something like that."

"They're mostly men. Are you gay?"

"No. I thought you meant the models would be female."

"Some. What are you doing now?"

"I quit college to join the army. I might go back to school, now that Uncle Sam's willing to pay for it."

"Is the war still on your mind?"

"A bit. Why do you ask?"

"This morning, at the café, you seemed tense. Before you sat down, you looked around. Checked the alley beside the building. You looked startled when a garbage truck dropped a Dumpster. And you ate with your head up. You reminded me of a cat sitting on a windowsill—eyes watching, tail twitching."

"Survival habits, I guess. Weird things have happened since I got back. Sometimes I get flashbacks, or I see someone on the street I know was killed in action. I see jungle where there are just trees. Dangling wires bother me."

"Really. I understand some of it. Why the wires?"

"Booby traps. A favorite of the Viet Cong."

"It must have been terrible."

"It's hard to explain how completely screwed up it was. Anyway, it can be disorienting, being here and there at the same time." He paused. "Sorry, I don't mean to run on. I just have to figure it out."

Mel tried to break the mood. "So now that you're home, what do you want to study?"

"I have no idea. Maybe photography or fly fishing."

"You don't sound like a serious student."

"I'm full of crap, mostly. I have no idea what I'm doing, so I pretty much need to start at the beginning and see where it leads me."

"Have you been to the admissions office?"

"I planned to go there today.

"After lunch, I'll point you there."

When they finished eating, George took the trays and bused the dishes. Mel took him outside and showed him a large sign with a map of the campus. "You're here," she said. "You're going there. I've got to run."

"Could I buy you dinner?" George asked.

"Not tonight. I've got a bunch of work to do. Stop by the bakery on Friday morning. I'll know what my work schedule will be for the weekend, and then we'll see."

"Do you live on campus?"

"I share an apartment with a couple of women just a few blocks away."

"Would you like a ride somewhere?"

"No, thanks. I'm headed for the library to do some research. Maybe I'll see you on Friday."

George watched Mel walk quickly away from him, going across the campus toward the library. He wondered if she was dismissing him, that Friday would never come. He turned in the direction of the admissions office, nearly colliding with some students walking toward him. He excused himself and kept walking.

"It's a bit late to enroll for the fall," an admissions assistant told him, "but if you're going to be a part-time student and you live off campus, we should be able to fit you into the class schedules."

CHAPTER TWENTY-SIX

On Friday morning Mel agreed to a dinner date that evening. "There's a nice Italian place within walking distance of my apartment."

The restaurant was full when they arrived. "It'll be about a half hour before a table opens," the hostess said. "If you wait in the bar, I'll come get you when your table's ready."

They stood near one corner of the bar and hailed the bartender. George ordered a beer, Mel a glass of Chianti.

"Really," George said. "What is your story? Are you married, rich, dating someone? Do you hate anyone who had anything to do with the war?"

"I'm here with you, aren't I?"

"Yeah, but for all you know, I'm a psycho veteran turned ax murderer."

"I thought that at first. Now I'm pretty sure you're just a male chauvinist."

"I assume you're a ballbuster, mad at all men."

"So why are you here then?"

"You're attractive and interesting. I like your blond hair and blue eyes. And the way you fill out a sweater."

Mel blushed. "So I'm just another pretty face with boobs?"

"Sorry," he said. "I didn't mean to insult you. It's been a while since I've been in the world, not to mention near a woman. I need some retraining."

"You should know," she said, "that I'm an active war protester."

George studied his beer glass, making designs with his thumb in the condensation on the side. She waited for him to look up at her.

"I'm telling you this because I don't want you to be surprised. I'm an organizer, and I lead the marches from the campus."

"Why?"

"We want to keep the pigs on alert."

"The police don't care. It's just another nuisance for them, but with some overtime pay."

"I mean the pigs in Washington."

The hostess came into the bar. "Your table's ready," she said. She ushered them into the dining area and gave them menus.

"There's a march next weekend. You'd be welcome to join us."

"I can't do that."

"Why not? You said yourself the war's a mess. It'll only change if we put pressure on the government. Since you were there, you should know that better than anyone."

"When I was in Nam, hearing about the protests just pissed me off. My team's still there trying to do its job. The protests aren't helping them."

"I'm glad you got home safe," she said. "But there are plenty who won't. It's a terrible waste of young lives."

George thought of Horse lying on his poncho before the medevac arrived. "You should have let me die," he'd said. Horse fulfilled that wish at the cabin, wheelchair bound, angry, and frustrated, jerking the trigger to get it over with. George stared off into the restaurant. His fist clenched, unclenched.

"George," Mel said. "You okay?"

George refocused. "Yeah, I'm okay."

"You drifted off there for a minute. Is there something going on?"

"I was thinking of my friend, Horse, who came back wounded, ended up killing himself."

"I'm so sorry," she said. "I didn't mean to touch a nerve."

"It's all right. He's just been on my mind." George's voice cracked, and he stopped to regain his composure. "The guy saved my life. He just couldn't save his own." He picked up his menu, tried to read it, then put it back down. "He left a kid brother who's stuck at home with his drunken father. I'm working on arrangements to let him live with me. I want to help, but I don't know the first thing about being a parent."

"Is that the kid you mentioned at lunch?"

"Yeah. His name's Hawk. He found his brother in a pool of blood, the gun still in his hand."

"How awful."

"Hawk told me he'd seen the gun and asked about it. His brother said he wanted it for target practice. Now, because he didn't take it, Hawk thinks he's responsible for Horse's death."

"Horse would have found a way if he was determined."

"You and I know that, but Hawk still feels guilty."

"Where's the rest of his family?"

"He's got a mom somewhere in Tulsa. She ran off a couple of years ago. His reservation home is a mess. So he can live in squalor with a drunk or with me. Some choice."

"That's a lot to consider."

George pushed his chair back from the table, put his head down, elbows on his knees. "I'm sorry, Mel," he said, "but I've lost my appetite. Maybe we should go."

She reached across the table for his hand. "Stay, George. We've got all evening, and I want to be with you." George raised his head, looked at her, then sat back up at the table.

"Do you like seafood?" she asked.

George nodded.

Mel waved the waiter over and ordered another round of drinks and two meals of linguini with clams. "Wait to put in our food order," she said to the waiter, "until after the drinks arrive." She turned back to George. "That's my favorite dish here," she said. "I think you'll like it."

By the time their meals came, George had mellowed, and Mel had changed the subject. "How did it go with the admissions folks?"

"Okay, I guess. I can start in the fall part-time."

"Do you have a place to live?"

"I've got my dad's house. There's plenty of room for Hawk, if he wants to stay there."

After dinner, they walked back to the campus quad and sat on a bench talking. "Have you ever seen the night sky?" George asked. "Without the streetlights?"

"Not for a long time. I'm a city kid. Once, at my grandparents' house, I did."

"Can't see anything here. You have to get out into the country, away from the light pollution."

"I'd like to do that sometime."

"Ever camp out?"

"I stayed at a Howard Johnson's once."

"Maybe you should go camping with me sometime."

"I'd have to think about that," she said. Mel leaned her head on George's shoulder. "Anyway, I'm glad I met you," she said, "even if you are a male chauvinist."

"I'm looking forward to hearing a bunch of feminist claptrap," he said, "and seeing what's left behind when the bra is burned."

CHAPTER TWENTY-SEVEN

The Wheelers' longtime housekeeper, Maggie, met George and Hawk at the front door. "This is Charles," George said, "our new houseguest. I call him Hawk."

"I'm so pleased to meet you, Charles," she said. "I've heard a lot about you." They walked through the house, giving Hawk the tour.

She had set the kitchen table in an alcove overlooking the backyard. "I've made some lunch," she said. "The rest of the soup is in the refrigerator. There's also milk and juice and other food in there, and bread and cereal in the cupboard."

"Where's the beer?" George asked.

"If you want to be a responsible parent," she said, "then there's no beer, at least as long as I'm shopping." Maggie puttered about the kitchen, making conversation while they ate.

"That was really good," Hawk said. "Thanks."

"Maggie's the best," George said. "She's always been there for me."

Maggie opened the dishwasher. "Your dishes go in there. Soap's under the sink." She untied her apron. "I'll leave you two to get settled. I'm off to an important bingo appointment."

After Maggie left, George made a mental inventory of the food stocks. There was a *Better Homes and Gardens* cookbook on the kitchen island, open to the tab "Soups and Stews."

"Can you cook, George?"

"I'm pretty good with C rations and carryout. I think we should learn together. That way, neither of us can blame the other if it turns out badly." He pointed to the cookbook. "Maggie's already thinking for us. How about beef stew tonight?"

They spent the afternoon lounging around the house, watching a football game. At halftime, they were back in the kitchen. Following the recipe, Hawk cut up and peeled vegetables while George sautéed the meat and then combined it all to simmer. "Smells good," Hawk said.

George surveyed the kitchen. Every counter was covered with pans, bowls, peelings, and assorted spills. "Looks like a grenade went off in here," George said.

"Based on the mess we've made," Hawk said, "I'm sure it will be great."

After dinner, they walked the neighborhood. George pointed out the route to Hawk's school. "It's not far," he said. "It'll take about twenty minutes. You'll want to get there early on Monday so you have time to check in with the office."

"I've never been to a school off the reservation. What's it like?"

"Probably the same as your school, just bigger, more complex. You'll be changing classes. There's a cafeteria, gym, and athletic fields. It'll take time to get oriented, but you'll be fine. You've got the home phone number and Christine's number. If you need something and I'm not home, give her a call. I'm looking at starting some classes at the university. They meet in the mornings, three days a week. Otherwise I'll be around."

The next morning after breakfast, George found a football, and they went outside to play catch. George threw while Hawk ran some patterns. "Maybe there's still a chance to try out for the team," Hawk said.

For dinner that night, George dragged a Weber grill out of the garage, found some charcoal, and showed Hawk how to start the fire and grill hamburgers. They opened some cans for side dishes and made a salad. "Maybe we should start a restaurant," Hawk said.

George laughed. "A sure path to bankruptcy."

CHAPTER TWENTY-EIGHT

On the morning of his first day at John Hay High School, Charles arrived early. He walked the almost silent halls feeling his way around. A few students leaned on their lockers, some chatted in small clusters of two or three, and all of them ignored him as if he were invisible. He strolled around, stalling, waiting for the office to open. Finally, when he saw a secretary unlock the door, he followed her in.

"I'm a new student," he said. "Charles Manawa."

"Well, welcome." She rummaged through a cabinet and pulled out a file with lists of locker numbers. "Here's your combination. I'll show you where you can find your locker. The teachers in each class will give you the books and bring you up-to-date on assignments."

She walked Hawk down the hallway, turned a corner, and showed him the locker at the end of the hall. She ran through the combination with him. Hawk dropped his jacket inside, took his empty backpack, and followed the secretary back to the office. She gave him a map of the classrooms and a class schedule. "Your first class is here," she said, pointing to a place on the schematic. "You can take it from there. Here's the list of classes, the teachers' names, and the room numbers."

Just before the bell rang, Hawk appeared at his first class and introduced himself to the teacher.

"Take a seat over there," she said, "at the end of that row. I'll bring you a textbook."

Most of the class was already seated, and Hawk felt all eyes on him. He slid into the seat and stared at the desktop until his teacher laid a book on his desk.

By lunch he'd made it through several classes feeling completely alone. No one spoke to him or acknowledged his existence. He bought a sandwich in the lunch line, wolfed it down, and then sat out on the front steps until the bell rang for the afternoon classes.

Midway through the morning of his second day, Hawk headed for the boys' restroom. Some of the older boys were already in there, zipping up, combing their hair. One of the bigger kids was holding court for the others. When Hawk walked in, the conversation paused.

"Well, what have we here," the kid said, looking at Hawk. "Looks like a new injun." Other kids snickered. The boy approached Hawk and put his arm around him. "Tonto, the name's Jake. Welcome to our school. Say, I'm a little short of lunch money today. How about spotting me some?" He squeezed Hawk's shoulder hard.

Hawk twisted away. "Sorry. I don't have any."

"Injun speak with forked tongue," Jake said. "I saw him buy lunch yesterday." Other boys crowded around Hawk. "Hold him, let me check." The boys grabbed Hawk while Jake stuck his hand in Hawk's pockets, coming up with a couple of dollars.

He waved the money at the others. "Lyin' injuns need a lesson, maybe get their head cleared." The boys shoved Hawk into a stall and forced his head down into a toilet bowl while another one flushed it. "There's a swirly for you, kid," Jake said. "Tomorrow, you bring more money. I'll need it for my lunch."

They all laughed and left the restroom while Hawk stood at a sink and washed his face.

When he walked into his next class, the teacher scolded. "You're late. This class starts at ten fifteen sharp."

"Sorry," Hawk said. "I had to wash my face." Several of the boys laughed but went silent when the teacher scowled at them.

At lunch, Hawk sat by himself again, this time without anything to eat. He pulled out a book and began working on an assignment. A tray slid down across the table. "Mind if I join you?"

Hawk looked up to see a head full of unruly auburn hair and thick glasses. She was dressed in an eclectic ensemble of unmatched layers. She smiled through her braces and pushed her glasses back on her nose. "I'm Gina," she said. "Really, it's Regina, but I hate that name."

Hawk waved for her to sit down. "I'm Charles," he said. "Officially Charles Soaring Hawk, but you can call me Charles or Hawk. Just don't call me Charlie or Tonto."

"We've got some classes together."

"Yeah, I saw you answer in math class today," he said. "You really know that stuff."

"I like math—anything to do with science, actually."

"I like art. I'm not much good at anything else."

"No lunch today?"

"Lost my lunch money."

"Sounds like Jake. He flunked a year, so he's older and bigger. Has a rep for picking on the new kids. He likes to lord it over everyone, trying to be the tough guy. He has a group of toadies who follow him around, sucking up." She slid a half sandwich over to

Hawk on a napkin. He looked at it for a few seconds, then picked it up. "Thanks," he said. "I'm starving."

"How's it going so far?"

"I'm feeling pretty stupid right now. I've got a lot to catch up on."

"I can help," she said, "if you don't mind hanging out with a freak."

Hawk laughed. "I'm the freak. You'd think no one ever saw an Indian before. You're the first kid to talk to me."

"I'm used to it."

A couple of other girls set their trays down. "These are my two friends," Gina said. "Traci and Patti. Meet Hawk. He's new." The girls were dressed like Gina, in a natural, unkempt sort of way. Patti had a large cloth purse over her shoulder with a big "Peace" button clipped on the side. Traci's long hair was crowned with a barrette of flowers.

"You look like sisters," Hawk said.

The girls giggled. "Maybe we are."

The last class of the day was physical science. When the class was dismissed, Hawk walked past Gina's desk. "Walking home?"

She nodded and got up to follow him out. The teacher was still at his desk, shuffling papers into a folder. As Gina went by his desk, she said, "Mr. Sanders, you didn't hear it from me, but Jake Slaker is shaking down kids for lunch money." She walked out of the room before he could respond. Together Gina and Hawk went outside. Other kids were gathered in clumps on the steps and out along the front walk. Gina and Hawk started down the steps. "Follow me," she said as she took a sharp right turn and headed across the lawn away from the others. "I hate them all. No sense taking any more insults."

As they walked past the athletic fields, Hawk could see the football team out practicing. "I'd like to try out for the team," he said. "But it's probably too late."

"They're desperate," she said. "They'll take anyone."

Hawk laughed. "I'm not that bad."

"Sorry, that didn't come out right. I'm sure you'd be a good player."

CHAPTER TWENTY-NINE

When he got home, Hawk told George about the incident with Jake. "What do you think I should do?"

"I can go with you to see the principal, or you can settle it on your own terms."

"What do you mean?"

"Guys like Jake don't care about authority. If you get him in trouble, he'll just find another way to harass you. Frankly, I think the best way is to take him on. If you rough him up, he'll find someone else to pick on."

"I'm not afraid to fight him, but he's a pretty big kid."

"When you're in a fight with someone bigger, don't back away. You'll never get out of his reach. You have to move inside to get the advantage and do some damage. Go for the groin. No guy can stand a kick in the nuts. Once he's grabbing his crotch, you can do some damage. Use short quick jabs. They're hard to block." He showed Hawk the motion. "Straight up, not from the side."

George held his hands out, palms up. "Try it," he said.

He got a lukewarm punch from Hawk.

"Hit my hands as hard as you can."

Hawk tried again.

"Harder, faster," George said.

They practiced some more, George walking him through some motions. "If you change your mind, tell me, and I'll go to school with you."

The next day, Hawk went to the restroom at the same break time. The boys were there again with Jake. "Hey, Tonto, you bring my lunch money?"

"Yeah, I have lunch money."

"Hand it over."

"You'll have to take it."

"I guess you didn't learn your lesson," Jake said. "Get him, guys."

One of the boys started to grab Hawk, but Hawk shoved him away. The kid tripped over someone's books and fell down. Hawk rushed at Jake, slamming him into a stall partition. Surprised, Jake swung his fist, hitting Hawk above the left eye; then he came at him, his hands around Hawk's neck, choking him. Hawk brought his knee into Jake's groin, doubling him up, then hit him with two sharp jabs to the face. As Jake staggered backward, Hawk pushed him through a swinging stall door, where he landed on the toilet. His hand triggered the flush lever. Blood streamed from his nose. Hawk swung the door open again and looked at Jake slumped over the toilet bowl. "My name's Hawk, not Tonto."

A smaller kid near the door slipped out and brought in the hall monitor. As the teacher entered, Hawk was pulling a paper towel from the dispenser, wetting it, then dabbing at the cut over his eye. "All right," the teacher said. "Everyone to the office, now."

A kid protested, "I wasn't involved."

"I said everyone."

At the office, the kids were all told to have a seat in the reception area in front of the secretary's desk. Jake sat across from Hawk and glared at him. Hawk's head throbbed, but he noted with satisfaction that Jake had stuffed his nose with toilet paper, and the blood was still seeping through the paper, running over his lip, and dripping onto his shirt.

"I need to see the nurse," Jake said. "That Indian kid broke my nose."

"Yep," Hawk said. He smiled at Jake. "I think you're right, Jakey. You should see the nurse, honey." Jake was on his feet then, heading for Hawk.

"Enough." A voice boomed from the hallway as Principal Bronson entered the room.

He was heavyset and balding, a formidable presence. He put a big paw in the middle of Jake's chest, pushed him back, and pointed his finger at him.

"Slaker, you go see the nurse, and you stay there until I release you." He looked at Hawk. The bleeding had stopped, but the area around his eye was beginning to swell. "You've got a rose starting to bloom." Bronson turned to the secretary. "Mary, go with Jake and ask the nurse to give you an ice pack to bring back for this young man."

"You sit here," Bronson said to Hawk, "until I'm done talking to the other kids." Then, one by one, he took the boys into his office and took statements from each. Finally, Bronson invited Hawk into his office. "Have a seat." Bronson sat on the corner of his desk across from Hawk. "What happened in there?"

Hawk was holding the ice to his forehead. He shrugged. "Jake's been stealing lunch money from kids." He looked directly at the principal without saying more.

"And?"

"That's it. I don't think he'll do it again, at least to me."

The principal got up and walked around behind his desk. Looking out the window, he said, "Violence is not a good way to solve problems. If something like that happens again, you should report it to me."

"I don't snitch."

"Not asking you to. I just need to know about these things. I'm sure I'll hear from Jake's parents, so I want to be prepared to answer any complaints."

There was a pause.

"A few of the other boys told me the truth. At least, their stories jibed, so I'm pretty sure I've got the picture. Jake's already got a rep for bullying." Bronson moved around his desk and sat down. "We have a rule about fighting on school grounds. First offense usually means a week's suspension. In your case, you're new, so I'll cut you some slack for the circumstances here. There'll be no suspension, but you'll have to serve a week of detention after school. If it happens again, whether you're right or wrong, you'll get two weeks' suspension." He paused and watched Hawk's composure. "Am I clear about that?"

Hawk nodded. "Yes, sir."

"You just started school here this week?"

"Yes, sir."

"So other than this incident, how's it going so far?"

"Pretty rough. One kid, Gina, has actually spoken to me, and I'm really stupid in class."

"Gina's a good student and can help. We can also get you some other tutoring if you need it. As for the other kids, they'll come around. Nobody warms up to the new guy until they see how he fits in."

"Is it too late to try out for football?"

"Never too late. I'll speak to Coach Barkley. He'll need a written permission slip from your guardian, and then he'll get you suited up. I'll call him today, and you can stop by after classes to get the information." Bronson paused. "Of course, there'll be no football until after you've served your detention."

He wrote out a pass and handed it to Hawk. "Get back to class, and give this slip to your teacher. You may stop by the nurse's office first and get a refresher on that ice pack."

Bronson followed Hawk back into the main office area and watched him head out the door to class. "Tough kid," he said to Mary. "Coach Barkley's going to like him."

At lunch, Gina joined Hawk. She looked at the area around his eye, which was now turning black and blue. "Well, I guess you fixed Jake. The word's out. Don't mess with the Indian. What'd you do to him?"

Hawk smiled. "The guy I'm living with," he said, "was in Special Forces with my brother. He taught me some stuff."

"Well, you shut Jake up for a while—at least until his nose is healed." She laughed. "You might have actually improved his appearance. I don't think he'll bother you again, but keep your guard up anyway." She reached up and gingerly touched Hawk's forehead. "Does that hurt?"

"A bit. Throbbing mostly. Jake's got a pretty good swing."

Traci and Patti walked by with their trays and sat at a nearby table. Patti waved. "Hi, Hawk. Nice shiner." She leaned in to whisper something to Traci that made them both laugh.

Hawk and Gina ate in silence for a few minutes.

"How come you're in this school?" Gina asked.

"I'm living with that friend of my brother's—he's a part-time college student. I go back to the rez on weekends."

"Where's your brother?"

Hawk looked off into the cafeteria, not answering. Finally, he said, "He died from the war."

"Oh, Hawk. I'm sorry. I didn't know."

"That's okay. How would you? Anyway, that's how I got here." He paused. "Mr. Bronson gave me a week of detention for fighting with Jake."

"What happened?"

"I wouldn't tell him much. Just said that Jake was stealing. Anyway, Bronson said he'll speak to the football coach. He thinks I can start practice after I serve out the detention if the coach approves."

"So what did Jake get?"

"I don't know. A broken nose, I guess. Do you mind if I don't walk home with you?"

"I guess you have no choice, but it's no problem. Some days I have afternoon stuff anyway. Violin lessons, or I have to babysit my little brother, Tommy."

"Maybe we could walk together in the mornings on the way to school. Like you said, twin freaks."

"Yeah. I like the sound of that. If we start early, I can help you with your homework."

CHAPTER THIRTY

When Hawk got home from school, George was in the kitchen preparing dinner. "How'd your day go?"

"There's good news and bad news," Hawk said. "The good news is that I can play football. The bad news is that I can't start until after I serve out a week's detention."

"What's that about?"

"I got punished for fighting when Slaker tried to take my lunch money."

"What did Slaker get?"

"A week's suspension and a broken nose."

George looked at Hawk's face. "Looks like Slaker got you once. Was it worth it?"

"Yeah, it was," Hawk said. "Although the principal warned me that next time I'd get two weeks' suspension, right or wrong. I don't understand why I should get punished for defending myself."

"I can understand the principal's standpoint. He doesn't want any violence in the school, but I'm proud of you for standing up for yourself."

Hawk opened his backpack and pulled out the football permission slip. "Will you sign this?"

"Of course. Have you met the coach?"

"I talked with him after class. He seems like a good guy. He said I can start practice as soon as I finish the detention. I've never really played on an organized team, just with the rez kids. Do you have any suggestions?"

"Yeah, sure," George said. "We'll work on it after dinner."

Later, out in the yard, they squared off in front of each other. "What position you going to play?"

"I don't know. Wherever I can. I'm probably too small for the line."

"Okay. Size is important, but speed and agility are better. Think angles."

"What do you mean?"

George put his hand on Hawk's shoulder. "Come straight at me."

Hawk lunged forward only to be repelled by George's long arms. When he tried to go lower, George pushed him down to the ground. "So this time, try to get by me by hitting me from the side, pushing me off-balance. Then you can spin out of my arms and get around me."

Hawk practiced the move a few times and eventually got around George.

"If you can get past the first lineman, then you can do some damage in the backfield. Same on offense. You can get past me by playing the angles and spinning away, not by hitting me head-on."

After serving his detention, Hawk met Coach Barkley and presented the permission slip. Barkley took him to the equipment room and fitted him for pads and a helmet. He dug out an old jersey from a box in the corner. "Sorry," he said. "This one's pretty ratty, but our supplies are limited, and you're a bit late to the party. The good stuff is taken."

"It's okay. I'm glad to have this. You should see what we play with on the rez."

"Get dressed and come out to the field. Just join in with the calisthenics. You'll catch on." On the way out to the field, Hawk saw himself in the mirror and realized that with his helmet on, no one could tell he was Cherokee. He looked like just another player.

After the basic exercises, Barkley had the boys all line up according to height. Hawk was at the short end. Barkley walked over and put his hand on Hawk's helmet. This is Charles Manawa," he said. "He's new. You can call him Charles or Hawk, not Charlie. I expect you to welcome him as part of the team, show him the ropes." Barkley walked back in front of the group.

"Sprints," he said. "Groups of five."

With each whistle, they ran fifty-yard dashes. Barkley took the winner of each group and raced them again. Hawk won in his group and finished well in the final race.

The rest of the afternoon was spent working on the basics of blocking and tackling and running through plays.

On Friday, Barkley gathered the players in a circle. "This is a new drill. We call this here 'bull in the ring.' I'll yell out two names. The second man called out has to try to tackle the first. The one still standing is the winner."

He called names of some of the older boys, the others cheering. The coach worked his way down into the newbies. Finally, he called, "Kleckner...Manawa." Hawk took a step forward, feinted one way, and rushed from the other side, easily tackling the boy and taking him to the ground. Hawk helped the boy up and returned to the circle.

A few minutes later, the coach hollered, "Grainger." A bigger kid stepped out. "Manawa." Surprised, Hawk looked around and realized he was the one called. Grainger grinned at him. Hawk ran toward him head-on, and Grainger shoved him to the ground. The other boys snickered. Hawk jumped to his feet and rushed Grainger again but spun at the last minute, grabbing Grainger's leg below the knee, catching him by surprise. Hawk drove forward, keeping Grainger off-balance but couldn't wrestle him to the ground. They danced around together, neither one giving in, until the coach blew his whistle. The boys let go and returned to their places in the circle. A boy next to Hawk gave him a punch in the arm.

"That's it for today," Barkley said. The boys began to jog back into the locker room.

"Hawk," Barkley said, "stop by my office after you get dressed."

In the office, Barkley said, "You did well today. I'd like you to think about playing in the backfield, maybe linebacker." He handed him a loose-leaf notebook. "There are some plays in there. Take that home and study them. I want you to start practicing with the varsity."

CHAPTER THIRTY-ONE

October 1969

On a Saturday afternoon, George, Earl, and Fuzzy gathered at Earl's to watch an Oklahoma football game. During halftime, Earl asked how things were going with Hawk.

"Pretty well," George said. "We've settled into a routine. I have morning college classes three days a week and get back in time to have supper ready when Hawk gets home from football practice. When Hawk has a Saturday game, his dad comes to watch, then takes him back to the reservation for the weekend. Hawk's playing some good football, mostly at linebacker on defense and halfback on offense. Even his grades have improved."

"So," Fuzzy asked, "have the dreams started yet?"

George paused, not sure what to say, but he was surprised to hear Fuzzy ask the question, that he would know about them. "Yeah, actually, they have, and they're becoming more frequent."

"I like the one with the evil house," Earl said. "I'm walking in the woods, and I come to this huge mansion. There's all kinds of people in there, like a party, so I go in. Everyone is milling around, and then I see the big dude. I can't describe him exactly, but I get this incredible feeling of dread. The guy gives off truly evil vibes. I walk the halls, going in various rooms, and then I realize there's no way out of the house unless I wake up."

"My all-time favorite," Fuzzy said, "is imminent capture. We're on a mission, and the choppers are coming for us. I can hear the rotors thumping, the engines roaring. Feel the dust kicking up as they land. The men are loading up, and I'm still in the bush, surrounded by trip wires. They're calling for me from the choppers, but I can't move without triggering an explosion, so they take off without me. Then I hear the VC coming, beating the bushes, taunting, 'GI, GI, you come out now. You die now, GI. Your time is here. Come out now.' My gun's jammed. There's nothing I can do."

"I've had similar dreams, but my specialty," George said, "is missing the flight home. The plane is on the tarmac and loading, but I'm still back at the armory trying to turn in my gear, or I'm missing my orders, or I'm in Saigon and don't have a ride back to the base. There's always some excuse, and I don't have time to fix the problem, so the plane takes off without me, and I'm still stuck in Nam. But I've had the other dreams too, the random scenes of burned villages, blown-up body parts, the whole nine yards."

"I have one like that," Earl said, "but in my case, I'm being sent back for a second tour."

"It's weird that we would all have basically the same dreams," Fuzzy said.

"Yeah," George said, "like the dream in high school where you can't remember your locker combination, and you're late for class. Or you've got a test, and you haven't cracked a book all year. You're not even sure where the class meets."

"Well, get used to it," Earl said. "They don't go away."

"I'm still jumpy about intruders," George said. "I wake up in the middle of the night, thinking I hear someone walking around, maybe Hawk, but I check on him, and he's asleep. I've set a few trip wires around to make noise. I know it's stupid, but I can't get it out of my head."

"Been there, done that," Earl said. "It takes a long time to get back home."

CHAPTER THIRTY-TWO

A few days after Hawk joined the team, Grainger invited him to a cafeteria table where the football players were having lunch. "C'mon, man, join us," he said. A table of cheerleaders sat nearby, which allowed easy interchange between the two groups. As the girls got their lunches and passed by the players, they flirted, making conversation. Susie, a petite blonde, paid particular attention to Hawk.

"I think she's hot for you," Grainger said. "And she's the pick of the litter." Hawk smiled but felt unsure how to react. Finally, he said, "I'm sure she'll cool off when her parents hear I'm from the rez."

Hawk was partway through his lunch when he saw Gina sitting by herself. He got up with his tray. "Later," he said and went over to sit down across from Gina.

"Well," she said. "I guess you're with the in-crowd now. They better not see you over here with me."

"I can do what I want."

"At least till Susie starts wiggling her little butt."

"She's okay," he said. "But she's not my girlfriend. I don't even know her."

"Look," she said. "I'm a freak and always will be. You're with them now."

"Are you blowing me off?"

"Maybe. Or maybe you're blowing me off." She got up, dropped her trash in the container, and left the lunchroom. Hawk sat staring at his tray until the bell rang.

Later in the day, he tried to talk to Gina again, but she ignored him. The next morning before school, he waited near her house to walk with her, but when she didn't show, he had to run to school to avoid being late. He tried talking to Patti, but she just shrugged. "Don't ask me. It's up to Gina."

Hawk defaulted to the players group then, surrounded by the cheerleaders, enjoying the attention. Gina refused to acknowledge his presence.

CHAPTER THIRTY-THREE

On a Thursday morning in early October, George met Earl and the other bikers at Earl's garage. Earl handed out the flags along with tape to mount them on the back of the bikes. Mel didn't have class that day and was planning another protest march. George had promised her that he would attend or at least be on the parade route to watch. George and Earl decided that the riders would join the protest on behalf of the POWs. They'd meet up with her at the city park afterward. They met Mel and the other protesters in front of the student union, where Mel provided placards and instructions to the marchers. As they began walking toward a city park, the riders, led by George and Earl, flanked the marchers on each side, separating them from the police who had lined the route. The bikers rode slowly along, revving their engines, keeping pace with the walkers. Earl and others were wearing their Angels colors, George his fatigue jacket. George rode up beside Mel as she walked. "Impressive display," she said, hollering above the roar.

When they got to their rallying point, a city park near the heart of the downtown, Mel took the bullhorn, stepped up onto a park bench, and assembled the group. There were loud chants and some singing. Toward the end of the gathering, she pointed down to George. "This is George Wheeler, a friend of mine, just home from Vietnam. I'd like to thank him and his friends for coming today." She paused, while the crowd cheered and applauded. "George," she said, "would you like to say anything?"

George looked around, shaking his head to beg off, but Mel reached down and pulled him up on the bench, pressing the bullhorn into his hand.

George looked out over the crowd. "I wouldn't be here if it wasn't for this good-lookin' woman beside me," he said. She punched him in the arm, but the remark drew some catcalls from the men there. "But since I am, I might as well speak my piece." He cleared his throat and looked out over the crowd. "I'm not the only vet in this crowd. Among the riders are Earl and Fuzzy, two men who also served in Nam." George pointed to them. "I know there are others." Then he spoke more directly to the crowd. "I respect your right to protest, but I don't agree with it. You're correct that the war is a mess. It's hard to describe how screwed up it is. But it's floundering because of the government's meddling, playing with it as if they even had a clue about it. There is a real conflict there between the North Vietnamese communists and the South Vietnamese, who want to be independent and free. Unfortunately, that purpose has become muddled by the Washington bureaucrats."

He paused, taking a breath. "For you, it's easy to protest. At the end of the day, you can just go back to your daily routine. For the soldiers, there is no end to the war. For them, every day is life or death. And when they get back home to the world, they're treated like crap by their fellow citizens, as if they're some kind of war criminals. These protests are demoralizing. But worse, those soldiers are spending a year in hell, and frankly, no one cares—not you or the people who sent them there."

The crowd got silent. Mel reached for the bullhorn, but George turned away and continued. "The worst is that there are dead and missing who will never see home again. That's why these bikers are here, not to petition against the war, but to make sure that no one gets left behind." He pointed to the bikes. "See those black pennants? We brought those today to show our resolve to find the missing and to bring everyone back. The government made this mess, and the government should clean it up. I hope you'll support that cause." He looked at Mel. "I guess that's all I've got to say, except...you are really looking fine."

The crowd chuckled as she snatched the bullhorn from him. George stepped down and walked back to his Harley. Mel tried to stir up the crowd again, but the protest mood had been broken, and the marchers were already drifting off. George looked over at Mel to offer a ride back, but she ignored him. As the other riders left, George followed behind them.

That afternoon, George called Mel's apartment. Her roommate answered. "Mel's not here," she said. "She was in a bit of a snit. Just grabbed her books and left."

CHAPTER THIRTY-FOUR

On Saturday morning, George stopped by to see Mel at the bakery. She let him sit for a while before she brought the menu and a cup of coffee.

"Yessir," she said. "What can I get for you?"

"Are you mad at me?" he asked.

"What do you think?"

"Why didn't you warn me?"

She turned toward another table. "I'm busy right now. I don't have time to talk. Do you want something to eat or not?"

George shook his head, drank the coffee, dropped a couple of dollars on the table and left. Hawk was back home on the rez for the weekend, so when George got back to his house, he packed his camping gear, a flask of Jack Daniels, some cigars, and some packaged C rations he'd brought back from Nam. He drove his truck to the Ouachita National Forest, southeast of Tulsa. He found a campsite, where he left his truck, and hiked back into the wilderness. By early evening, he had reached a small clearing at the top of a hill overlooking the forest. After eating, he smoked a cigar and nipped at the flask, watching the sun go down and listening to the night close in. A great horned owl called in the distance. Another answered. George recalled how, in the jungle, Horse heard every animal sound, every birdsong. The wilderness, in all its nuances, seemed to be embedded in Horse, telling him many things, including the presence of the enemy. George wished Horse were there with him now.

Partway into the flask, George wondered about Mel and whether the damage was reparable. He shouldn't have teased her about her looks in front of the crowd, but he was dead serious about his opinions on the war. He didn't know if she could accept that in him. He lay back on his poncho, soaking up the darkness. Finally, he crawled into his sleeping bag and slept the night under the stars.

A week later, Mel left a message on his answering machine. "There's a special tomorrow morning on day-old glazed doughnuts, two for one."

The following morning, George stopped by the bakery. She brought him two doughnuts and coffee without asking. When her customers were all served, she stopped back by his table.

"I'm sorry I flipped out," she said, "but you surprised me, that's all."

"I think that's my line."

"I've had other vets speak, and they were all dead set against the war. With everything you've been through, I expected the same reaction from you."

"It's a mixed bag," George said. "I'm glad to be out of the war, and I'd like it to end; but I'm still thinking about my team, back there in harm's way, doing their job. I'm not prepared to let that go."

"I guess I asked for it. I was afraid that if I mentioned it beforehand, you wouldn't come on the march."

"It's okay. I'm glad you let me speak. The protesters also need to hear about the soldiers who are still over there."

"Can we agree to disagree?" Mel asked.

"I can agree that neither of us has the right to dictate to the other."

"That's close enough," she said. She circulated among the tables again, taking care of customers.

As she passed by his table again, he said, "I was thinking of cooking a big steak on the grill tonight. It's too much for one person. Would you like to join me?

"Pick me up at six," Mel said. "I'll bring vegetables."

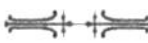

At the house that evening, George poured Mel a glass of wine and opened a beer for himself. "Let's go out on the patio," Mel said. "It's a nice evening."

George had forgotten to remove his intruder alert, so when Mel slid open the patio door, a string of tin cans clattered onto the patio.

"Holy crap, George. You scared the bejeebers out of me."

George hurriedly collected the cans. "Sorry," he said, "I've been worried about someone breaking in."

"Seriously?"

George gave her a brief explanation, talking about noises around the house at night.

"You can't get the war out of your head, can you."

"It's nothing. It'll go away."

She took his hand. "Come with me."

In the living room, she took their drinks, set them on an end table, and helped him move the coffee table aside, leaving a space in the middle. She turned the lights down. "Take off your shoes and socks," she said.

"That's it? Nothing else?"

She laughed. "Just do as I say."

She led him through some simple yoga exercises, stretching, breathing, ending with some basic poses—the sunbird, the warrior. Finally, she sat in a lotus position. "Just sit cross-legged for now. You've got to get loosened up before you can move up to an advanced pose." Eyes closed, they practiced breathing. "As you're sitting here," she said, "I want you to imagine that you have a large safe beside you. Now open the door."

"This is a bunch of crap," he said.

"Pay attention."

"Okay, it's there. The door's open."

"Think of the worst memory you have of the war and mentally put it into the safe. Then close the door and lock it." She waited quietly.

"Okay, I did that."

"Now control your breathing and focus on something pleasant, maybe the river where you and Hawk have fished. Concentrate on that scene until you're not thinking of the war anymore." After a few minutes, she asked, "What's happening?"

"The door to the safe is coming open."

"Close and lock it again," she said. "Concentrate."

When the session was over, she asked, "How do you feel?"

"Relaxed," George said. "I feel good."

"I go to yoga three times a week," she said. "I want you to come with me. It may not be a cure-all, but I think it will help settle you."

"Is the class for men or women?"

"It's mixed, but more women than men."

"Do all the women wear leotards?"

"Yes, and tights in the cool weather."

"I'm in, then."

"Whatever it takes." She crawled over and embraced him.

"We've done the warrior position," he said. "How about we try the missionary?"

She slowly twisted out of his embrace, taking maximum advantage of his caress. "First, we're fixing dinner," she said. "I'm starving."

For the first time in weeks, George slept through the night.

CHAPTER THIRTY-FIVE

One morning in the middle of football season, Hawk was in the hallway between classes when he saw Jake and two other kids coming toward him. One of them said, "There he is." Hawk moved aside, but they crowded him.

Jake chest-bumped him up against the hallway wall. "Hello, Tonto."

"Jake, get lost, man. I'm done with you."

"Yeah, well, I'm not done with you. You sucker-punched me, remember?"

"You just got some of your own medicine, that's all."

Jake yanked at Hawk's books, spilling them on the floor. "Oops! Looks like you dropped your books." Other students began to notice and slowed up to watch the proceedings.

Hawk bent down to gather the books and scattered papers. "I told you," Hawk said. "I'm not fighting you."

"Well, then, I guess I'll just kick the crap out of you anyway." He slammed Hawk against the wall, spilling the books again. He took a swing at him.

Hawk ducked, moved away from the wall, held his hands out in front of him. "Knock it off, Jake."

Jake came at him again. "I'll knock it off, all right." Hawk sidestepped him, blocking him sideways, but one of Jake's friends grabbed Hawk. Jake punched Hawk hard in the stomach, then as Hawk was doubled over, hit him again in the face. The boy holding Hawk shoved him to the ground.

Jake started to walk away, but Hawk got back up and tackled him from behind, banging Jake's head on the floor. When Jake rolled over, Hawk was on him, banging his head repeatedly against the floor.

Two teachers came around the corner. The teachers pulled them apart. "Get your books together," one said. "You're both going to the principal's office."

The other kids faded away, heading for their classes.

Bronson's action was swift. "I warned you, Charles," he said. "You've earned a two-week suspension starting now."

"Jake started it. I told him I wouldn't fight, but he just kept coming at me."

"Doesn't matter. I'm calling your guardian."

"He's not home. I'll tell him when I get home."

"You bring him here tomorrow morning, eight o'clock sharp."

"What about Jake?"

"You worry about yourself. I'll see to Jake."

Hawk left the office, went to his locker to collect his things, and went home. Hawk dropped his books on the coffee table, turned on the television, and sat down on the couch. *So much for football,* he thought. *So much for this whole freaking school and living off the rez.* He stewed for a while, watching some stupid soap opera. Then he went to his room.

George got home about three o'clock. He'd been to class and had lunch with Mel. The front door to the house was unlocked, the television on. Hawk's books were on the coffee table. George walked through the house, calling for him. He found Hawk flopped on his bed, staring at the ceiling.

"What's up, man?"

"I'm going back to the rez. I'm done with that school." Hawk explained the incident, how he got suspended. "I was just defending myself. No one bothers to deal with Slaker."

"Come on," George said. "Let's go out and get some dinner tonight. We'll talk about what to do."

CHAPTER THIRTY-SIX

The next morning, George took Hawk back to the school, and they met Bronson in his office. Coach Barkley was there in the outside office, talking to one of the secretaries.

Hawk introduced George to the coach.

"Hawk," he said. "When you didn't show for practice, I found out you'd been suspended."

"It wasn't my fault."

Bronson came out of his office. George introduced himself.

"Hawk said you wanted to see me."

"I've suspended Charles for two weeks. He has to understand that fighting is not allowed."

"What are you doing about the other kid?" George asked. "This is the second time he's assaulted Hawk. Surely you're not saying Hawk can't defend himself."

"Slaker's not your concern."

"He is when he's bullying my ward."

"Jake has lots of problems. We don't need to get into that."

"I appreciate your concern about one kid," George said. "But now it's personal, and I won't stand by and see my kid abused by a misfit."

"Well, the punishment stands. I hope Hawk will learn something from it."

"What he's learned so far is that the school has a bully, and no one's willing to do anything about it."

"Is there anything else, Mr. Wheeler?"

"Not now, but if this doesn't come to an end, you can expect some legal action, including criminal charges against Slaker."

"Thanks for coming." Bronson showed them the door. Barkley hung back. "Wait outside for me," he said to Hawk and George.

A few minutes later, Barkley emerged from the office, and they all walked together toward the school door. "Mr. Bronson won't budge," the coach said. "You've got two weeks off, so don't waste it." He handed Hawk a slip of paper with a list of exercises and a regimen for running. "Stay in shape. We have some important games left when you return."

"I'll talk to his teachers to get his assignments." George thanked the coach, and they left the school building.

"You're toast for two weeks," George said, "so you can hang out with me."

"I'd rather just go home to the reservation."

"Barkley knows you got shafted, but he respects that you stood up for yourself. You've still got a place on the team."

"So what? I can't play."

Instead of going back to the house, George drove to the campus. "There's someone I want you to meet," he said.

George parked at the Art Center. They went up to the second floor of the building and stopped outside a studio room. The sign on the door read CLASS IN PROGRESS. DO NOT ENTER.

George looked at his watch. "They'll be finishing soon," George said. "Have a seat."

As the class ended, the door opened, and students filed out. George took Hawk in and went over to an easel, where Mel was collecting her art supplies. The drawing on the easel showed a nude woman, sketched in charcoal. "Nice," George said, nodding to the picture. "This is Hawk, the kid I've been telling you about. Hawk's got a few days off school, so I thought maybe you could give us a tour."

Mel extended a hand. "Hi," she said, smiling. "I've heard a lot about you. I'd be glad to show you around."

Mel walked them through the studios and showed him the student work in progress and on display. "I understand you're an artist."

"I do some drawing."

"I've seen a couple of your things. They're good. Have you ever worked with watercolors?"

"Not really," Hawk said. "I've done mostly pencil sketches."

"I've got an open day tomorrow. If you'd like to come back, we could work on some things together here in the studio."

"That would be great," Hawk said. "I'd like that."

"Have you ever been to the Gilcrease Museum?"

"What's that?"

"The best collection of Native American artifacts in the country. It's at the edge of the campus."

Mel looked at George. "Time for a field trip," she said.

On the way out, Hawk asked George, "So is she your girlfriend?"

"Maybe."

"She's nice."

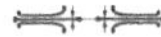

During the two-week suspension, George and Hawk worked out together in the early morning, then Hawk went on campus with George and studied in the library during George's classes. Mel devoted some free time in the studio, showing Hawk some basic techniques with watercolors.

On Mel's day off, they visited the Gilcrease Museum. "Bring your sketchbook," Mel said. "I want you to copy and study some of the Indian designs." They spent the afternoon at the museum. George walked briskly through the exhibits, trying to get an overview of the collection.

Mel, on the other hand, paused at various exhibits, and she and Hawk sketched what they observed. "Look at these symbols," she said, "Notice how different tribes shared common designs." They went into a particular room, and Mel asked one of the guards if they could open some of the artifact drawers.

"You have to have an appointment for that," he told her. "But you can arrange it through the curator's office."

"I never knew this was here," Hawk said. "It's an amazing collection."

Back in the studio, Mel showed Hawk her embossing tools. "I think it would be cool if you'd learn to enhance your drawings with these techniques," she said. "You could draw ordinary objects but finish them with designs embossed on the paper to illustrate your heritage." At the end of the day, she gave Hawk an old toolbox that had a mixture of art supplies: some tubes of water-based paint, some brushes, and a couple of her embossing tools. "Take this home and practice. When you've got some stuff finished, we'll review it together."

Hawk was excited.

"Remember this," she said. "Art has to have content. The more you know, the richer the content will be. So you can draw what you see and get a picture, or you can take what you see and draw it in a way that adds meaning beyond the simple re-creation of the image."

"I'm not sure I understand."

"You'll see it as you practice. If you want to draw a flower, look up the flower and understand it, how it's used, its characteristics. Your drawing will be improved by that knowledge."

CHAPTER THIRTY-SEVEN

November 1969

The last football game of the season was at home. Hawk's suspension was over, and he had earned a starter's jersey, playing linebacker and a bit role as a halfback on offense. As the players came out onto the field, Hawk looked into the stands and saw Mel and George. A few rows over, he saw Gina sitting with Traci and Patti. Traci jumped up, yelling, "Yo, Hawk. Kick some butt." Hawk laughed. He waved before putting on his helmet.

Hawk's team, the Renegades, were up against the Rockets, the best team in the league. They were expecting a rough night.

The game started badly for the home team. The Rockets took the kickoff and marched easily down the field for a touchdown. When Hawk's team got the ball, they went three and out, punting it back to the Rockets.

The trash talk had already started, but on the next series, as the Rockets quarterback dropped back to pass, Hawk slipped through the line and tackled him for a ten-yard loss.

"You won't do that again," a lineman told Hawk, but on the next play, Hawk dodged a different lineman and tackled a runner in the backfield just as he took the handoff. The Rockets seemed flummoxed. Their coach called a time-out.

Barkley told his guys. "They'll double-team Hawk this time, so Grainger, this is your chance to come at them from the other side. Hawk, you just keep the pressure on them."

On the next play, the quarterback faded back again and was crushed, this time by Grainger, who forced a fumble recovered by the Renegades.

Barkley called a pass play, and his quarterback faked a pass to Hawk along the sideline and hit the left end, who scampered untouched into the end zone.

Energized, the Renegades played above their heads all night, holding the Rockets at bay until a last ditch effort led to a Rocket field goal and victory.

In the locker room, Barkley gathered the team. "You showed me tonight that we've got the makings here of a very good team. We're going to work hard to get ready for next season, and then we'll cause some serious damage in this league." He singled out some of the players for their efforts, including Grainger and Hawk. "Look around you. These are your brothers. This is your team."

The locker room erupted in a loud cheer, followed by the excited banter of kids on a high. Hawk didn't want to leave. For the first time, he felt part of something good, and he believed he was more than just a poor Indian kid.

Outside, George and Mel were waiting. As Hawk came out of the school building, one of the cheerleaders ran up and gave him a hug. "You were really great. We almost won," she said. "We're all going to the Sugar Shack. Come with us." Hawk looked up to see Gina standing off to the side with her friends. "Uh, no thanks," he said. "I can't, not tonight."

After the cheerleader ran off to join her friends, Hawk saw George and Mel.

"Great game," George said. "Let's go out and celebrate somewhere."

Hawk followed along, looking over his shoulder and hoping to see Gina, but she and her friends had disappeared into the crowd.

CHAPTER THIRTY-EIGHT

In early December, Hawk noticed that the school orchestra was giving a Christmas concert. "Could we go?" he asked.

"That sounds good," George said. "Of course we can."

The audience was sparse, mostly parents, and they ended up sitting close to the front. Hawk wanted to be there because he knew that Gina would be playing in the orchestra, but they were surprised when she got up to play a solo. She had fixed her hair and was wearing a straight black dress, the orchestra uniform.

After the concert, Hawk and George walked up to Gina and her parents. Traci and Patti were also there, talking with Gina. When she saw Hawk approaching, Gina had a surprised look on her face. Traci and Patti said hi and then wandered off.

"You were really good," Hawk said.

George spoke to Gina's parents and introduced Hawk.

Gina's dad extended his hand. "I'm Fred. This is my wife, Sarah. Pleased to meet both of you."

"Your daughter is an amazing violinist," George said.

"So you're Charles—or is it Hawk?" Fred said to Hawk.

"Either."

"I've heard about you from Gina."

Hawk wasn't sure if that was good or bad. "Yes, sir."

Gina said little but seemed pleased that Hawk had come to the concert.

George rescued him. "C'mon, Hawk," he said. "You've got some homework left. It was nice to meet you folks." He waved to Gina. "Keep it up."

The next day, Hawk was sitting on a large rock on the school lawn. Gina walked up the sidewalk. "Oh hi," she said. "Thanks for coming to the concert last night. I didn't know you liked orchestra music."

"I don't. I didn't know you liked football."

"Sometimes I like it."

"I tried to see you after the game, but you took off."

Gina leaned against the rock. "I'm sorry I've ignored you."

"It's okay," Hawk said. "I'm used to it. Like twin freaks, remember?"

Neither spoke as they watched the kids file past them into the school.

"Don't be mad because I have some other friends," he said.

As the last of the kids passed them, Hawk slipped off his backpack. "I have something for you. I've been carrying it around for a few days."

He pulled out a package wrapped in brown paper.

"What is it?"

"Go ahead, open it."

Gina carefully pulled the paper back. It was a framed watercolor of a red prairie flower.

"Hawk, this is beautiful."

"The flower's called Indian paintbrush."

"I've seen it before."

"Did you know that you can eat the blossoms?"

Gina shook her head.

"Sometime I'll tell you our legend about how it was created."

They stood quietly, Gina looking at the painting. "I like the way you embossed it with the picture of a hawk."

"George's friend Mel is an art student at the college. She showed me how to make that imprint. I think I'll use that as my signature."

Hawk looked at his watch. "It's late. We better get to class." Gina slipped the picture into her pack and grabbed his arm, pulling him toward her. She kissed him on the cheek. "Thanks, Hawk." They ran together into the school just as the bell rang.

CHAPTER THIRTY-NINE

On a Saturday morning during his Christmas vacation, Hawk was sitting on his dad's front porch, talking to his friend Zeke. The old dog, Sooner, sat between them.

"What's your school like?" Zeke asked.

"It's okay. Big. I played football this fall. We had a decent season."

"It must be different having an actual league and playing other schools."

"Yeah, and they have a band. I don't much care about that—I just want to play."

"Is the schoolwork hard?"

"About the same, at least for me. My grades are still crap."

"I miss having you around."

They watched a '58 Oldsmobile come up the road and turn in the driveway. "That looks like my mom," Hawk said. "What's she doing here?"

Zeke got on his bike. "I've got to get going. Good to see you."

Hawk got up off the porch, looked the car over as Florence got out. The car was tricked out with a Continental kit attached at the rear, custom hubcaps, a long radio antenna, and dice hanging off the mirror. Florence had her hair tied up in a blue bandanna and was dressed in jeans and a western shirt. She gave Hawk a big hug. Hawk did not return the favor, his arms at his side. "You've grown so much," she said. "You remember Richard?"

Richard Holdress got out of the car then. Hawk thought Richard looked like some eastern dude: creased jeans and silver belt buckle, pressed western shirt, turquoise stone bolo tie, and a Stetson cowboy hat pulled down low over his eyes. Without his snakeskin boots, he would have been shorter than Florence. Hawk nodded toward Richard but said nothing.

"Richard has a good job now with an oil-drilling company. We've bought a house. We'd like you to come see it." She handed Hawk a box wrapped in Christmas paper.

"What's this?"

"Go ahead and open it," she said. As he pulled back the paper, he saw it was a Sony transistor radio. "I thought maybe you would like it. All the kids are using them."

"I can't go to your house," Hawk said. "I'm busy."

Albert came to the door. "Who is it?"

"Hello, Al," she said.

"Well, well. You must be out of money to come here with your no-good husband."

"Back off, old man," Richard said.

Albert came across the porch, steaming, but stumbled down the steps. Hawk helped him up. "I'll kick your butt," Albert said to Richard, his voice slurred by alcohol.

Richard laid his hat on the hood of the car. "Come on, then. Let's get to it."

Hawk stepped between them. "It's okay, Dad. They're just visiting. Go on back in the house. I'm fine."

Albert dusted himself off, paused, and went back up the steps. Sooner followed him back inside.

"You want to live like this the rest of your life?" she said. "You could come with us. Get a new start."

"I'm fine. I've got a new life. I don't want to live with you."

"You may not have a choice if the courts get involved."

"What's that mean?"

"I know you're not living here during the school year. I'm your mom. If you're going to be away from here, I've got first right."

"I haven't seen you for almost two years."

"I know. We've had some rough times, but we're back on our feet. Now that I'm settled, you belong with me."

"I don't belong to anyone."

"I didn't mean it like that. Come on. Get some things packed. You can come with us now. Get away from this dump."

"It's not a dump. I like it here. I'm not leaving."

Holdress walked toward him. "Obey your mother," he said. "Get in the car." He turned to Florence. "We'll get him some new clothes at Penney's."

Hawk backed away slowly, looking for an opening. Holdress kept pressing. Hawk ducked around him and took off running down the farm lane.

"Damn. Get in the car, Florence. We'll catch him."

At an opening in the fence, Hawk made a sharp turn and headed cross-country toward the river. By the time Holdress had backed out and followed him, Hawk was out in the field running through the grass.

"Ain't wrecking the car to get him," he said. "You're gonna need a court order." He turned the car around and drove back to the highway.

CHAPTER FORTY

February 1970

The custody hearing was held in early February. In the courtroom, Florence and Richard sat on one side with their attorney, David Grabel. Christine was seated beside Hawk. Also present were Principal Bronson, Coach Barkley, Three Songs, George, Albert, Gina, and her mother Sarah. Before the evidence was presented, the magistrate set the tone for the hearing. "I want the parties to know," he said, "that the state's primary interest is making sure that a child lives with one of his parents. If one parent is found unfit, or if the circumstances of the current custody are not appropriate, then the child, by Oklahoma law, must be placed in the custody of the other parent. The court may not consider custody of a nonparent when there is a suitable parent available to assume custody."

He looked at both counsel. "Am I understood?"

Grabel nodded.

Christine spoke up. "I understand the basic concept you're proposing," she said, "but the law is also clear that a child's well-being is not determined solely by the immediate parental guardianship, but the larger context of his environment and how he is achieving success in that environment."

"You're not listening," the magistrate said to Christine. "I don't care about the total environment. My job is to place the child with the appropriate parent. Now, in this case, I'm led to believe by the investigator's report that the father is an unemployed alcoholic. The mother, on the other hand, is married to an employed oilfield worker who makes a good living. The mother is a capable, responsible parent who is entitled to custody."

"With all due respect, Charles has not seen his mother in two years. She walked out and abandoned him. Her so-called responsible husband has been the subject of several complaints of abuse from the mother."

"Irrelevant," Grabel interjected. "Besides, they've all been dismissed."

"Charles is getting along well in school. He is a good student and athlete, and the tribe has made him an apprentice to the medicine elder. This proposed change of custody would disrupt all of that opportunity for him."

The magistrate interrupted again. "We have a limited time to hear this matter, so we're going to excuse the witnesses from the courtroom and begin hearing evidence. Just understand that I will not allow extraneous testimony about custody arrangements or environments that don't involve parents."

Grabel called the court's investigator as his first witness. "We've seen the report," the magistrate said. "Confine your inquiry to questions of clarifications about the report."

"The report is clear on its face. I have no further questions," Grabel said.

On cross-examination, the court investigator admitted she had not checked the criminal records and police reports regarding Richard Holdress, nor had she considered complaints of abuse that had been filed by Florence and then dropped. "The actions of the mother's spouse are not relevant," the investigator said. She had not talked with any of Charles's teachers, nor George, nor Coach Barkley.

"I did hear," she said, "that Charles has been living with a Vietnam veteran, not a relative."

On the witness stand, Florence gave a tearful account. "I left my husband because of his alcoholism and verbal abuse. I did not want to leave my son, but after I remarried, the tribe created an atmosphere that made it impossible for me to visit or even communicate with Charles. We have made a good home in Tulsa, and it is in his best interests to join us there."

Under Christine's questioning, Florence admitted that she had made no contact with Charles for the past two years—no letters, no phone calls, no visits. "You have to understand," she said. "I was just so intimidated by his father."

Christine asked the magistrate to privately interview Charles regarding his preferences. The magistrate refused. "He hasn't reached the age of consent," he said. Christine then proffered the testimonies of Principal Bronson, Coach Barkley, Three Songs, and George.

"Your proffer is denied," the magistrate said. "I explained at the outset that I will not consider any nonparental custody arrangement when there is a fit parent able to assume custody."

At the conclusion of the evidentiary hearing, the magistrate recessed for a short period. He returned to render his decision. "Charles's custody will be changed to Florence Holdress, effective immediately. I expect the parties to work out some reasonable arrangements for visitation between Charles and his father, which will be part of the order." He banged his gavel and left the bench.

Hawk sat at the counsel table, stunned. He leaned toward Christine and whispered, "Does that mean I have to go with them?"

Christine nodded. "Unfortunately, there's little chance of appeal, and even if we're successful in getting a rehearing, you're going to have to stay with your mom until the court is willing to review the matter."

Florence and Richard approached the counsel table. "Let's go, kid," Holdress said. "You're with your mother now." He grabbed Hawk by the arm to move him from his chair. Hawk spun out of his grasp and stood. "Don't touch me," he said. He looked at his mother. "Why did you do this to me?"

"Oh, honey," she said. "I love you. You belong with me."

"I'm not anyone's property," he said. "Especially not yours."

Holdress snapped, "Keep your mouth shut. Respect your mother."

Christine intervened. "Please, folks," she said. "Give us a minute here. Charles will meet you out in the hall."

By then, Gina, Sarah, and the other witnesses had come into the courtroom. Christine recited the short version of the outcome. Gina slipped her hand over Hawk's fingers. When it was time for Hawk to leave, Gina gave him a brief hug, slipping a small photo into his shirt pocket. "Write me," she whispered, but he turned away, angry at the world.

George tried to offer some solace, but Hawk exploded. "See what you did? You should have left me on the reservation." Hawk walked to the courtroom door, then turned and looked back. He swept a hand around in the air, pointing to all of them and the courtroom in general.

"All of this," he said, "is just a bunch of crap, treating me like I'm a piece of meat." He shoved the courtroom door open and stalked out into the hall. Sarah wrapped her arms around Gina.

"Is there anything we can do?" George asked.

"There's virtually no chance for a rehearing," Christina said. "While the magistrate was completely arbitrary in his refusal to hear the evidence we offered, the supervising judge won't just overturn the decision. He'll take the easy way out. So Charles really has no choice but to go with his mother."

"Hawk's right. I should never have taken him from his dad's custody. This would not have happened if he was still on the reservation."

"Don't second-guess yourself," Christine said. "You did what you thought was in his best interest. Even his dad agreed with you. Florence could have made a strong case for change of custody based on Albert's alcoholism. The courts often favor the mother in these matters, anyway."

CHAPTER FORTY-ONE

When he reached the hallway, Hawk ignored Florence and Richard and walked past them toward the exit stairway. They fell in behind him. "The car's just outside," she said. "I think you'll like your new room. We've painted it nice just for you." When they got to Richard's car, Hawk got in the backseat and slammed the door. "Fasten your seat belt," Richard said, but Hawk sat, his arms folded across his chest, staring down at the floorboards.

At their home, Florence took him upstairs to show him his room. She had new clothes laid out on the bed—some jeans and western shirts. "I figured you wouldn't have anything with you, so I bought these for you. We'll get your things from home when you have your visitations. There's a backpack, too, for school."

After a long pause, Florence said, "Well, I'll let you get settled. I'm going down to start dinner. I'll call you when it's ready."

She pointed to an empty basket in the corner. "I forgot to tell you. I got a puppy for you from a friend of mine. Thought maybe that would help. He's outside in a pen in the backyard. You can bring him in at night when it's cold. When he's housebroken, he can stay in the house. You can name him." She left him then and went downstairs.

Hawk closed the door, swept the clothes onto the floor. "I'm not dressing up like some freakin' cowboy," he said to the wall. He lay down on the bed and stared at the ceiling. He wondered what would happen now—starting over at a new school, the same crap all over again, trying to fit in. He hated George, his parents, and everyone else who had been in his life—not necessarily in that order. "Dammit," he said to himself. "Dammit to hell."

He got up and looked out the window. His room was over the sunporch, about a four-foot drop from his window. From there he could shinny across the tree limb overhanging the porch and be down on the ground and gone. He knew now was not the time to try it. They would be suspicious, afraid that he would bolt, so he would wait them out and build up their confidence that he was doing okay. Let them get careless while he took time to plan. But he'd practice while they were out of the house so that he could make the escape seamlessly.

Then he saw the puppy. He went downstairs and out the back door, and picked him up from its pen. It had the face of a Lab, but was smaller, all black except for a white patch on his chest. He seemed glad to be held but was restless. He put the dog down in the grass and watched while the dog went over near a bush and relieved himself. The dog came back to him and nuzzled him. They played on the lawn together until Florence came to the door. "Dinner's ready," she said. "Did you name him?" Hawk shook his head, put the dog back in his pen, and went inside.

Dinner was uneventful. Florence forced small talk, mostly about the dog, but Hawk stayed sullen and ate quickly. When he finished he picked up his dishes and put them in the sink.

Richard said, "Sit back down. You didn't ask to be excused."

Hawk glared at him and walked out of the kitchen. Up in his room, he flopped on his bed. He brushed up against his pocket and then found Gina's photo. He had forgotten about it. On the back, she had written, "Write me," with her address below. He memorized the address, then got up and looked around the room, pulled open a drawer to his desk and felt around inside until he found a seam where he stashed the photo. No reason to leave a trail back to her. He wondered then if Gina would consider running away with him.

He went back outside and played with the dog. "I think I'll call you Bear," he said.

CHAPTER FORTY-TWO

At dinner the next night, Richard said, "You need to get a job after school, maybe a paper route. You could help with the expenses around here, instead of wasting your time."

"I'm not wasting time."

"You mean, you're not wasting time, sir."

Hawk looked at him directly. "No, I don't." Richard's hand came flying in a wheelhouse swing at Hawk, but Hawk saw it coming and ducked, causing Richard to hit a glass of milk, sending it crashing onto the floor. "Now look what you've done," he yelled at Hawk. Florence was on the floor with paper towels picking up the glass, sopping up the milk.

"Make *him* clean it up," Richard said.

Go to hell, Hawk thought. He got up from the table and left the room.

"You get back here," he heard from the kitchen as he took the stairs two at a time to get to his room, slamming the door behind him.

A while later, Florence came in with a plate of food that she put on the desk. "I'm sorry about what happened," she said. "Richard's never been around kids much, so he needs some practice." Florence picked up some of the clothes Hawk had thrown on the floor and hung them in his closet.

"Charles, I know I haven't been a good mother to you," she said, "especially during the past two years. It was wrong the way I just left you there with your dad. But I want you to know that a day hasn't gone by when I didn't think about you. I know this change is hard, but I'm trying to do the right thing now for both of us."

"I was getting along fine with George," Hawk said. "You could have come to visit me at his house. He's a good guy, and he would have worked with us. You didn't need to go through the court and cause all this."

"It's not right that you would be living with someone else," she said. "Like it or not, I'm still your mom. Someday, you'll understand that."

She approached the door to leave.

Hawk said, "Bear."

She stopped, puzzled.

"My dog. I named him Bear."

She laughed. "That's a good name. I just hope he doesn't grow that big." She went over and looked out the window. "He seems like a good dog," she said and headed for the door.

"Mom," Hawk said. "Did you know that Horse was a hero in the war?"

Florence paused, leaning into the edge of the open door. "No, I didn't. All I heard was that he took his own life. No one would tell me anything else."

"It was George Wheeler, the guy I was staying with. He told us. He served with Horse in the same Ranger unit. After George came home, he brought Horse's medals. The tribe gave Horse a military funeral and the name 'Stalking Bear' for the afterlife. I named Bear after him."

Florence was in tears now and came over and sat on the bed next to Hawk. "I'm so sorry," she said. "He meant a lot to both of us. Thank you for telling me."

CHAPTER FORTY-THREE

On his way home from school, Hawk passed by Big Lou's Motorsports, a motorcycle dealership. He walked through the outside lot, looking at the bikes. A salesman approached him. "Can I help you with something?"

"No, just looking."

"Come over here," the salesman said. "We've got some street bikes that would fit you."

They walked over into another section of the lot. The salesman held a bike for him. "Get on. See if the size is right."

Hawk sat on the bike, grinning. "Only one problem. No money."

"Do you have a job?" Hawk shook his head. "You can buy these on credit if you have some income, and if your parent will sign for you." Hawk got off the bike. "Thanks," he said. "I want to find a job, but I don't really know where to start."

"What's your name?"

"Charles."

"I'm Al." He handed Hawk a card. "When you get ready to buy, give me a call." He set the bike back on its kickstand. "Sometimes the boss hires kids to do odd jobs on the lot. He's not around today, but stop by tomorrow. Maybe you could talk to him. Lots of grocery stores also have jobs for kids after school."

The next afternoon, Hawk told Florence he was taking Bear for a walk. He found a piece of rope for a leash, took his backpack, and walked Bear to Big Lou's.

Before he went inside the showroom, he put Bear into his backpack.

"I'd like to speak to someone about a job," he said to a woman seated at a desk.

"Sure," she said. "Cute dog." She picked up her phone and pushed an extension. "Hey, Lou, you got a visitor."

A giant of a man appeared behind Hawk. His voice boomed, "What can I do for you, son?"

"I'd like a job. I could work after school and on the weekends."

"What can you do?"

"Whatever you want. Clean up, run errands."

"Cherokee?"

Hawk nodded.

"How come you're living out here, instead of on the reservation?"

"My parents are divorced. The judge ordered me to live with my mom, and she's here in Tulsa. I need to help her with expenses."

"How old are you?"

"Fifteen."

Lou laughed. "More like fourteen. But I'll take that. Will your mom give permission?"

"Yes, sir, I think so."

"The thing is," Lou said, "I don't have a current opening. I already have a kid working here after school."

Hawk looked down at his shoes. "Well, thanks, anyway."

"Tell you what," Lou said. "Let me think about it. You give Grace your name, address, and phone number. I'll let you know if something opens up."

⟜⟝

A few days later, Hawk stopped by and spoke to Grace. "I just wondered if Lou has changed his mind."

"He's out in the lot," she said. "You stay here, and I'll check with him."

A few minutes later, she came back. "No decision yet," she said. "Thanks for checking."

Hawk went back the next day, but Lou wasn't there. He returned every day over the next week. On Friday, Grace told him Lou was in a meeting. "It'll be a while," she said.

"Do you mind if I wait for him? I'll stay outside."

Grace smiled. "Sure, go out and look at the bikes. When he comes out, I'll tell him you're here."

After a few minutes, Grace came out to the lot and found Hawk. "Lou said he'll see you now."

In his office, Lou stood up and reached across his desk, extending his hand to Hawk. "I guess you really want this job."

"Yes, sir, I do."

"Well, you're persistent, I'll give you that."

Lou picked up his phone and dialed the extension of his service manager. "Hey, Frank," he said. "Has that kid, Jason, showed up this week?"

"Haven't seen him."

"Has he called in?"

"Nope."

"Okay, if he shows up again, tell him he's fired. I've got a replacement." Lou turned back to Hawk. "Here's the deal. Come every day after school until six o'clock, then on Saturdays from seven thirty until six. I'll give you a trial period. You'll have to bring your own lunch on Saturdays."

"What will I be doing?"

"Your job is to wash the bikes—keep everything clean. I'll pay you by the hour, in cash, once a month. I don't want any more employees, so you won't be on the payroll. You'll just work for me. If you steal, screw up, or don't show up for work, you'll be done. Got it?"

"Yes, sir," Hawk said. "When could I start?"

"How about tomorrow morning? You can't bring the dog, though. What's his name, anyway?"

"Bear. I named him after my brother. He died from injuries he got in Nam."

"That's a good name. Your brother would like that. What branch was he in?"

"Army Rangers."

"Tough guys, those Rangers. I'll bet you're proud of him." He got up from his desk, pulled a photo off the wall, showing some marines in combat gear, kneeling beside a Higgins boat landing craft.

"You know," Lou said, "I served with the marines in the Pacific during World War Two—Iwo Jima, Peleliu, all of those ugly islands. Have you ever heard of the code talkers?"

Hawk nodded. "They were Navajo. They used their own language to convey secret messages so the Japanese couldn't decode it."

"I worked with the code talkers," Lou said. "They were good men. Tough soldiers."

Hawk looked at him, but could think of nothing to say.

"They all had Indian names that they preferred."

"My full name is Charles Soaring Hawk."

"I like the name Hawk," Lou said. "So Hawk it is."

He took Hawk to the service area. "You'll report every day to Frank here. He'll tell you what to do."

The next morning, Frank gave him a tour of the dealership, showroom, service bays, and body shop. "This is the wash area," he said. "When we get a bike in on trade or a customer brings one in for repair, we always wash and degrease it. So you'll start here. Then use this degreaser. Rags here. If the bikes are all cleaned, then you patrol the lot for trash and sweep the outside walks. Sweep the service bay at the end of the day. Lou says you're fourteen? You can get a scooter permit at fourteen. We'll help you so that you can run errands for parts needed for the service department. If you go on an errand for someone, tell me so that I'll know where you are."

They went back to the wash area, where several bikes were standing. "These are heavy," Frank said. "So don't try to move them without help until you get the hang of it. If you tip one over, you'll scratch the paint, and Lou will take the repair out of your pay."

Frank went back to the service bay, and Charles started washing. After getting the mud off, he flushed it down the drain and sprayed the pavement clean. He dried each of the bikes, and then used the rags and old brush and the degreaser to clean the parts. He found some chrome cleaner and worked on the trim. As he was working, the salesman Al walked by. "Heard you got the job," he said. "Glad to have you on board."

After a couple of hours, Frank stopped by. "Looking good," he said. "Did you bring a lunch?"

Hawk shook his head. "I didn't have time. And there was nothing at home."

Frank handed him a handful of change. "Vending machine over in the corner. Take a break and get yourself a candy bar."

On Saturday, as the service bay closed up, Hawk stayed on, sweeping and cleaning up. Finally, Frank came over. "That's it for today, Hawk. Good job. See you next week."

"I'm not quite done," Hawk said. "Can I come back tomorrow?"

"Service bay's not open, but the salesmen will be here. One of them will let you in there if you decide to work. I'll let the manager know you might come in."

By the time he got home, Richard and Florence had finished dinner.

"Where you been?" Richard asked.

"I was at work. I left a note."

"Well, next time, get home on time if you want any dinner."

"I have to work until six."

"How much you making, anyway?"

"Don't know for sure. Lou said he'll pay me once a month."

"Whatever it is, you give it to your mamma. Time you started pulling your own weight."

Florence set a plate on the table. "Sit down, honey," she said. "I'll dish you up some food."

CHAPTER FORTY-FOUR

The dealership showroom was open on Sunday from noon to four. Hawk was there a few minutes before noon.

The manager let him in. "Frank said you'd be here. Let me know when you're finished, and I'll lock it back up behind you."

When he finished the sweeping, Hawk surveyed the work areas, hung loose tools back on the racks, coiled the hoses, and straightened up each of the bays. Then he walked through the lot, spot-checking the bikes on display, wiping the fingerprints off with a rag and some spray cleaner. He found some trash blown into a corner of the lot, got a trash bag, cleaned it up, and threw it in the Dumpster at the back of the lot.

The sales manager approached him. "Hey, kid," he said. "What's your name?"

"Charles, sir."

"Well, Charles, you're out of uniform. If you're going to be working here, you're going to have to look the part."

He handed Hawk a hat and a windbreaker with a Big Lou's logo on them. "See if these fit."

Hawk tried them on. "Yeah, thanks. Thanks a lot." He curled the brim of the hat, shortened the headband, and took them to the locker Frank had given him. "See you next week," he hollered to the manager as he left for home.

The next day, Hawk wrote a short letter to Gina. "Got a job," he said. He mentioned Bear and his new school. "If you want to write to me, you could send it to Big Lou's. Just put my name on it.

The next Saturday, Hawk finished the washing by noon. He approached Frank. "I'm done with the cleaning. Would it be okay if I watched some of the mechanics, maybe helped a bit until you have something else for me to do?"

Frank smiled. "Tell you what. We just got this old Vespa in on trade. We'd usually just junk it, but we could probably fix it, and it'd give you something to ride on errands. I'll talk to Lou and get his approval. If Lou's okay, we'll fix it up together, and you can use it to get around."

Hawk was grinning from ear to ear. "Cool."

"It's actually not in too bad shape," Frank said. "It needs new brakes and some engine work. Jimmie, over in the body shop, will help you give it a new paint job. We'll put a dealer plate on it when it's done."

CHAPTER FORTY-FIVE

When they had finished the repairs to the Vespa, Frank helped him wheel it over to the body shop area where he introduced Hawk to Jimmie.

"Yeah," Jimmie said. "I've been seein' you around. Nice to meet you."

"Jimmie got out of trade school a couple of years ago," Frank said. "He's doing a good job. He'll be running our body shop soon as he gets more experience." Frank turned to Jimmie. "I'd like you to work with Hawk to repaint the scooter. I want him to learn how to take it apart, prep it, and paint it. Don't take up regular customer time to do it, but we'll need to get it done soon because Hawk will start using it for errands."

"I'm actually caught up with work at the moment," Jimmie said, "so we'll get started right away. It won't take long to get it ready."

Hawk pulled a pencil sketch out of his pocket and unfolded it. It was a picture of a hawk diving, talons down. "I'd like to paint this on the rear fender after we get the new coat on."

Jimmie took the sketch and showed it to Frank. "This is great. I've got some color tabs there on the shelf. We can match it with the body paint."

Jimmie went to his workbench and found some hand tools. "Before we start, you look it over and see if you can figure out how it comes apart. Then I'll help you. Some of the bolts and fasteners will be tough because of rust, but I'll show you how to get 'em loose."

As they started working, Jimmie said, "You got some talent. Over lunch break, I'll show you my pickup. I'm working on it now, getting ready to paint—maybe you could do a design for me as well. Maybe some pinstripes."

At lunch Hawk and Jimmie went across the lot and looked at Jimmie's '55 Ford pickup. He'd patched all the holes, sanded the filler, and primed the spots. Hawk walked alongside the truck, trailing his hand across the patches, feeling the smoothness. "It reminds me of a pinto horse we had on the rez. Kind of the same coloring. Maybe a horse design would be good."

"Yeah, that would be cool. Could you work up some sketches?"

"I'll bring some in."

"Ain't never met a real Indian before—except for maybe Crazy Harry."

"Who's that?" Hawk asked.

"Some old hermit my dad and I met one time hunting in the Ozarks. We don't know his real name. Dad just started calling him Harry. Anyway, he's got this cabin in the woods at the edge of the national forest just on the other side of the line into Arkansas. His truck was broken down by the side of the road, and we stopped to help him. Took him home. He can hear and understand words, but can't speak. He waves his arms around, points to stuff. But he was a good cook. We stayed overnight in his cabin and then helped him get his truck fixed and back home. Harry's like a real hermit, you can't see his place from the road. It's well hidden. He sneaks into the forest and poaches game. Does everything—tans the leather, makes his clothes like an old mountain man. Dresses like he's Indian, but Dad's not sure if he is. Just lives on his own."

"Could we go up there sometime?"

"I guess so. I think I could find it again. He's a pretty weird dude, though."

"I could speak some Cherokee to him. Maybe he'd understand."

"Why do you want to go there?"

"I need to get away from my stepdad. I'm looking for some place to go."

"How are you going to get away?"

"I'm not sure yet, but I'll be able to work it out soon. Maybe we could go up sometime this summer when I don't have school."

As they walked back from their lunch break, the receptionist motioned for Hawk to come to her desk. She handed him a letter. "Came today," she said. "We're not supposed to get personal mail here at the dealership. Is there another address your friend could use?"

"Not really. I don't want her letters coming home where my stepdad can see them."

"Okay," she said. "For now, I'll just drop them in this side drawer here. I'll let you know when they come. Lou likes your work. You're doing a good job."

"Thanks," he said. "You've been real nice to me."

CHAPTER FORTY-SIX

With Hawk staying at his mom's, George revised his routine to spend more time on campus with Mel. He attended the yoga sessions with Mel, mixing the routine with workouts in the campus fitness area, did his studying in the library. It took a while for George to get comfortable with the yoga class. There was only one other male in the class who was much older than George, but fit.

George wondered aloud if people would think he was weird.

"You don't have to wear leotards," Mel said. "Just do the work."

"I just hope Earl and Fuzzy don't find out. I'll never live it down."

"Don't be so sure," Mel said. "Sports coaches are now using yoga as part of their training regimens. It teaches balance and helps build muscle tone. It's just that the teacher goes there to the gym where the players can be together."

Eventually, George found the workouts useful. He even bought his own mat and set up a place at home where he could practice.

Hawk had cooled down from his courtroom tirade and let George take him to the reservation on occasional Sundays for visits with his dad and Three Songs. After dropping Hawk at home, George would go to Nancy's house for Sunday dinner.

One Sunday, Albert and Three Songs met Hawk, Mel, and George at the museum. Hawk showed them through the exhibits, describing what he had learned.

"This is a good display," Three Songs said, "but don't forget, these artifacts were recovered by whites desecrating our sacred burial sites."

"I never thought of that," Hawk said, "but you're right. These rightfully belong back where they were found."

"We can't change that now. Just don't forget it. It's up to us to preserve our heritage. No one else will do it for us."

CHAPTER FORTY-SEVEN

On the last Saturday of the month, Big Lou called Hawk into his office. "I was going to pay you a buck an hour," he said. "But you're a good worker, so I'm adding a bonus of fifty cents an hour. I'm not paying you for Sundays, although my sales manager says you've been coming in on some days, doing extra work. I like that. You want to get ahead. I'll put the bonus in an envelope here for you, like a savings account. At the end of every quarter, I'll give you the savings from the previous three months. That'll be an incentive for you to stay working. If you leave before the end of a quarter, you'll forfeit the bonus for that quarter. Sound like a deal?"

"That's okay," Hawk said, then hesitated. "Sir? I was wondering if I could put that extra money toward the Vespa. I've got my permit now. At the end of the school year, I could work more hours if it'd be okay."

Lou hefted the envelope, thinking. "What do you think it's worth?"

"I don't know, but Frank said you would probably just junk it. So whatever you say. I'll even keep it here at work until it's paid for, so you'll know I'm only using it for work."

"Well, I gave a hundred and fifty dollars on trade for it, but that was just to make the deal on a new bike. How about a hundred?"

Hawk nodded. "Yes, sir, that'd be okay."

"Deal." Lou stuck out his hand to shake. "Frank tells me you've been helping in the shop, and Jimmie really likes your artwork. He's going to put some samples up on the wall in the body shop. If people start seeing your art, they'll want special paint jobs. We'll get some more things for you to do."

Hawk rode the scooter home that night. He took out thirty dollars from his pay and hid it with Gina's picture. He gave the rest to his mom.

At dinner, Richard mentioned the scooter. "Where'd you steal that from?"

"It belongs to Big Lou. It was going to be junked, so we fixed it up for me to use running errands. Lou said I could use it on my own time."

"Kind of a wimpy two-wheeler, if you ask me. Something a girl would ride. When I was a kid, I had a real dirt bike."

"It's transportation, and it helps me do my job."

"Just keep it out of the way, unless you want me to back over it with the car."

Hawk installed an eyebolt on the floor of the scooter. On Sundays, he put Bear on his leash and snapped it into the eyebolt, letting Bear ride between his legs on the floor of the scooter. To get him used to the movement, he took Bear for test drives around the neighborhood and then gradually on longer trips. Bear poked his nose around the foot guard to feel the breeze and learned to lean into the curves with Hawk while keeping his footing. Passersby smiled at the odd pair.

CHAPTER FORTY-EIGHT

Hawk had finished his homework and was lying on his bed with Bear. He had the radio on softly, listening to a rock 'n' roll station. He could hear the television in the living room, turned up loud for a sitcom. He heard Richard's voice. "Florence, get in here." Hawk turned off the radio, quietly opened his bedroom door. He could see Richard standing in the living room, a bundle of clothes in his arms.

His mom came into the living room.

"When are you doing the laundry?" Richard said.

"I already did it. Your clothes are in your closet."

"Squaw, I told you I like my western shirts starched," he said. "You call this starched?" He threw the clothes on the floor in front of her. As she gathered them up, he kicked her, toppling her over onto the floor. "You never seem to get it right," he said. "It's all about that kid of yours now. It's time you started taking care of your man."

Florence got up, gathering the clothes. "I'm doing everything same as always. I don't know what you're complaining about."

He grabbed her by the front of her shirt and sent her sprawling across the floor into a wall. "If you don't know what I want," he said, "then you'd better find out before you get hurt."

She rose up slowly, gathering the clothes against her chest.

"Now, bring me some bourbon, and it better be fixed the way I like it."

Florence stood for a minute, gathering her wits. She dropped the clothes and went to the kitchen for the liquor.

Hawk closed his door. He switched the radio back on and turned it up louder.

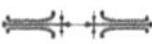

A few days later, when Hawk got home from work, dinner was over. Richard was still at the table, smoking a cigarette, nursing a glass of bourbon neat.

"Hi, Mom," Hawk said. He looked at the plate sitting at his place. "Is there any food left?"

"Don't matter," Richard said. "If you're not home on time, you don't get to eat."

"I had to work late. Lou had a bunch of cycles come in today. They needed cleaning."

"Sit down, honey," Florence said. "There's plenty of food."

Richard reached across the table and sent Hawk's plate sailing across the kitchen. It smashed against the wall. "I said there's no food for anyone who shows up late."

Hawk grabbed his empty milk glass and slid it hard across the table, smashing it into the bourbon glass, shattering both.

Richard jumped up. "You little punk," he said. Hawk was already leaving the kitchen, heading for the stairs. He turned to see Florence barring the doorway, holding a candlestick in one hand, threatening Richard. "Back off!"

Hawk continued upstairs, slammed the door to his room, and heard more arguing.

"Settle down, Richard," his mom said.

"It's time that kid learned some discipline."

"What, you want him to be like you, a drunk, a bully? You touch him, I'll kill you."

"Bitch, it's time I taught you a lesson."

Hawk opened his door and stood there listening. He was slapping her with his belt, then shoved her down to the floor. As Florence screamed at him, Hawk ran down the stairs. By the time he got to the kitchen, the back door had slammed shut, and he heard Richard's car squeal out of the driveway.

Florence was crumpled in a corner of the kitchen. "Mom, Mom," he said. "You okay?"

Florence nodded and tried to get up. Hawk helped her get to her feet. He got her to a chair. Her face was a blotch of red. She was in pain, holding her ribs. Hawk went to the refrigerator for some ice, wrapped it in a tea towel, and brought it to her. He had her hold it to her face.

"Why do you let him do that?" he said.

"He's just drunk. There's no stopping him when he's that way. I'm glad he left. He'll come back tomorrow, but maybe he'll be sobered up by then."

"Shouldn't we call the police?"

"I've called before. They wouldn't do anything. It just made him mad, and he beat me again."

"You can't let him do that."

"Come here," she said. She held him close in her arms and started to sob.

The next morning when Hawk left for school, Richard was at the kitchen table, nursing a cup of coffee. When he kissed his mom good-bye, Hawk could see the black-and-blue bruises on her face. He gave her a hug, grabbed his backpack, and stormed past Richard without comment.

CHAPTER FORTY-NINE

During the last week of March, over Hawk's spring break, George and Mel picked him up for a week's visitation with his dad. By prearrangement with Albert, Hawk spent a couple of nights at George's house before George took him to the reservation. George also arranged a visit with Gina.

George dropped Hawk and Bear at her house and left him for the afternoon with the plan that George and Mel would come back and have dinner with Gina's family.

It was a sunny day, but still chilly. Gina, Hawk, and Bear walked together back to the high school.

"What's it like with your mom?" she asked.

"School's okay. Everyone just ignores me, leaves me alone. I go to my job every day right after class and work there most of the weekend. My mom is nice, but her husband is a real creep. He beats her up whenever he gets drunk."

"That must be awful."

"She won't do anything about it. I don't get why she takes it."

"Patti's dad is like that. She says her mom is getting a divorce."

They stopped at the front lawn of the school.

"Watch this," Hawk said. He led Bear over by the rock and unclipped the leash. "Sit, Bear," he said. Hawk walked back a few steps. Bear started to get up, but Hawk said, "Stay, Bear." Bear sat back on his haunches, watching. Hawk continued to back away until he reached Gina. He knelt down. "Come, Bear," he called. The dog jumped up and trotted over and took a treat from Hawk.

"I've been training him," he said.

"That's amazing," she said. "Where did you learn to do that?"

"Mom helped me. She trained my other dog, Sooner. Bear's really smart and catches on quickly."

Gina got up. "Follow me." She took his hand, and they walked back into a small alcove behind the main building. When they were out of sight of the street, she said, "I've been thinking about this for weeks." She put her arms around his neck, pulled him close to her, and kissed him. Hawk was surprised, not sure what to do. She kissed him again. "I've missed you so much."

"Me too," he said. Hawk held her tight, smelling the cool air in her hair, mixed with her perfume. They separated as they heard a car pull into the parking lot. They saw a teacher get out and enter the building. "Come on," Gina said. "Let's go back. Dinner will be ready soon."

CHAPTER FIFTY

After his spring break, Hawk returned to a worsening situation. Whenever Richard was in the house, Hawk could hear the arguing, which usually ended in Richard calling his mom names and hitting her. One evening in May, Richard arrived home late, drunk. Florence had kept food warm for him. When she served him, he threw the plate full of food across the kitchen.

"I'm tired of eating your slop," he said. From his bedroom, Hawk could hear the crash of chairs being thrown around. His mother screamed as Richard beat her. Hawk called the police from the upstairs phone and reported his stepdad to the dispatching clerk. A short time later, Florence opened the door to the responding officer.

"We had a call," the officer said.

"I didn't call," she said.

"Who else is in the home?"

"My husband. And my son's upstairs in his bedroom."

"Is there a phone up there?"

Florence nodded.

The officer studied the bruises on Florence. "Well, I'm here. Do you want to make a report?"

Florence shook her head. "I'll be all right. Thank you for coming."

After the police left, Hawk was in his room, lying on his bed, Bear beside him. Some music was playing on the transistor radio at the end of his bed.

Richard came to the door and rattled the knob. Finding it locked, he yelled through the door, "Open it!" When Hawk didn't respond, Richard kicked it in. He stood in the doorway, looking at Hawk.

"Time for show and tell," he said. He pointed to the radio playing on the bed beside Hawk. "You should stop listening to that crap." Reaching around behind his back, Richard pulled a pistol from his waistband. He held it in one hand, stroked the barrel with the other. He swayed a bit, unsteady. "You know what this is?"

"A gun."

"Not just a gun. A Smith and Wesson, snub nose, thirty-eight caliber. It's good protection—reliable and effective. There are millions of them in circulation, all unregistered." He spun the cylinder, looked it over, and snapped it back into place. "Holds six shots. Enough for you, your mom, and that scruffy mutt lying beside you. I use hollow points. One shot does a lot of damage." He walked toward the bed.

Hawk lay there, holding Bear close to him, staring at Richard, saying nothing. He could feel droplets of sweat under his arms.

"I know what you're thinking—that I'm just bluffing, trying to scare you. You're thinking I wouldn't do anything that would land me in jail." He pointed the gun at Hawk.

"Let me tell you something, kid. I've been in the joint before. Ain't nothin' there I'm worried about, and that's even assuming the dumb cops caught me before I got to Mexico or Canada or

Alaska—wherever I'd get to before they found the bodies." He walked around to the side of the bed.

"So, you think on this. You interfere again, you're gonna hear a pop. Then you'll come downstairs and see your mom lying there on the floor. Then there'll be another pop, and you'll be lying next to her. Then the dog will join you."

He grabbed the pillow from behind Hawk's head. "Consider that before you try to play the hero again." He pulled the hammer back, put the pillow on top of the radio, and stuffed the gun into it. There was a muffled shot, silencing the radio. He held the pillow up, showed Hawk the powder burns over the bullet hole, and threw it in his face.

"See how easy that was? Your mom didn't even hear it over the TV, and no one else will either."

He walked back to the door and then turned. "Pay attention, boy, if you want to live long enough to see next year. Even then I might drop you for the fun of it." Richard moved the door on its hinges and looked at the broken panel. "See what you've done?" he said. "You're going to have to pay for that." He stalked out into the hallway, down the stairs, and out the front door. Hawk heard him back out and drive off down the street.

Hawk looked at the pillow. He heard his mother coming up the stairs. He put the pillow behind his head and pulled Bear closer.

Florence appeared at the door. "I thought I heard a gunshot."

"Maybe a firecracker outside."

"Why, then, am I smelling gunpowder?"

Hawk shrugged. "Don't know."

"What'd he want?" she said.

Hawk sat up on one elbow, looking at her. "Nothing," he said. "He was just mad I called the cops."

"I know you want to help, honey, but you should just stay away from him when he's like that."

"He's always like that."

"Not always."

"Why didn't you file charges with the police?"

"I've done that before. They won't do anything. It just makes things worse. It's not worth the hassle."

She started to leave, then saw the door. "You said nothing happened. Who broke the door?"

"It was locked. He wanted in."

She picked up the radio, examined the smashed front. "So, did he put a bullet in this?"

"I told you no," he said.

"Tell me the truth." She stood beside him. "I'm not leaving this room until I get an honest answer."

Hawk stalled.

"Well?"

"He threatened me," Hawk said. "I didn't want to make you worry."

"What'd he say?"

"That if I called the cops again, he'd kill all of us, Bear included."

Florence slumped down on the bed and put her hand on Hawk's.

"He's just bluffing," Hawk said. "But don't tell him I told you."

"Hawk," she said. "He's a very dangerous man. I want you to stay clear of him. I'll find a way to deal with him. Promise me you'll stay out of it."

"Okay," he said. "But it's not right. If I have to, I'll call the cops again. I'll file the charges myself."

After she walked out of the room, Hawk lay there wondering how he got in this mess, why his brother had left him alone. He wrapped the radio in the pillowcase and stuffed it into his backpack.

CHAPTER FIFTY-ONE

May 1970

On a Sunday, Jimmie agreed to take Hawk to find Crazy Harry. When they got near the forest, they took a couple of roads without finding the cabin, then came to a small convenience store with a double gas pump.

"Okay," Jimmie said. "Now I know where I am. We had stopped here just before we found Harry up the road. I think I can find his place from here."

They discovered the track then. It was barely visible from the road, just a couple of wheel ruts leading up a slight grade, around several bends, then ending at a small cabin surrounded by woods. Jimmie honked as he came up the drive, and stopped well short of the house. "We'd better walk from here," he said, "so's he'll recognize me."

Crazy Harry came out on his porch in leather pants, a T-shirt, and a headband tied around his gray hair. He was barefoot.

"Harry," Jimmie said. "It's me, Jimmie, remember?" Harry smiled and came off the porch. "This here's Charles Soaring Hawk."

Hawk raised his hand and said hello in Cherokee. Harry looked at him for a minute. He came closer and started dancing around them, waving his arms.

Hawk imitated him with a few parts of a war dance Three Songs had taught him. He reached into a pocket of his backpack, pulled out some jerky, and gave him a piece. Crazy Harry looked at it, tilting his head. Then he bit off a piece, chewed it, and broke into a broad smile. Waving his arms, he motioned them into the house.

The cabin was well built, sturdy. It had a small cookstove in one corner, and the only furniture was a table and two chairs, handmade. A cot, covered by a wool Indian blanket, had been built into another corner.

There was a shotgun propped up next to a longbow and a quiver of homemade arrows. Fantails, which Hawk recognized as grouse and wild turkey, were tacked to the wall. The only light was a kerosene lamp hanging on a hook over the table. Leather leggings and a jacket hung on pegs on the wall by the door. The place was sparse, but immaculate.

Harry brought out some flat bread, put a jar of jelly and a knife on the table, and motioned them to eat.

Hawk noted an eagle feather tied to the quiver. He pointed to it, saying the word *eagle* in Cherokee. Harry reached up on a shelf and pulled down two pieces of bone. He blew into one, making an eagle cry. He handed a bone to Hawk, who imitated it, but not as well. Harry called back and then smiled. He nodded to Hawk to try again. Hawk blew into it several times before getting the sound right. Harry clapped his hands and did a few dance steps.

Jimmie said, "We can't stay. Just wanted to stop and say hello." They started to leave. Hawk spoke again in Cherokee. Harry nodded and waved his arms.

Back in the truck, Jimmie asked, "What did you say to him?"

"I asked him if I could come back and stay with him awhile."

"What about your mom—would she allow that?"

"I'll tell you more about that. I hope so. For now, I don't want anyone to know I was here, so keep it to yourself."

CHAPTER FIFTY-TWO

June 1970

One Saturday in mid-June, Hawk went to Big Lou's office. "I have to go back to the rez for the summer, so I won't be able to come into work for a while."

"Sorry to hear that," he said, "You're a good worker. As soon as you're back, you come see me." Lou opened up his desk drawer. "You want your bonus?"

"Is the Vespa paid for?"

"Yeah, and some left over."

"Then, if you don't mind, I'll take the cash so that I have something to get me through the summer. I'd like to leave the Vespa here. I have no way to get it home, and there's no place to ride it there anyway."

"Tell you what," Lou said. "Let's leave the Vespa titled in the dealership. That way, when you get back, you can use a dealer tag, and you won't have to pay for insurance."

"Thanks for everything," Hawk said. "You've helped me a lot."

On the way home, Hawk stopped at a pay phone and called Gina's house. Her mom answered the phone. "Just a minute," she said. Hawk heard her call for Gina. "I think it's Charles," she said.

When Gina picked up, Hawk asked, "Is your mom still on the line?"

"She went outside. I heard her hang up the extension."

"I want to tell you something," he said. "But you have to promise that you won't tell anyone, not George, not even your parents."

Gina paused. "Why?"

"When I tell you, you'll know why. Promise?"

"Okay," she said, "I'll keep it to myself if you promise me that you're not going to do something to hurt yourself."

"I won't. It's just that I'm going away," he said. "I've got to get out of my house. I can't stand living there."

Gina started to choke up. "Where are you going?"

"I've found a safe place. There's someone there, another Cherokee. It'll work out."

"Where is it?"

"I can't tell you any more right now. You won't hear from me for a while, but I will come back." More silence.

"I don't know, Hawk."

"Please trust me on this," he said finally.

He could hear Gina crying.

Another pause. "I have to go now. I think I love you," he said. He hung up.

CHAPTER FIFTY-THREE

The following Sunday, Jimmie met Hawk at the dealership. Hawk parked the Vespa in the body shop and put a tarp over it.

"Don't you want to take it with you?" Jimmie asked.

"It's still titled in the dealership," Hawk said. "Lou thinks I'm going home to the rez for the summer. I told him I'd leave it here. I don't want anything to happen to it. If I don't come back, Lou can resell it if he wants."

Hawk had Jimmie drop him and Bear on the road at the entrance to Harry's drive. "Don't tell anyone where I am. I'll never let on that you brought me here. I don't plan to go back home." He pulled a package from his backpack addressed to George and handed it to Jimmie. "One more thing," he said. "Please wait a couple of weeks, then put this in the mail. He gave Jimmie a five-dollar bill. "This should cover the postage."

"What is it?"

"Just some things I want my friend to have."

"All right," Jimmie said. "I hope you know what you're doing. If things don't go well, call me from the convenience store, and I'll come get you."

As Jimmie drove off, Hawk slipped on his backpack, put Bear on his leash, and started up the drive. A couple of times he thought he saw something move off to the side of the road, but decided it was his imagination. By the time he got to the cabin, Harry was standing on the porch, cradling a shotgun.

Hawk waved and walked toward Harry, calling, "Osiyo."

When Harry recognized Hawk, he cracked the gun open and propped it by the door. Harry came off the porch and danced around Hawk. Bear barked at him, and Harry stopped. He let Bear smell his hand, then petted him.

Inside the cabin, a pot was simmering on the stove filling the room with the rich smell of stew cooking. Harry set two plates down, served the stew, and put some in a pan to cool for Bear. He laid some flat bread on the table and poured two glasses of water. He made eating motions with his hands.

"Venison?" Hawk said in Cherokee. Harry nodded.

"Can I stay here awhile? I've run away from home, and I don't want to go back."

Harry got up and walked around the table, thinking. Then he waved Hawk outside. He pointed to Hawk's footprints in the dirt. Harry went to the edge of the woods, broke off a sapling, and came back, brushing the ground to erase the tracks. They returned to finish their meal.

CHAPTER FIFTY-FOUR

The following morning, George got a call from Florence. "Charles has come up missing," she said.

"I haven't seen or heard from him," George said.

"I've called the dealership, but he's not at work. His boss told me that Charles was going back to the reservation for the summer. I'm going to drive out there and see. He should have said something. He's supposed to be with me."

"I doubt that he's there. I don't know how he'd get there, but it's worth checking."

"Al can be a bit volatile, so I'm worried about just dropping in."

"I'll meet you there. If Albert is upset, just wait until I get there, and we'll talk to him together."

As George arrived at the reservation, he passed an EMS vehicle leaving, sirens sounding. At Albert's home, he met Florence on the front step, talking with the tribal police officer.

"Richard drove me here," she said. "As soon as we arrived, Al came out of the house, yelling at us to get off his property. I tried to ask him about Charles, but he picked up a pipe and smashed a headlight on Richard's car. Richard wrested the pipe from him and coldcocked him. The EMS just left."

"Where's Richard now?"

"I don't know. Headed home, I guess. I refused to go with him. I'm done living there. I just want to find my son."

After the tribal police left, Florence and George went inside.

The dog came over and nuzzled her. "Hello, Sooner," she said. "You look like the rest of us, haggard and worn-out. Anybody fed you today?" She saw a bag of dog food in the corner of the kitchen, fixed him a bowl, and gave him some clean water. She slumped in a kitchen chair, head in her hands. She sat back up, smoothing her hair back. "What a dump," she said. "No wonder Charles moved in with you."

Together, George and Florence began collecting the trash, emptying ashtrays, clearing out the rotten food from the refrigerator. Florence went back to the bedroom, stripped the bed, and collected laundry. She found a box of Tide under the sink and started a load. Then she returned to the kitchen, where she washed everything down.

"What do I do now?" she said. "I don't have a car, and what money I had is in my purse in Richard's car."

"For one thing, you witnessed an assault. You should file charges."

Florence laughed. "That's a joke. White man accused of assaulting Indian. Most people around here, Richard included, think it's their right to beat up on Indians."

"Regardless, you need to speak with a lawyer," George said.

There was a knock on the door. Florence let a woman in.

"Martha," Florence said. "Come on in here, girl."

A woman entered the home and gave Florence a bear hug. "Heard there was a ruckus."

"That's putting it mildly," Florence said. "Meet George Wheeler. He's a friend of the family."

"I saw the EMS truck," Martha said.

"They took Al to the hospital. Richard hit him in the head with a pipe."

"What're you going to do?"

"I don't know. I refused to go with Richard, so I'm on my own."

"Got a place to stay?" Martha asked.

Florence shook her head.

"I've got a spare bedroom," Martha said. "You can bunk with us while we figure this out."

CHAPTER FIFTY-FIVE

Hawk awoke with Bear licking his face. Harry was already at the stove, warming breakfast. Hawk rolled up the blanket and tucked it into the corner. They ate the rest of last night's stew. Then Harry motioned for Hawk to put on a jacket, and the three of them struck out toward the woods. He showed Hawk a latrine he'd built about fifty feet from the cabin. On the opposite side of the cabin, he'd fenced in a garden near a spring where he got his water. He'd built an enclosure there, like a small springhouse where he kept some things cool. There was a tin cup hanging on a nail by the door. He filled the cup with the water and handed it to Hawk. Hawk drank it, refilled it, and gave some to Bear.

Hawk followed Harry on a small trail into the woods. As they walked, Harry made some small blazes on the bark of trees behind them. He stopped occasionally to let Hawk get his bearings. When they reached a hillside with a view of the surrounding area, Harry stopped again and let Hawk look around. They heard a rustle off to one side and watched a deer appear and then slide back into the woods after seeing them.

By noon, Harry motioned to Hawk to take them back to the cabin. Slowly they made their way home, following Harry's blazes. Bear was already comfortable and knew where to go. They made another trail away from the cabin in the afternoon and continued the practice for several days as Hawk learned his way around. Harry showed Hawk where he had set snares, and they made the rounds of them, checking them. They harvested a rabbit he'd caught. Hawk looked at a nearby pile of wood Harry had cut.

"Would you like help splitting that?" Hawk asked. Harry nodded. "Show me how you want it done."

One morning, after their hike to check the snares, they returned to Harry's cabin. Harry went over to the driver's side of his pickup. Opening the door, he motioned for Hawk to get in. Bear jumped in first, and Hawk sat behind the wheel. Harry got in on the passenger's side, closed the door, and handed the keys to Hawk.

Puzzled, Hawk asked, "You want me to drive?"

Harry nodded.

"I don't know how."

Harry took Hawk's hand, put the key in the ignition, and made a turning motion. Hawk turned the key, and the truck jumped and stalled. Harry smiled, pointed to Hawk's left foot and the clutch pedal. He made a motion for Hawk to depress the clutch and then turn the key again. This time, with the clutch in, the truck started and idled. Harry moved Hawk through the gears, holding up one finger for first, then moving the shift to second gear and holding up two fingers. In reverse, he pointed backward out the window. He moved the gearshift back to first, then indicated for Hawk to release the clutch while depressing the gas. Hawk let the clutch out too quickly, and the truck stalled again.

Harry grinned, slapping the dashboard. He made the motions again, showing the friction point, when both pedals were roughly even. Hawk started the truck and tried again, this time inching the truck forward without stalling. He pressed the brake to stop but forgot to put the clutch in, and the truck stalled again. They kept practicing, and Hawk began to move the truck in a wide circle in front of the cabin, getting the hang of the gearshift and use of the clutch.

When they got out of the truck, Harry danced in front of it, making herky-jerky movements the way Hawk first drove. Bear was chasing him, barking. Hawk joined in the dance, mimicking Harry, laughing. Hawk went inside the cabin and found a piece of charcoal in the woodstove. He returned and sketched an eagle on the hood, feathers trailing over the fender. Harry clasped him on the shoulder, proud of the decoration. Harry prepared dinner for them, and then Bear and Hawk retired for the night.

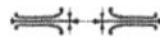

After a few days, Harry took the truck to go buy supplies. When he got back to the cabin it was empty, but within the hour Hawk and Bear came in from the woods. Hawk was carrying another rabbit. "Checked the snares," he said.

That afternoon, they walked a long distance from the cabin, down into a ravine. Harry stopped near a large brush pile and pulled a couple of branches away. Behind the branches was a three-sided Adirondack-type lean-to lodged up against the wall of the ravine. There was a low bunk built along the back, a fire pit in the center. He took Hawk up a short trail along the side of a hill and showed him another spring. He knelt and cupped his hand to drink and motioned to Hawk. All three drank there. Harry first pointed to Hawk and then the shelter as if to say, you will stay here. He gave Hawk the bone whistle and motioned him to blow it. Then he held up three fingers and pointed to himself.

When they were back at the cabin, Harry motioned for Hawk to get his gear packed. Harry also filled a wicker pack basket with a small cast-iron pot, a knife, a hatchet, and some food. Hawk gave Harry a pencil sketch of an eagle soaring. "I drew this while you were getting supplies." Harry danced again, then found a nail in one of the timbers and stuck the picture there.

Gathering their gear, they hiked back to the shelter. Harry helped cover the bed with pine boughs. They gathered firewood. Harry had Hawk shinny up a tree with a rope, and they created a food cache to keep the food away from wild animals. They built a fire, Harry showing him how to keep it small and hot to avoid smoke that would disclose his location.

By evening, Hawk and Bear were settled in, and Harry returned to his cabin.

CHAPTER FIFTY-SIX

On his first morning in the shelter, Hawk awoke to the smell of bacon frying. He could hear some low singing. Harry was squatting by the fire, cooking with his back to Hawk. Bear was lying beside him. Hawk closed his eyes and listened to the song, finally realizing that it was a Cherokee cradle song, sung by mothers to their babies. *So Harry can speak?* he thought. *Why would he pretend to be mute?* Hawk stretched, making some noise. Then he waited. The singing stopped. Hawk rolled on his back, stretched again, and sat up. Bear came over to him, tail wagging. "Good morning," he said to Harry while hugging Bear. The air was cool. Hawk retrieved a sweatshirt from his pack and moved over to the fire beside Harry. Harry gave him a piece of bacon from the frying pan. Hawk blew on it to cool it, then gave a portion to Bear. Harry scrambled some eggs in the grease and then warmed flat bread he had brought from the cabin. Together, they ate the breakfast.

"I heard you singing," Hawk said in Cherokee.

Harry replied in Cherokee, "I will speak with you, but only in Cherokee. I will never speak the English. Do not tell anyone that I can speak at all."

"I will honor that. But why won't you speak?"

"When I was a small boy, all the children in my tribe were required to go to the white man's schools. They took us by force and made us live at a school far from our home. I never saw my family again. They tried to make us forget our Cherokee language and insisted we learn English. I refused, so they beat me in front of the other children."

Harry stood up and lifted his shirt, revealing deep scars that crisscrossed his back. "They beat me many times, but I would not speak the English. When the school closed, I was adopted by a white family who owned a large cattle ranch. I was good with horses and worked hard there. They treated me well, but I was still a prisoner. When I became a man, I tried to find my tribe, but I had no idea where they were. That's when I moved here."

"What's your name?"

"I am White Owl. The whites gave me another name, which I won't say."

After breakfast, they moved the branches back to conceal the lean-to and then left to explore the area. Bear seemed excited, running off following a scent, then coming back. By afternoon, they were back at the shelter. Harry showed Hawk how to carve a deadfall trigger for trapping small animals. The first time Hawk set his version under a large rock, Harry tried to trigger it, but the rock wouldn't fall. Harry studied the trigger and showed Hawk how he had cut the bevels incorrectly. Hawk carved another one and this time, with only slight pressure on the bait stick, the rock dropped instantly. Harry did his war dance, smiling. They walked back to the cabin, checking traps along the way, and found a snared rabbit.

Harry knelt by the rabbit and said a prayer. "You should always thank the animal's spirit, or you will have bad hunting."

Behind and away from the cabin, Harry began to clean and skin the rabbit with a penknife. Partway through the process, he handed the knife to Hawk and motioned for him to complete the job, helping him get the hide off intact. When they finished, Harry braised the rabbit parts with butter in his iron skillet, and Hawk cut up some potatoes, a few wild onions, and some greens that Hawk didn't recognize. They put the vegetables together with the rabbit in the skillet and let them cook slowly.

While the food was cooking, Harry brought out a bow and arrows he had made. They went to a clearing, where he showed Hawk how to shoot. Harry tied a rabbit hide to a string he hung from a branch, and Hawk practiced. At short range he missed a few times, but as his accuracy improved, Harry moved him back to challenge him. While Hawk practiced, Harry fashioned a crude quiver with a piece of canvas. He fitted a strap to go over Hawk's chest.

After cleaning up the dishes, they walked up a hill toward a clearing. Together they watched the stars emerge into the night sky. Remembering Three Songs' lessons, Hawk pointed to some of the constellations, naming them in Cherokee. By midnight, they decided to make their way back, and Harry pushed Hawk ahead, letting him find his way back to the shelter.

CHAPTER FIFTY-SEVEN

July 1970

Big Lou ushered Christine and George into his office and closed the door. "You're George Wheeler?"

George nodded. "Yes, sir, and this is Christine O'Donnell, the lawyer who's helped me with Hawk."

"Hawk thinks a lot of you," Lou said. "He told me that you put his brother on the medevac after he was wounded. Made things right for him with his tribe."

George nodded and shifted a bit in his seat.

"Reason I'm mentioning that," Lou said, "is that I think if Hawk was hiding, he'd come out for you. Course, we'd have to find him first."

Christine explained about the package Hawk had sent to George. "It was full of sketches he'd made of his mother's injuries after her husband beat on her. There was also a radio wrapped in a pillowcase. Hawk's note inside said that his stepdad had put a bullet in it to threaten him."

"Sounds like it was pretty rough for him," Lou said. "Funny thing, he never mentioned it. Just came in to work, did his job. He's a good worker and liked it here. The problems at home must've just been building up inside until he decided he couldn't live there anymore."

"It's important that we find him before the authorities put him into the juvenile system," Christine said. "We'll have a better chance of working things out privately. Unfortunately, the system is somewhat prejudiced against Indian kids."

"I asked around before, but no one seemed to know anything. Let's try again. There's one guy here who might know something. He worked closely with Hawk in the body shop."

They left Lou's office and walked to the body shop. Jimmie and a couple of others were dismantling a wrecked car. "Take a break," Lou said to the others. "We need to talk to Jimmie a minute."

As the workers were cleaning their hands, Lou asked Jimmie about the car, killing time until the others were out of the shop. He then closed the door.

Jimmie had his hands in his pockets. "What's up, boss?"

"This here's Christine O'Donnell. She's Hawk's lawyer. This is George Wheeler. George served in Nam with Hawk's brother. Hawk was living off the rez with George before the court ordered him transferred to his mom's place."

Jimmie adjusted his ball cap, snugged it down a bit.

"As you know," Lou said, "Hawk's come up missing. I'm wondering if you've heard anything."

"Nope," Jimmie said looking down at the floor. Lou walked around a bit, thinking, then saw the rear fender of a motor scooter under a tarp back in the corner of the shop. Lou walked over and pulled the tarp back. "Funny thing," he said. "Hawk told me he was going to the reservation for the summer, but said he'd leave the scooter here. At the time, I didn't question him, but it seemed odd to me. Now, it makes sense. He really didn't plan to go back to the rez at all. He couldn't get anywhere unless someone helped him, say someone with a pickup truck and time on his hands."

He walked back and stood in front of Jimmie. He pulled the brim of Jimmie's hat up, exposing his face. "You like your job here?"

Jimmie nodded.

Lou leaned in, closer to Jimmie's face. "Well then, it's time you come clean because if I find you've been holding out on me about Hawk, you'll be on the bricks so fast your head'll spin." Lou backed off, and Jimmie stumbled backward onto a stool.

Jimmie's shoulders slumped. "I promised him I wouldn't tell. He couldn't stand it at his mom's. I found him a place to live and took him there. I'm sure he's okay, just hiding out."

When the story was out, George spoke up. "Okay, let's not spook him. We could ride up there and see if we can talk to this Harry guy."

"The thing is," Jimmie said, "Harry can't speak. But he can understand you. Maybe if you took him a note to give to Hawk, he'd let Hawk decide. Harry knows me. I could go with you."

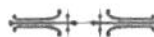

The next day, Lou took his Lincoln Continental, and they all drove across the line to Arkansas. Stopping at the gas station/convenience store, George went in to talk to the owner.

"Haven't seen a kid with Harry," the storekeeper said, "although a funny thing happened. Harry came in and bought some dog food. When I asked him about it, he got real nervous, ripped open the bag, and popped some in his mouth as if it was for him. Old Harry's crazy like a fox, so I figured he'd got a dog but didn't want to tell anyone."

From the convenience store, Jimmie directed them to the track leading to Harry's place. They drove slowly up the lane, dodging the worst of the ruts, then stopped at the edge of the woods.

"Jimmie and I will walk from here," George said. "You folks stay back, out of the line of fire, in case Harry really is crazy."

George and Jimmie got out, started walking toward the cabin. Harry came to the door, cradling the shotgun. "Harry," Jimmie said. "We came to see Hawk."

Harry waved the gun at them, threatening.

"We're peaceful," George said, "and we're friends of Hawk. I have something for him." George walked forward slowly, carrying the tomahawk in its hide sheath and a sealed envelope addressed to Hawk. He stopped a few feet below Harry's front porch, laid the items on the ground, then backed away slowly. Harry knelt down and picked up the tomahawk, pulled it from the sheath, and studied it, turning it over in his hands. He cracked the shotgun open then and cradled it, motioning them to come inside his cabin. George waved Christine and Lou up to the cabin.

"We're friends of Hawk," George said. "We need to talk with him. Could you take him the note and the tomahawk? He'll know it's from us."

Harry's dinner was simmering. He put the pot of stew on the table and filled a plate with flat bread, motioning for them to eat. Then, with his wicker basket, the note, and the tomahawk, he left the cabin.

"I don't know about you," Lou said. "But I think this smells pretty good, and I'm starving."

"What kind of critter do you suppose he's got in there?" Christine asked.

"Better not to know," George said. "I agree with Lou." He broke off a piece of the bread and dipped it in the stew. "By the way, that's Hawk's drawing pinned to the wall there."

Hawk was practicing with the bow and arrow near the lean-to when he heard the eagle-bone whistle. Hawk replied, and Harry emerged from the woods.

They went back to the lean-to. Harry stirred the remaining coals of Hawk's fire, building it up a bit to provide some warmth. Hawk pulled a piece of jerky from his pack. He gave some to Harry and a piece to Bear. Harry gave Hawk the tomahawk and the letter.

"How many came?"

Harry held up four fingers spread.

"Jimmie?"

Harry nodded. "There were two other men and a woman with red hair," Harry said. "One of the men brought this note and the tomahawk. The other was older and much taller.

"That'd be George and Christine," Hawk said, "and probably Big Lou. Jimmie must have brought them here."

Hawk opened the envelope and read the note aloud while Harry petted Bear. "Do you think I should go?" he asked.

Harry seemed noncommittal. He walked around a bit as if contemplating the situation but then nodded yes. They packed Hawk's things, watered out the fire, camouflaged the lean-to, and headed down the trail.

Outside the cabin, Hawk was warmly greeted. "Both you and Bear have grown," Christine said. Lou pointed to the stew and spoke to Harry. "Thanks for the food. We left some for you and Hawk." Christine walked Hawk through the details of his mother's divorce action. An attorney in Christine's office was working with Florence, and she was now back at the reservation, staying with her friend Martha. It was still summer, so there would be time to work out final living arrangements before school started up again.

"You've still got a job," Lou said to Hawk, "as soon as you're back on your feet."

"Could I come back to visit Harry again?"

"I'm sure we can work that out," George said. "Earl and I wouldn't mind some R&R in the woods, and we'd be glad to bring you back.

Hawk turned to Harry and spoke in Cherokee. "They said I can come back and visit you." Harry war danced around the group. Hawk gave him the bow and arrows. "Keep these for me," he said.

Harry went inside and brought out a leather pouch. He gave it to Hawk and pounded his chest once, extending his fist to Hawk. Hawk bumped his fist and pounded his own chest. "Osiyo," Hawk said.

"Let's get going," Lou said. "We're burnin' daylight."

CHAPTER FIFTY-EIGHT

Toby Jamison, a young associate in Christine's office, secured a pretrial divorce order allowing Florence to recover her personal belongings from Richard's residence. Earl, George, and a deputy sheriff accompanied Florence to Richard's home, to help her pack and remove her clothes.

"You ain't getting any furniture," Richard said. "It's all mine."

"Keep it," she said. "It's all crap anyway."

Richard started in on her then, deriding her in front of the deputy. The deputy took Richard by the arm and ushered him outside. "You sit here on these steps. You can watch from here what she takes out. But if you get to jawing again, I'll cuff you and take you for a ride downtown. Now are we clear about that?"

Richard jerked his arm away from the deputy's grasp and sat down on the steps. He lit a cigarette and looked out onto the street, ignoring the deputy.

Hawk slept at his dad's while Florence stayed at Martha's. Florence stopped in from time to time to check on Albert and help with cooking and housekeeping. Without asking, she had the junk hauled away from the front yard, and the place began to look more habitable. Hawk appreciated his mom's help. He said to her one afternoon, "Would you ever consider moving back home? I'm sure it would be okay with Dad."

"I really can't stay here," she said. "Your dad needs to get some help. It would be too easy for him to get dependent on me again." She put her arm around Hawk. "You and I will be moving back into town soon. I've got my own place, and I'll find a job. With Richard out of the way, there's no reason your dad and I can't be friends."

CHAPTER FIFTY-NINE

Hawk accompanied his mom to the alimony pretrial hearing. Richard was snarling. His lawyer, David Grabel, was combative.

Florence's lawyer, Toby Jamison, walked the court through the allegations of Richard's abuse and how Florence had been forbidden to leave the house without him. She was not allowed to drive—or even shop—without Richard accompanying her. Florence testified, showing the radio and the sketches made by Hawk, and identified the signature on the pages. He called Hawk to corroborate the information.

The judge refused to admit the radio but accepted the sketches into evidence. Grabel declined to present evidence on behalf of Richard. The court granted a temporary restraining order, awarding Florence temporary alimony, pending the final divorce hearing. Richard was allowed to stay in his house and have the use of his truck and the checking account.

On the way out of the hearing, he spoke to Florence under his breath. "Bitch, you can fight me until hell freezes over, but you'll never see a dime." Overhearing the comment, Jamison said to Grabel, "You might remind your client that the restraining order prevents him from disposing of any assets until the divorce is final."

"We can read," Grabel said, taking Richard by the arm and ushering him into the elevator.

By the end of the summer, Florence and Hawk had moved into her apartment near Big Lou's. Lou had found her a job at another dealership where she processed car titles and sales documents. "The guy owed me one," Lou said of her new employer. "Just don't let me down."

Lou met with Hawk. "You've got your job back," he said. "The scooter's yours—you paid for it, but I want to tell you one thing." Hawk shuffled his feet, embarrassed, but finally looked up. "I'm disappointed that you lied to me. I didn't know you were in trouble. If I'd known, I could have helped. You have to learn to trust people who are important to you. If you lie to me again, you've lost your job. Am I clear?"

"Yes, sir. I'm sorry."

"You're young," Lou said, "and we all make mistakes. We can start with a clean slate. I just want you to know where I stand. Do we have a deal?" Lou stuck out his hand.

"Deal." Hawk shook Lou's hand. "Thanks for giving me a second chance."

"Good. Now get on over to see Frank. He's got things for you to do." Hawk started toward the door. "Hang on," Lou said. He went to a box in the corner of his office and pulled out a hooded sweatshirt. He tossed it to Hawk. "We got a new logo," he said. "Now get to work."

After work, Hawk called Gina's number. It rang a few times, and he was about to hang up when Gina's mom answered. "Gina's not here right now," she said. "Where are you?"

"I'm back with my mom, and things are settled a bit. I was wondering if I could come visit Gina on Sunday afternoon."

"Of course. Why don't you come over for lunch, and then you'll have the afternoon to visit."

"Do you mind if I bring Bear?"

"Not at all. By the way, Charles, is everything okay?"

"It's a long story," he said. "But things are better."

CHAPTER SIXTY

It took a while for Hawk to find Gina's house. He had a Tulsa map, but he still had to work his way across town through the traffic. As the slowest vehicle on the road, he had to contend with the exasperation of drivers stuck behind him. Eventually he found his old school and then knew where he was. Within a few minutes, he pulled up to Gina's house. He beeped a couple of times as he pulled in. By the time he unlatched Bear, Gina was there with her arms around him. "Hi, Hawk," she said, hugging him. Bear barked.

Gina laughed and knelt down to pet him. "Hello, Bear"—she ruffled his fur and let him lick her face—"I've missed you."

Fred's voice came from the porch. "Mom's got lunch ready," he said. "Come in and wash up."

"Can Bear come in?" Gina said.

"Bear's welcome anytime."

As they came in the door, Gina's two-year-old brother, Tommy, shrieked and toddled over to Bear, hugging him. Bear licked him and lay down, letting the boy fall over him.

"I think Bear likes him," Gina said.

During lunch, the parents were circumspect, not asking too many probing questions about Hawk's summer. They mostly asked about his drawing and plans for the fall.

"My mom's getting a divorce," Hawk said. "She's moved to a new place near my school. That's where I'm living now. She's kind of made up with my dad. At least, they seem to be friends, so things are better there. But I won't be coming back to John Hay."

"Well, I'm sure that things will work out for you," Fred said.

After lunch, Hawk and Gina sat in the front yard with Bear and Tommy, talking and playing with them. "It was brave of you to leave," she said, "I don't think I could have done that."

"Why would you even want to? You have great parents. Everything about my home was a mess."

Gina touched his arm. "At least your stepfather is gone."

"Yeah, but he keeps calling. I'm afraid Mom might take him back."

"Really, why?"

"Don't know. There's an attraction there, or maybe she's afraid to live alone. I hate him. If he comes back, I'll leave again."

Gina lay back on the grass. "I'm really glad you came to see me. I'm sorry you won't be back at my school."

"I just noticed," Hawk said. "You got your braces off."

"Finally." She gave Hawk a toothy grin. "What do you think?"

"You're pretty."

Hawk lay back on the grass beside her, watching Tommy clamber over Gina, jumping on her.

"Maybe we could get together more often. Would your parents let you ride on the scooter? I'd get a helmet for you."

"I doubt it. They're pretty strict. They don't want me going out on dates, but maybe they'd let me go for short trips. I guess I could ask."

"If they won't, I'll come here…if it's okay with you."

Gina rolled on her side to face him. "If you don't mind spending time with a freak."

CHAPTER SIXTY-ONE

September 1970

A few days later, when Hawk got home from work, his mom was standing by the stove stirring a pot. Richard was sitting at the kitchen table, his back to Hawk. Behind Richard's back, Hawk pointed to Richard and mouthed, "What's he doing here?" He sat down at his place. Florence dished up some food for him.

"How was work, honey?" she said.

"Okay, same as usual." He looked over at Richard, then back at his food.

"Richard stopped by to talk about us getting back together."

Hawk looked down at his food. "He's not supposed to be here. Isn't that what the court order says?"

"It's okay," Florence said. "I let him in. He's stopped drinking and has a new job as a serviceman for a heating and cooling contractor. He's handy with mechanical things. It's a good job."

"But what's he doing here?"

"I came to apologize," Richard said. "I know I've treated you badly, but I'm back on my feet now. I think we could get a fresh start."

Hawk looked at Richard then, studying his face. When Richard looked away, Hawk wolfed down the rest of his food, got up from the table, and rinsed his dishes.

After he put them in the dishwasher, Hawk turned back to look at Richard. "You need to leave here *now*, or I'm calling the cops."

"Say again?"

"There's a court order. You're not supposed to be here. I'm calling the cops."

"She let me in."

"I don't care. This time, I'll file the complaint."

Richard glared at Hawk, his fists clenched. Florence intervened, putting her arm around Hawk. "Please," she said. "Settle down. Go to your room, and I'll be up to talk to you in a bit."

As Hawk left the kitchen, he looked back and noticed the bulge under Richard's shirt above the hip pocket. He looked again at his mom. He left the kitchen and went toward his room but stood in the hallway, listening.

"You know I want to come back," Richard said. "I still love you. I've got my head straight, and we can make it work."

"I've heard that before."

"Well, I can make it right."

"Before we talk about you coming back," Florence said, "you need to pay the alimony like the court ordered."

"What's the point if I'm coming back?"

"The point is that you owe me that money for all you put us through, and we can't start clean unless you do what you've been ordered to do."

"What about the kid?"

"What do you mean, 'What about the kid?'"

"You saw that."

"He's young. Things don't always make sense."

"Well, he don't belong here. He's a runner. Just trouble. He was part of the problem—why we weren't getting along. Our coming back together ain't goin' to work if he and that dog stay here."

"We're a package, Richard. Me, Charles, and Bear. I've already lost one son. I'm not going to lose the other one. If that's not good enough for you, then there's no point in talking."

There was a long silence when the only sound was Richard's spoon stirring his coffee.

Florence spoke again. "You need to get three things right. Stay sober, pay up, and get comfortable with the idea that Charles is staying with me. There's no negotiation. Those are the terms."

Hawk could hear Richard's chair scraping backward as he got up from the table.

"Sounds to me like maybe you've got a new boyfriend, reason why you're making it so hard on me to come back."

"Boyfriend?" She laughed. "You've got to be kidding me. Where'd you get that idea?"

"I know how it works," he said. "Woman leaves her man, finds someone else to replace the one she left behind."

"Richard, there's no boyfriend. You just need to do what's right by me and Charles. Then we can talk about getting back together."

"I'll think on it," he said. "If I'm back here next week, I'll settle up."

When Hawk heard the door close and the car leaving the driveway, he came back into the kitchen. "I don't trust him."

"Honey, can we talk about this?"

"About what?"

"You know what. About getting this family back together."

"Why do you want to do that? Do you like getting beaten up?"

"He only does that when he gets drunk, and he's quit drinking."

"Do you believe that? Dad has said that he'll quit drinking a million times, but he never does. He can't. You know that. You know how hard it is. Why do you think Richard is any different?"

"He's a good provider when he's sober. I can get along with him."

"Has he paid the alimony?"

"No, because he's been laid off, and now he's back to work."

"So, if he moves in, does he have to pay?"

"He has to pay the past amount owed. But if he moves in, he'd take care of expenses—it'd be the same."

Hawk went to the sink and got a glass of water. "I think Richard wants to move back so that he won't have to pay."

"Now you're just being petty. If we're back together, it won't matter."

Hawk finished the water and set the glass on the counter. "Sounds like you're going to do it anyway. Why do you want my approval?"

"You're right, Charles. I don't need your approval, but I'd like you and Richard to be friends."

"That won't happen. And I don't think it's the right thing for you to do. But I can't stop you." Hawk started to go back to his room. "By the way, Mom, did you notice he had the gun with him?"

"I didn't see it. Are you sure about that?"

"Yeah. He carries it in a holster at his back. When he was sitting at the table, I could see it sticking up against his shirt."

"That can't be. Why would he bring that here, especially with the court order?"

"Mom, I saw it. Richard doesn't care about court orders. He told me himself. He's not afraid of going to jail, either. You shouldn't trust him, regardless of what he says."

CHAPTER SIXTY-TWO

The following Saturday, Hawk worked late. Lou had received a truckload of bikes at the end of the day, and Hawk stayed to help get them unpacked and set up.

When he got home, he was surprised that the front door was locked. His mom's car was in the parking lot, and he could hear the television. He knocked, but got no answer. He didn't have a key but knew the manager kept a spare for them in case Florence forgot hers, so Hawk went to the manager's apartment. His wife answered the door.

"Sure, honey. I'll get it for you."

She went to her kitchen, took a key off a board on the wall, and gave it to Hawk. "Just bring it back once you get in."

Back at the apartment, Hawk unlocked the door and went into the kitchen. The television there was blaring, and he shut it off.

"Mom," he called. He walked back into the foyer toward the living room. She was lying on the living-room floor. Bear was beside her, whimpering. There was a gun in her hand, and blood pooled beneath her in a large stain. Hawk placed a hand on her neck to feel for a pulse.

"Mom! Mom!"

He grabbed the barrel of the gun and slid it away from her hand, dropping it beside her, then ran back in the kitchen, picked up the phone and dialed the operator. "Call the police," he said. "My mom's been shot."

The operator connected him with the police dispatcher who began asking for details, and his name and address.

Hawk snapped, "Just get an ambulance. Hurry!" He tried George's number but got no answer, so he called Christine.

"I'll be right there," she said. "Don't touch anything."

"I already did."

"What did you touch?"

"I pulled the gun from her hand, and my hand's all bloody."

"Okay, I understand. Don't touch anything else, and don't wash your hands. Stay out of the room until I get there, and don't tell the police anything except your name."

The EMTs arrived first, and when no one answered the door, they entered cautiously and found Hawk huddled with Bear on the kitchen floor. A medic approached the body, took a pulse, and shook his head to the other. "Check the boy for shock."

The police arrived shortly thereafter. Tenants, hearing the commotion, were beginning to gather in the hallway, and the officers moved them back from the door.

An older, plainclothes officer entered the apartment, went into the living room, and studied the scene for a few minutes. "Get the forensics team over here." The detective knelt beside Hawk and showed him his ID.

"I'm Jack Darles," he said. "I'm a detective with the Tulsa police. Can you tell me your name?"

"Charles—Charles Manawa."

"Is the woman in the living room your mom?"

Hawk nodded.

"Did your mom own a gun?"

"No."

"Can I ask you some more questions?"

Hawk shook his head. "I just called my attorney. She said not to say anything until she got here."

"Okay, we'll wait for her. Just stay here in the kitchen."

Christine arrived.

An officer at the door raised his hand to stop her. "Crime scene," he said, but she showed him an ID and her attorney registration.

"I'm the boy's attorney." She went past the living room and saw the body, then came over to Hawk, knelt beside him, and hugged him. "I'm so sorry," she said. "So very sorry." She turned then and recognized Darles.

"Hello, Christine," he said.

Christine got up and shook his hand. "Hello, Jack."

"It's been a while since you were in the DA's office."

"Almost ten years," she said. They talked briefly, confidentially. Christine explained why she was there.

"I started to ask him some questions," Darles said. "But he wanted to wait until you arrived. Can I talk to him now?"

"Let me talk to him first."

"Okay," Darles said. "I'll give you a few minutes while I work with the forensics folks." Darles went into the living room.

"It's Richard's gun," Hawk said. "It's his thirty-eight."

"Where did you find it?"

"It was in Mom's hand, but loose. Not like when Horse shot himself and I had to pry the gun out of his fingers. Richard must have put it there."

"Where did you touch it?"

"I grabbed it by the barrel and took it out of her hand. I left it on the floor beside her."

"How did you get the blood on your hand?"

"When I saw her there, I put my hand on her neck to try to feel a pulse. Her face was covered in blood."

"So you picked up the gun after you got blood on your hand?"

Hawk nodded.

"Can anyone verify where you've been all day?"

"Big Lou. I was helping him until I left for home around seven o'clock. The door was locked, and I had to get a key from the landlord."

Christine left him then and talked with Darles. "The gun belongs to his mom's husband, Richard Holdress," she said. She relayed what Hawk told her. "Run powder residue tests on her face and hands. Also, I'd like you to test Hawk now before he washes his hands."

"Will do," Darles said. "Do we have any proof that it's the husband's gun?"

"Holdress is a real snake. He regularly abused Florence. Even threatened Charles with the gun. He shot out a radio to make his point. We have the radio and the bullet. The ballistics will match up."

"Do you know where he lives?" Darles asked.

"I think he's over on Forty-Eighth Street, where they lived before the divorce, but I'll check with Charles." She went back to the kitchen with Darles.

Hawk confirmed the address. "I don't know where he's working. I heard Mom say he was a repairman for a heating and cooling contractor. We moved here after she filed for divorce and got the restraining order."

"There was a restraining order?"

"Yeah," Hawk said. "But Richard didn't care. He was here last weekend. He wanted to get back together with Mom, end the divorce, but Mom told him he'd have to pay her the back alimony he owed her. He had the gun with him then. I saw it under his shirt, where he carries it. He told Mom he'd be back this week to settle up."

The detective picked up his radio and called his department. "Get someone on Richard Holdress. His address is 3932 Forty-Eighth Street. He apparently also works at a heating and cooling company. If he's not at home, start calling contractors.

"She was shot on her left side," Darles said. "Was your mom left-handed?"

"No, sir, right-handed. There's no way she shot herself. It was Richard. I'm sure of it."

Darles pulled Christine into the foyer and spoke softly. "We're going to have to treat the boy as a suspect."

"You've got to be kidding."

"Until the forensics comes through, he's the only one with a connection to the crime scene."

"Well, then, you can't ask him any more questions."

"Will you let us do the powder residue tests, take his fingerprints, and check the blood on his hand?"

"Only if I'm present and you test both hands thoroughly, particularly the back of his hands."

Christine went back into the kitchen to talk with Hawk, who was sitting at the kitchen table, and explained what was happening.

"What do you mean, test me? I didn't do anything. It's Richard. Why would I kill my mom?"

Christine sat down next to him. "Hawk, listen to me. Until the forensics have been completed, we know that you're the only one, beside your mom, who has left fingerprints on the gun. I want them to do a gunpowder residue test on your hands, because that will show that you did not fire the weapon. They'll do the same with Richard, when they find him, but he's likely already scrubbed his hands clean or was wearing gloves. We need to collect all of the physical evidence we can, so I want the police to test you as well."

"Who's to say I didn't wash my hands?"

"The blood there says it. If you had washed your hands, the blood would be gone."

"I can't believe it," he said.

"Will you go along with it? I think it's in your best interests."

Hawk stared at the table, thinking. "Okay," he said. "As usual, Richard gets his way."

Darles came back into the kitchen. "Your attorney will take you to the police station where we can do the tests, but before you go, I need to give you this warning." Darles pulled a card from his wallet. "You have the right to remain silent and to refuse to answer questions. Anything you say may be used against you in a court of law. You have the right to consult an attorney before speaking to the police and to have an attorney present during questioning now or in the future. If you cannot afford an attorney, one will be appointed for you before any questioning if you wish."

CHAPTER SIXTY-THREE

With the investigation pending, Florence's body could not be buried promptly according to Cherokee custom. Christine reviewed again the importance of the forensics tests in terms of building an evidentiary case against Richard.

"It's not fair," Hawk said, "that everything has to revolve around Richard, without concern for our traditions."

"The trial process won't always seem fair," Christine said. "But the prosecutor has to make sure that he has all of the evidence together."

In the meantime, George talked to Hawk's principal who agreed that Hawk should have a few days off. He and Earl proposed taking him to Arkansas to spend some time with Harry, thinking time away would be helpful. Albert agreed as long as they drove a vehicle and didn't take Hawk that distance on a motorcycle. Earl packed his truck with camping gear and groceries, and they set out.

Following their usual pattern, they parked at the edge of the clearing around Harry's cabin and walked toward the cabin to give

Harry plenty of notice of their arrival. As soon as Harry appeared at the door, Bear ran toward him. Harry crouched on his porch, letting Bear nuzzle him.

"We came to visit," George said. Harry came off the porch to shake their hands and then war danced around them, imitating a crouching animal. Hawk joined in, and they chased and sparred with each other like tiger cubs.

"We can stay a few days," Hawk said. "Earl and George have a tent. If it's okay, Bear and I will stay with you in the cabin."

Harry showed them a flat grassy area beside the cabin as a site for the tent. Earl walked back and brought the truck up and unloaded some of the groceries. He set the groceries on the kitchen table and pulled a chicken from a cooler. "If we could build a fire outside," he said, "we thought we'd cook this chicken." Harry clapped his hands, excited. They went outside, where Harry showed them an area for the fire and pointed to a stack of wood beside the cabin.

While they set up camp, Harry played with Bear. When the fire was ready, George produced a dutch oven, put the chicken in it, and placed the oven in the coals. He and Hawk cut up some onions and potatoes and put them into a packet of aluminum foil that they buried in the coals beside the pot. Harry went into the cabin, mixed up dough for flat bread and, while the food was cooking, fried up a serving of bread. Hawk was beside him in the kitchen, helping with the bread. He spoke without looking up.

"My mom got killed," he said. Harry looked at him, puzzled. "Her husband shot her while I was at work. He's been charged with murder."

Harry pulled the pan off the fire, went to a chest in the corner of the room and pulled out a black shirt. He laid it on the table, took a knife, and sliced open the collar. He tore the shirt in half and cut a strip of cloth from the body of the shirt, folded it into a band, and tied it around his head. He followed with two other strips, one for Hawk and one for Bear, then made two more, which he laid on the table.

"For George and Earl?" Hawk asked. Harry nodded.

Hawk took the headbands outside to where George and Earl were sitting by the fire. "Harry made these in honor of my mom. You don't have to wear them, but you can if you want to."

"Of course we'll wear them," Earl said. He tied his on, and George followed suit. Harry and Bear joined them.

"Three Songs taught me a song we sometimes sing at funerals," Hawk said. "Could we sing it now?"

"I think we should," George said. Harry held up a hand. He went to the cabin and brought back a small packet of tobacco from the cupboard. He crouched by the fire and sprinkled the tobacco over the coals, making a cloud of light smoke. Hawk held out his hands and, in a soft voice, began singing,

> We n' de ya ho
> We n' de ya ho
> We n' de ya ho
> We n' de ya We n' de ya
> Ho, ho ho ho
> He ya ho he ya,
> Ya ya ya

Harry stood mute, his eyes closed as he swayed slightly to the song. When Hawk finished, Earl asked, "Can you translate it?"

Hawk said, "I am of the great spirit. Ho, I am of the great spirit. Ho, it is so, it is so. Great Spirit, Great Spirit, Great Spirit."

"I see why it would be sung to honor someone," Earl said. "It's a good song."

"I think I caused Mom's death," Hawk said.

"What do you mean?" George asked.

"The first time I called the cops on Richard for beating my mom, he threatened that if I ever did it again, he'd kill us all, even Bear. The week before he killed Mom, he was at our apartment. I told him to leave and that, if he didn't, I'd call the cops again. I know that's why he killed her. He'll be coming after me next."

"I hear where you're coming from, Hawk," George said. "But you're wrong. Richard's a psycho. He was furious that your mom wanted a divorce. That's why he killed her. It had nothing to do with anything you said."

They all sat quietly by the fire, occasionally stirring the coals. Finally, Earl took a pair of pliers from his pocket and lifted the lid of the dutch oven. "It's done," he said and pulled it from the coals.

By the time they finished dinner and cleaned up, it was dusk.

"Going to be a clear night," George said. "We should go up on the ridge and watch the stars."

Harry led them to a spot behind the cabin, gave each of them a rock to carry and then they set off together. Harry led them to an open clearing with a good view. At the clearing, Harry arranged some other stones into a cairn. Then he placed his stone on the pile.

George went next. "In memory of your mom."

"Rest in peace," Earl said.

Hawk knelt and placed his stone last. "I love you, Mom," he said. Bear was beside him, and Hawk stayed silent for a long time, stroking him.

George broke the silence. "Hawk, do you remember the night the elders met with us—when they gave Stalking Bear his name? It was a sky like this—clear. There's Orion in the same position as it was that night. And there's Ursa, the Bear."

Hawk repeated the name of the constellations in Cherokee for Harry.

They all sat on the ground a long time, watching the stars. Coyotes yipped in the distance. "What do you remember most about your mom?" Earl asked.

"She was a good person," Hawk said. "I'm just sorry she ever got mixed up with Richard." Hawk lay back on the ground and looked up at the sky. "I asked her why she stayed with him. She knew it wasn't right, but she thought that Richard would get better. She treated everyone that way."

They stayed quiet awhile. "I hope they fry him," Hawk said finally.

"I know how you feel," Earl said. "When we were in combat, we just wanted to trash everything and everyone whenever one of our guys got waxed. But there's no satisfaction in it. No amount of revenge brings someone back."

"Earl's right," George said. "The revenge just eats away at your insides. No good comes of it."

"I hate him," Hawk said.

It was late when George stood up. "Time to head back. Tomorrow's another day."

CHAPTER SIXTY-FOUR

In the week following completion of the forensics and ballistics examinations, the prosecutor presented the evidence to the grand jury, and Richard was indicted for murder. Hawk moved in with George on the condition that he would visit his dad regularly. Christine initiated proceedings to have custody transferred back to Albert. Three Songs convinced Albert to let Hawk stay with George temporarily on the basis that fewer disruptions would suit Hawk at the moment. Hawk had his scooter and could get back and forth to school and to Big Lou's for work. Bear stayed with him at George's house.

George occasionally visited Hawk at work. In a conversation with Lou, George explained about Earl and his working on controls for the disabled. "He designed hand controls for motorcycles so that paraplegics can still ride."

"We get some requests for that sort of thing," Lou said. "Maybe we could work something out with Earl's shop to customize some of our bikes."

"Earl's got a great operation," George said. "I'm sure he'd be glad to talk to you."

George arranged to meet Lou at Earl's, and after some discussion, Earl agreed to equip several of Lou's new bikes with the hand controls. Together, they worked out the details and priced the accessories.

"My lawyer thinks the VA might even pay some of the cost of the modifications," Lou said.

Lou funded work on several models, allowing Earl to experiment with concepts to develop the best controls. Hawk provided artwork to be painted on the bikes to give them a distinctive flair. Earl would come in on Sunday and meet with George, Hawk, and Lou to work out the concepts for the art. Lou liked patriotic themes and thought they would sell well to the vets. Hawk worked out sketches of screaming eagles and streaming stripes and stars. Jimmie painted the designs on one of the bikes in Lou's body shop.

Lou was impressed. "Let's get several models finished," he said. "Then I'll do a big weekend display. We'll put up a huge tent in the parking lot and have everyone there—Earl's choppers, the Angels. We'll serve free food. We'll also paint some of the regular bikes with Hawk's designs. Midafternoon, we'll auction off one of the bikes and donate the proceeds to the POW group."

Lou held the bike display on a Saturday in October. He ran full-page ads the week before with pictures of Earl, George, and Hawk standing with Lou behind one of the bikes. The ads proclaimed free food, demos, and the auction to benefit the POWs. Earl and George distributed flyers to the veterans' groups and the local motorcycle clubs. By nine that morning, Lou's dealership was decked out in red, white, and blue bunting. American flags were displayed throughout the lot, with Earl's black pennants attached to the masts below the American flags. Earl had designed some flag standards to be mounted on motorcycles, and every visitor received a small black pennant.

Hawk was standing inside the showroom beside one of the bikes that featured his designs. Lou had also put up a display of Hawk's sketches of other designs. A customer was describing a design he wanted Hawk to create, and Hawk was taking notes on a pad.

"I was a helicopter gunner," the man said. "We nicknamed our chopper 'Mad Dog.' I'd like a picture of a helicopter looking like a flying bulldog, something like that."

"I think we could work that out," Hawk said. "I'll need to spend some time on it, and then Lou will call you to come in and look at it."

"That'd be great, man," he said. "I really like your stuff."

As the biker walked away, Hawk heard, "Hello, Hawk."

Gina grabbed him in a giant hug. "I'd like something with Bear on it," she whispered.

Hawk saw her dad then and was embarrassed by Gina's embrace. "Wow, what are you doing here?" he said. He pried himself loose and shook Fred's hand.

"We couldn't miss it with all the publicity."

George showed up then, followed by Big Lou. Fred began talking with them. Gina interrupted, "Dad, do you mind if Hawk shows me around? I'd like to see where he works."

"Sure, Gina, go ahead. We'll be right here."

Hawk took Gina's hand, led her on a tour of the shops, introduced her to Frank and Jimmie. "These guys are all really great," he said. Coming back out into the parking lot, Hawk saw Earl over by a bike, explaining the controls.

When Earl looked up, Hawk pulled Gina forward. "This here's Earl Schlemmer. He builds motorcycles. He's the guy who made the hand controls for disabled riders."

"Whoa, Hawk," Earl said. "You never said anything about no Gina." He turned to her. "What you doin' hanging around with a bum like Hawk, anyway?"

Gina laughed. "We're twin freaks," she said. "Two of a kind."

"Well, Hawk's getting the best of that deal. Real nice to meet you."

Lou was on the loudspeaker now, inviting everyone under the tent for the ceremonies and the auction. When the crowd was gathered, Lou asked for silence, then called for the presentation of the colors.

A four-man team from the VFW marched in with the American flag and a large black flag. They posted the flags in stands by the podium. A local minister gave a prayer of remembrance for the lives lost in all wars and particularly for those who were still missing in Vietnam.

Lou introduced Earl. He explained his work and that he would be available for more demos after the auction. He called up Gale Dalpo, a local auctioneer, who proceeded to sell an off-road bike painted with Hawk's design.

Midway through the bidding, Dalpo stopped the auction. "Now, there's an added bonus," he said. "If you're buying the bike for someone who's disabled, then Earl and Lou will equip the bike with the proper controls at no extra charge. All proceeds go to the National League of Families of American Prisoners and Missing in Southeast Asia."

By the time Dalpo called "sold," the price had reached $3,500. Lou had a big blank check made out to the league. When the auction closed, Lou took a thick Magic Marker and wrote the amount on the check. He held it up for the newspaper reporter to photograph.

Hawk walked Gina and her dad to their car. "I didn't know you liked motorcycles," he said to Fred.

"I don't," he said.

CHAPTER SIXTY-FIVE

Richard stood at the end of Hawk's bed, holding the pistol. He was wearing orange coveralls and looked unshaven. Richard stroked the barrel with his left hand, spun the cylinder, and snapped it back into the gun. Grinning, he pointed the gun at Bear. Hawk tried to call out to George, but no words came out. There was a gunshot and then laughter.

Hawk struggled to get out of bed but was caught in the covers. By the time he was free, he saw Bear beside the bed, sleeping. He got up and stroked Bear and went to the kitchen with Bear padding behind him. Hawk opened the refrigerator, got out the orange juice, and poured himself a glass.

A sleepy George appeared at the kitchen door. "What's up, Hawk?"

"Bad dream. I thought I saw Richard by my bed, holding the gun. I thought he'd shot Bear."

"Don't worry," George said. "He's in jail awaiting trial." George sat down at the kitchen table. "Pour me some of that, will you?"

Hawk set a glass on the table and sat down across from George. "What if Richard doesn't get convicted?"

"I doubt that will happen," George said. "Christine says that they've got some strong evidence putting him at the scene of the crime."

"Yeah, but what if the jury doesn't believe it? What then?"

"Let's not focus on negatives. Anyway, not even Richard is dumb enough to come after you."

"He told me he's not afraid of prison. I think he'd rather get revenge, even if he gets caught. Even if he doesn't get me, he'll come after Bear."

"Let's talk to Christine. I think we just need to be careful for a while." George paused. "And let's not think up a bunch of scenarios that might not happen. The prosecutor has a good case. Richard had a motive. The ballistics prove it was his gun. There are also the threats he made against you."

"But it's just my word against his about the threats. He's smart. He'll have an answer for everything. I'm just afraid he'll get out. Then he'll come after me."

"Try not to worry. You'll have to testify, but the lawyers will get you ready for that. You'll have to be prepared to do your best in court and let the prosecutor handle the trial."

CHAPTER SIXTY-SIX

November 1970

The morning of the trial, Hawk and George sat with Detectives Darles and Larson in the witness room while the judge presided over the jury selection. Christine stayed in the courtroom to watch the jury selection process. After about an hour, she came back.

"The jury's been chosen," she said. "The court has recessed for a bit. After that, they'll start with opening arguments."

"What's the jury look like?" George asked.

"Two housewives, the rest men, mostly blue-collar types, all white. There's one older man who has a college education. He'll likely be chosen foreman."

"Is it a good jury for the defense?"

"It's hard to say. Holdress only needs one in his corner, a stubborn loser type like him who wouldn't be swayed by circumstantial evidence."

After the recess, the judge called the jury back for opening arguments. The presentations finished about eleven thirty.

Christine came back into the room. "The judge recessed the jury until one o'clock. Then he asked the attorneys to go back into his chambers. I assume he's going to discuss the possibility of a plea bargain."

"How did the opening arguments go?" George asked.

"I'll walk you through them," she said. She paused and looked at Hawk. "You're not going to like what I'm about to tell you, but I won't sugarcoat it. You okay with that?"

Hawk nodded.

"The prosecutor," she said, "did a good job telling your mom's story, about the abuse, the threats made to you. He explained the physical evidence and clearly linked the gun to Holdress. While the killer tried to make it look like a suicide, the forensics are clear that Florence did not pull the trigger. The lab found no gunpowder residue on her face or hands, only evidence of fibers in her wound, which matched the fibers on one of the couch pillows in the living room. So, clearly there was no suicide."

"Did they find a pillow with a bullet hole in it?" Hawk asked.

"There were matching pillows. One is missing. It appears that Holdress used the same method of shooting that he demonstrated for you when he shot out your radio. He probably took the pillow with him and threw it away. As you know, he owed your mom several thousand dollars in back support and knew she wouldn't take him back unless he paid. So he had a motive for killing her."

She paused again and looked directly at Hawk. "Here's the weak part of the case. Holdress did a good job removing any fingerprints or other evidence that would indicate he was there that day. The only fingerprints on the gun match yours and your mom's. Your prints were on the barrel consistent with what you've said, but not consistent with someone pulling the trigger. The only evidence linking Holdress to the killing, besides the gun, will be your testimony. Holdress's attorney admits that his client was there the week before and had the gun with him, but he claims that your mom was worried about intruders, and so he left the gun there for her protection."

"That's not true," Hawk interjected.

"Of course not," she said. "You talked with your mom about the gun. He took it with him. Unfortunately, it's his word against yours because there's no one else to verify that information."

"I'm telling the truth."

"Yes, but that's a judgment that the jury has to make. I can tell you this, however, from my experience as a prosecutor. Juries are very reluctant to convict someone of murder only on circumstantial evidence. They have to believe, beyond any reasonable doubt, that Holdress had the intent to kill her. The only live testimony is from you, and you're a teenager."

Hawk hung his head. "And an Indian."

"You're right," Christine said. "We have to consider that some of the jurors will be prejudiced."

"But they'd believe a creep like Holdress," Hawk said.

"Nothing's certain until the evidence is in and the jury has rendered its verdict. The judge is talking with them now about a plea bargain. Holdress knows the risk of going forward, so don't be surprised if he cops a plea to a lesser charge."

At precisely 1:00 p.m., the judge called all of the parties back into the courtroom. Hawk, George, Christine, and the detectives took seats in the front row of the spectator section behind the rail.

"I understand that the defendant has offered to plead to some of the charges," the judge said.

The prosecutor and defense counsel both nodded.

"Mr. Holdress, please rise." The judge then walked him through the charges and the offenses he was pleading to. "You've consulted with your counsel, and you understand your pleas?"

"Yes, sir."

"The pleas are accepted, and a finding of guilty on charges of manslaughter and aggravated assault will be entered. Sentencing will be set in two weeks after the presentence investigation. The bond is revoked, pending final sentencing."

The jury was then excused, and the judge left the bench.

As the spectators stood up, a deputy approached Holdress and handcuffed him. When the cuffs were on, Holdress looked back at Hawk and winked. Hawk exploded and started to climb the rail, but George caught him and pulled him down. "Come on, man," he said. "It's over."

By then, Holdress was leaving the courtroom escorted by two deputies, one on each side.

The prosecutor met George, Hawk, and Christine back in the witness room.

"The pleas were recommended by the judge," he said.

"What does he get?" Hawk asked.

The prosecutor explained the sentencing possibilities.

"So he could be out in five years?" George said.

"Sooner if he qualifies for probation."

"You're kidding."

"No, that's what we agreed to. We have no evidence to place Holdress at the scene, only Charles's testimony of past abuse and that he was there the week before."

"So," George said, "you thought the jury would not believe Hawk?"

"That was a consideration. Even the judge was skeptical that we could get a conviction of murder. He recommended the plea bargain."

Hawk was on his feet. "That's why he winked at me. He killed her. He said he'd get away with it. And he did. He'll be coming for me next." Hawk stormed out of the room and ran down the courtroom stairs toward the street. By the time Christine and George got to the sidewalk, Hawk was gone.

"Come on," Christine said. "I'll get the car. We've got to find him.

CHAPTER SIXTY-SEVEN

Hawk knew the city now, after driving all over town running errands for Lou. He also knew the route back to the reservation. As Hawk came out of the courthouse, he saw a line of cabs waiting at the curb. He walked quickly up to the closest one and climbed in the backseat.

"I need to get to Wagoner," Hawk said.

"That's a ways," the driver said. "Gonna cost you about twenty dollars."

Hawk pulled out his wallet.

"I've got ten," Hawk said. "If you can get me to Route 51, I can hitchhike from there."

"That'll do," the cabbie said.

"Great, thanks."

Hawk slouched down in the backseat as the cab pulled away from the curb. The rush-hour traffic was starting up, and they immediately were stopped in a jam of cars merging onto the Broken Arrow Expressway. Hawk watched the meter ticking, wondering how long his money would last. The cabbie reached up and shut off the meter. "I'll start it again when we're moving."

After they left the Broken Arrow, the cabbie drove a couple of miles down Route 51. He pulled over at a gas station.

"I can make it from here," Hawk said. "Thanks a lot."

"It's nine bucks," the cabbie said.

Hawk handed him the ten. "Keep the change," he said. Outside the cab, Hawk stripped off the tie and tossed it into a garbage can. He kept the coat. It was November now, and the wind was getting colder. He pulled up the collar and started up the road, dragging his thumb for a ride.

A pickup slowed. The driver rolled down the window. "Where you going, son?"

Hawk recognized him. "Broken River."

"Lucky for you. Get in. I'll drop you there." When Hawk climbed in, the driver said, "You look like Albert's boy."

Hawk nodded. "I'm Charles. Thanks for the ride."

When Hawk got home, he found his dad parked in front of the television, drink in hand. "What are you doing here?" Albert asked. Hawk explained about the trial.

"I'm done with those people," Hawk said. "They let Richard get away with murder. If they call, don't tell them I'm here. I'm not going back. I belong here."

"Told you not to get your hopes up," Albert said. "White people is white people. Simple as that."

Hawk went to his room and closed the door. In his closet he found Stalking Bear's military rucksack. He took some warm clothes and packed them along with Stalking Bear's sleeping bag, his KA-BAR knife, and military poncho. He set out his hiking boots and slid a folding knife into his pocket along with his pouch of fire-building materials. He put the pack back in the closet. In the top drawer of his dresser he found Horse's wallet. He looked through it and found a driver's license and some miscellaneous papers. He put the license in his own wallet, got his winter jacket and a wool hat from the closet, and walked back through the living room. "Going for a walk," he said. "I'll be back at dinnertime. Don't forget—don't tell anyone I'm here."

CHAPTER SIXTY-EIGHT

George and Christine cruised the block around the courthouse, and then made a wider surveillance but came up empty. "Crap," George said. "We've lost him."

"Let's go to my office," Christine said. "I'll call the police and have them keep an eye out for him."

"Wimp prosecutor," George said. "No wonder Hawk's mad."

"The lawyer is not all to blame. It's the system. He's being practical, making sure he got a conviction. Holdress is smart. He left no prints anywhere. The only tie to him was the gun. The prosecutor could see that a jury might not believe Hawk and would side with Holdress. There's a lot of prejudice out there against Indians."

"Still, it's not right."

When she reached the police department, Darles was not yet back from the court. "Have him call me when he returns," she said. She then called the school and talked to the principal. Finally, she reached Lou and explained the situation.

"Damn courts, lawyers, they can all go to hell," Lou said. "What'll we do now?"

"Tomorrow, George and I will go out to the rez. I suspect that's where he went. We'll see if we can cool him down, get him back to his routine. He's pretty frosted right now. Can't say I blame him."

"I don't know. Hawk's been through some rough stuff. I wouldn't be surprised if he's on the run again."

CHAPTER SIXTY-NINE

It was late afternoon as Hawk walked the trail to the river. At the cabin, he sat on the porch looking out over the river. *How could they do that? That creep is laughing all the way to prison.* Hawk would find a way to get even someday.

He pulled out his pocketknife, picked up a stick, and whittled angry strips off it, making a sharp point on the end. Then he stuck it in the ground and headed back home.

When he walked back in the house, his dad was putting dinner on the table, from a can of Dinty Moore beef stew. Hawk buttered some bread, and they ate together.

"That lawyer woman called here, looking for you," Albert said. "I told her I hadn't seen you. I'm not sure she believed me. Said she and George might come out tomorrow."

Hawk gathered up the dishes, put them in the sink, and ran some hot water over them. Albert fixed another drink and went back to the TV. It was getting dark outside, the winter evening beginning to close in. At about nine o'clock Hawk woke Albert. "Dad, why don't you go to bed and sleep there?" Albert, roused out of the chair, stumbled to the back bedroom followed by his dog, Sooner.

"See you in the morning," Hawk said.

Hawk went back to the kitchen and selected some cans of food. He opened a box of matches and put some in a plastic bag. He gathered up a small pot, a frying pan, a plastic coffee cup, and some silverware, and took them to his room. He pocketed his cash savings. He added a flashlight, soap, toothbrush, and a roll of toilet paper to his pack. He found the truck keys hanging on a nail on the back of a cupboard door. Then he lay on his bed, thinking. He needed to leave that night; otherwise, George would be there tomorrow and try to talk him back to Tulsa. He didn't want to go back, he was sure of that. He'd have to explain it later to Gina and the rest of them. He wondered if there was a way he could pick up Bear and take him along but decided that was impossible. Anyway, he could travel more easily alone. George would take care of Bear for now.

Around midnight Hawk got up, dressed warmly, and picked up the pack. He could hear his dad snoring loudly in the back bedroom. Hawk eased out the door and started the truck without the headlights. He backed out into the road. It was a moonless night. No one was outside. It was a good time to leave. He drove west on 51, following the road back toward Tulsa. He remembered a truck stop near Wagoner. He'd drop the pickup and maybe find a ride with a trucker from there.

At the truck stop, he parked at the back of the lot, dropped the keys on the floor of the driver's side, and locked it. There were a couple of trucks idling while their drivers were inside getting coffee. When one came out, Hawk asked for a ride.

"Where you headed, son?" the trucker asked him.

"Away from here. North, mostly."

"You running away?"

"Not really. I'm leaving here to look for a job. I'm sixteen now."

"I don't usually pick up hitchhikers."

"I'm in a jam. If you'd take me for a while, you can drop me up the road a bit, and I'll look for another ride. I promise I won't be any trouble."

"All right, then, get in. But if you change your mind, sing out, and I'll let you off."

As they headed north on Highway 69, the driver said, "Name's Ed, by the way." He stuck out his hand.

"Charles," Hawk said. "Thanks for the lift. I won't tell anyone you gave me a ride."

"I ran once myself," Ed said. "That's how I came to trucking. Learned along the way."

He looked over at Hawk's gear.

"That's a nice pack you got. Military issue?"

"It was my brother's. He had it when he was in Nam."

"What's he doing now that he's back?"

"He's dead."

"That's tough. Sorry to hear that. I was in Korea. Lost some good buddies there. I felt lucky to make it home alive."

They drove awhile in silence. "Look, Charles, I'm on a two-day run to Duluth with a few stops along the way. So I suggest you get some sleep. I'll wake you up north of Kansas City when I stop for breakfast. How far north you going?"

"Far as I can."

"It's getting to be winter up there. You got warm clothes?"

"I'm pretty good, but I'll get some better boots and gloves when I get up there."

"We'll talk along the way. For now, get some rest."

"Thanks," Hawk said. He curled into the corner and was instantly asleep.

CHAPTER SEVENTY

The next morning, Christine and George drove out to the reservation. They knocked on Albert's door but got no answer. They knocked again, louder.

Roused out of sleep, Albert came to the door, growling. "What the hell do you two want?"

"We're looking for Charles," George said. "Did he come back here?"

"He ain't here. I just looked in his room. It's empty. You can come in and look for yourself if you want to."

"Any idea where he might be?" George asked.

"Hah, that's a laugh," Albert said. "Who the hell you think you are? You come here and pump my kid full of ideas about a good education, playing sports, all that crap, and now you want to know if I have an idea where he might be?"

"Well, do you?"

"No." He pointed at George. "You. You're supposed to be his guardian. Lotta good you are. Can't even keep track of him."

Christine described the trial and what happened. "He got out the door before we could stop him."

"Well, you'd better find him, and when you do, I want him back home here where he belongs."

"Where's your truck?" George asked.

"Well, it was here yesterday. He must've taken it. At least now you know what to look for."

Albert went back inside, slamming the door. He watched from the window as they pulled away.

"Let's call Darles and get an APB out on the truck," George said. "That's a start."

CHAPTER SEVENTY-ONE

Ed woke Hawk outside Kansas City when he stopped for breakfast. At Ed's prodding, Hawk talked about his brother, his dad's alcoholism, and the events surrounding Florence's death.

"That's a lot of bad," Ed said. "I can understand your wanting to leave. Is there anyone who'll be looking for you?"

"I was close to our medicine elder, Three Songs. He was teaching me a lot about Cherokee ways. And there's George. He served with my brother in the army. I was living with him before my mom got custody."

"What are you going to do when they find you?"

"I'm not going back there."

"You can't run from things forever. That's what I tried to do and ended up trucking. Never did get settled down."

"Maybe I'll go back someday, but not now."

"What you gonna do when you get up north?"

"I haven't thought that far. Just start looking for work, I guess."

"You don't want to stop in Duluth. You'll just end up on the streets, homeless. Then the cops will pick you up. I'd go a bit farther north into the smaller towns. Winter help is scarce. I used to vacation at a lodge up there. Route 61 runs right up along Lake Superior, near a big wilderness area. There's good hunting and fishing, lots of camps and lodges."

"I'm pretty good in the outdoors."

"Well, you might find some work at a lodge. There's not much else going on during the winter in Northern Minnesota. You'll have to get up past Duluth, near Ely, to find the places that might hire. You got any ID?"

"Got a learner's permit. A library card. That's about it. I can drive a stick shift. I'm good with dogs and know how to canoe and camp."

"When we get to the terminal in Duluth, I'll look around for a driver going north to International Falls. Maybe he can drop you up around Silver Bay. At least get you in the neighborhood of the Boundary Waters."

"I'm a hard worker," Hawk said. "I'd be a good employee."

"Sure you would," Ed said. "The problem is finding someone who'll hire you without asking too many questions. Someone who won't insist you go back to school or turn you over to the cops."

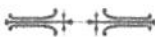

When they arrived in Duluth, Ed told Hawk to stay in the truck, out of sight, until he could find someone who might take him up north. He eventually came back to the truck. "Get your gear," he said. "I think I found someone who can drop you up the road."

As he was getting out of the truck, Ed handed him some cash. "Hide this somewhere on your person where it'll be safe. It's your emergency money. Don't never use it unless you absolutely have to. It's your only parachute."

Hawk started to count it. Ed put a hand over it. "Put it away now. Don't let anyone see it, otherwise it'll be gone next time you're asleep." Hawk stuffed it into his front pants pocket, then followed Ed to a panel truck idling at the edge of the lot. A tall Nordic-looking man was standing by the truck, smoking. His worn wool shirt was open, missing some buttons. He was wearing a red-and-black wool hunter's cap that made him look like Elmer Fudd. "This here's Olie," Ed said. "Olie, meet my nephew, Charles. He needs a ride up to the Silver Bay area. Going to work for an outfitter there on 61, just above Silver Bay."

"You betcha," Olie said. "Get in. I'm ready to go."

Hawk turned to Ed. "Thanks for everything."

Ed slapped him on the back. "Good luck, kid. Stay warm."

They pulled out of the parking lot, Hawk in the passenger seat with his pack between him and Olie.

"Nice pack," Olie said. "How much you want for it?"

CHAPTER SEVENTY-TWO

George and Christine drove 51 back toward Tulsa. "Well, counselor," George said, "where do we go from here?"

"Sure seems like he's disappeared. We could have a needle in a haystack."

"Hard to think he'd leave Bear behind," George said.

"He's desperate, upset. He knows you'll take care of Bear. But he's also street-smart. He could get away from here quickly, especially with the truck."

"If he's out on the highway, he could be in another state by now."

They stopped for a cup of coffee on the way back into Tulsa. Christine found a pay phone and called Darles.

"I reached Darles," she said after the call. "He'll put the word out, but there must be a million 1960 Chevy pickups in this area."

A couple of days later, Christine called George. "We got a make on Albert's truck," she said. "It was locked and parked at the back of that truck stop where we had coffee."

"That makes sense," George said. "He would have known that route well. I'll go over there and see what I can find out."

At the truck stop, George sat at the counter and ordered a cup of coffee and a piece of pie. George thought the waitress, Lillian, might be Cherokee.

"Live close by?" George asked, while she poured his coffee.

"Near Stilwell over in the territory. My husband works construction."

"Do you know Albert Manawa? Has a son Charles."

"Everybody knows them, what with the murder trial in the papers. Too bad about Florence. She was a nice person. She just couldn't pick a good husband."

"I came out to see Charles, but his dad says he's gone. Doesn't know where he is."

"I thought he was living in town."

"Yeah, he was living with me. I served with his brother in Nam."

"Okay, I know who you are now. I thought you looked familiar. It was a good thing you did for Horse."

"Well, Hawk's taken off, upset about the death of his mom. The police found Albert's truck parked out back. I'm wondering if maybe he came in here and hitched a ride somewhere."

"Haven't seen him, but I'll ask around."

"Were there trucks through here two nights ago?"

"I was off, but let me check with Lucie. She worked that shift. I can call you when she comes in."

George wrote his number on a napkin. "That would be great," he said. "Anything would help."

George called Christine back. "The waitress here knows the family. She didn't work the night Hawk took off, but she'll talk to the night staff and call me later today."

CHAPTER SEVENTY-THREE

Traffic was light on Minnesota Route 61. Hawk shifted a bit in his seat, rested his arm on his pack, pulled it closer to him. The cab was filthy, the floor cluttered with food wrappers, the ashtray overflowing with cigarette butts. Olie played with the radio, then finally turned it off. Between cigarettes, he sucked on a big coffee mug he kept in a holder draped over the transmission hump.

"How far you going, kid?"

"Silver Bay," Hawk said. "You can let me off anywhere in town there."

"Ain't nothin' in Silver Bay. Why you going there?"

"I've got a job."

"Silver Bay's a crap town. I grew up around there."

"This your regular route?"

Olie's truck struggled as they started up a small hill, making him downshift. "You betcha. Haul stuff to International Falls. Pick it up at Duluth, bring stuff back."

"You work for yourself?"

"Yeah. Used to drive for somebody else. Bought this truck so's I could be my own boss. Quit taking orders from numbskulls."

As they came to a longer hill, Olie downshifted again, moved into the slow truck lane, letting other vehicles pass. At the crest, he moved back into the regular lane. The truck picked up speed going downhill, but its suspension caused it to sway as it accelerated, making Olie brake to keep it under control in the wind. They followed this pattern down the highway.

Olie finished his coffee. "You're a good-looking kid," Olie said. "You getting any?"

Hawk had been looking out the window, watching the scenery. "Getting any?"

"Yeah," Olie said. "You getting any with the girls?"

"No, I'm not getting any."

"I bet you are, you just don't want to say." They drove for a while in silence. "There's a whorehouse up here off the road a ways. We could stop there."

"No, thanks," Hawk said. "I don't have any money anyway."

"You sell me that pack, I'll throw in the cost of a whore. They might even give you a freebie, it being your first time and all."

"No. You want to pull off, that's up to you. Just let me out along the road."

"You queer?"

"What do you mean?"

"You like boys? Maybe that's why you don't go for girls."

"I'm not queer."

"I bet you are. I seen pretty boys before. They try to hide it, but I can always pick 'em out."

Hawk was watching the road now, trying to figure out how he could ditch Olie and find a ride with someone else. When they got to Lighthouse State Park, Olie pulled into the park drive. A sign said WINTER HOURS: SATURDAY 9–4.

Olie stopped the truck. "Time to take a leak," he said. "You better go, too. There's not much on this road." They got out of the truck, went over to the grass at the edge of the pavement. When Olie finished but was still hanging out, he turned to Hawk. He pointed down. "You ever seen one this big?" he said.

Hawk looked at him. He shook his head.

"I'm thinking a kid like you would like to suck this." He waggled it at him. "Kinda like payment for the ride."

Hawk started back toward the truck.

"Hey, kid, I'm serious. You wanna go any farther, you got to suck me off, or I take your pack and leave you here. Your choice."

Hawk reached the passenger side door. "Okay, but not here out in the open. Let's drive down the road a bit, where it's secluded."

Olie laughed. "I knew you was a queer. I can always tell. You gonna enjoy it. It'll be the biggest one you ever licked." Hawk waited until Olie was on the driver's side, then grabbed his pack and started running toward the woods.

Olie jogged after him, yelling, "Come back here, you little faggot," but after about fifty yards, Olie was winded. He bent over, gasping for breath. Hawk was in the woods now, gone. Olie pulled a cigarette pack out of his pocket, took one out, and lit up. He staggered back to the truck and hollered into the wind, "Good luck, kid. I hope you freeze to death."

Hawk hid at the edge of the woods until he saw Olie's truck back out and turn onto the highway, headed north. He looked around. Away from the wind, it was comfortable there, but the sun was starting to go down, and it was getting colder. He found a spot among some pines, crawled under the branches, and spread out the poncho. There was no good place to start a fire, and he didn't want to draw attention to himself. He pulled out a can of ravioli and ate the contents cold. As darkness came, he crawled into Stalking Bear's sleeping bag, wrapped himself in the poncho, and went to sleep.

CHAPTER SEVENTY-FOUR

George got a call from Lillian about eight o'clock the following evening.

"Sorry I couldn't call last night. Lucie was off, but I talked with her when she came on today. She didn't see Charles. She said it was a light night, only a couple of long-distance trucks. The rest were mostly local stuff. She knows one of the long-distance guys. Name's Ed. Drives for Intercon Express. He's a regular. Makes runs through here with stops in Joplin, Kansas City, and other places en route north to Duluth. He won't be back for a couple of weeks. He never deadheads, so he'll stay in Duluth until he gets a load to bring back. He was by himself, though. She didn't see anyone in the restaurant looking for a ride."

George thanked her. "I'll be out to have dinner sometime," he said. "I owe you a big tip."

She laughed. "I'll be looking for you. I work four days a week, Tuesday through Friday, twelve-hour shifts. I like big tips."

George called Christine. "We might have a lead," he said. "The waitress there said a long-distance trucker passed through that night on a run to Duluth. It's his regular route. He's probably still there. Doesn't leave his destination until he's got a load to bring back. Could we get a cop to go talk to him?"

⟿

A couple of days later, Darles called George. "I heard from a detective in Duluth, name of Smedley. I'd teletyped him a photocopy of Hawk's picture and some details. Smedley went to the Duluth terminal, found the driver who'd taken Charles there. The driver said he hooked Charles up with a short hauler to drop him in Silver Bay."

George called Christine. "Okay, I think we've got solid information. At least we have a general idea where he might be, but he's got a few days' head start. I'm going to drive up there and look for him."

"That's a long drive."

"I could fly, but with the truck, I can take Bear and some personal gear. Winter's coming, and I'd like to have some outdoor gear with me."

Before he left Tulsa, George called Mel. "I'll be gone for a while. I'm going north to Minnesota to look for Hawk."

"Minnesota? How'd he get way up there?"

"Seems he caught a ride with a trucker headed that way."

"I guess you don't have any choice. Is there something I can do?"

"No, unless you want to go along and keep me company."

"I really can't go right now, with work and my projects due after the break. I'm sorry."

"I'll keep you posted."

"Be safe. Call me when you get there."

"Will do."

"George," she said. "I'll miss you."

CHAPTER SEVENTY-FIVE

At first light Hawk awoke, stiff and a bit cold. There was a light frost on the ground around him. He stretched, packed up, ate a bit, and got back on the road. He walked toward Beaver Bay. Just outside the town, he stopped at a roadside restaurant and got some breakfast. After he finished, he noticed a cork bulletin board in the foyer covered with want ads and business cards. He saw a handwritten note. "Wanted: Winter Help. Colton's Wilderness Lodge, SR 1, Silver Bay." Hawk borrowed a pen from the cashier and copied the phone number down. He got back on the highway and started walking north.

By noon he was in Silver Bay. He stopped at a gas station, used the restroom, bought a candy bar and a Minnesota road map, and got change for the phone. John Colton, the lodge owner, answered his call.

"I'm calling about the job," Hawk said.

"Just drive on Highway 1 until you see the sign for Colton's Wilderness Lodge. Take that road all the way to the end. That's where we are."

"I'm in Silver Bay," Hawk said. "But I don't have a vehicle. How long a walk is it?"

"It's a few miles, take you all day. Where are you now?"

Hawk looked around him. "I'm at a Shell station and convenience store on 61 across from the IGA."

"I know the place," Colton said. "I got to come in for supplies anyways, so I'll pick you up there. What's your name?"

"Charles, Charles Manawa."

"All right, then. Don't leave there. I'll be by in about an hour. I've got a green truck, the lodge name's on the door. My name's John."

Hawk went back into the station and talked to the clerk. "I have a ride picking me up in a while. Do you mind if I wait outside?"

"Suit yourself," she said. "If you get cold, come in here. Nobody'll care."

Hawk found a spot beside the store with a view of the highway, ate the candy bar, and studied the map.

After an hour, Hawk began to worry that Colton wouldn't come. He went back in the store to get warmed up. "Didn't show yet?" the clerk asked.

"Not yet," Hawk said. "Probably got held up."

"Everything's a bit slower around here, especially in the winter. I'm about to throw out that coffee, make some fresh. You want a cup? On the house."

"Yeah, thanks," he said. She poured two cups and dumped the rest.

"Help yourself to cream and sugar if you want it."

Hawk stood by the store window, allowing the steam from the coffee to rise up and warm his face.

"You from around here?" she asked.

"Not here, exactly. I came up from Duluth. Wanted to find some work with a lodge."

"You've come to the right place. Most folks move south to the cities for the winter, so there's lots of jobs if you don't mind the cold."

"I'm okay with that. But I'll need to get some warmer boots. Is there a store around that sells used stuff?"

"Yep. You go up the road a bit, you'll see a rough-looking place called Hugh's Useds. He sells stuff on consignment. You might find something there. I know he's got some snowshoes."

A green pickup pulled into the station. "I think this is my ride," Hawk said. He picked up his pack and started out the door. "Thanks," he said. "You've been real nice."

"Good luck to you, hon."

Outside, Hawk walked to the truck as Colton got out. "Mr. Colton?"

"I thought I was picking up an adult. How old are you, anyway?"

"Sixteen. But I'm a good worker. I know my way around the woods."

"Indian? I haven't had much luck with the Indians around here."

"People say I look Indian, but my parents are Mexican. My dad works for a dairy farmer outside Minneapolis."

"Well, get in. I'm John Colton. After I get the supplies, I'll take you out to the lodge, see what you can do."

John fueled up. He drove across the road to the grocery, and Hawk got out of the truck with him and followed him around the store. After he paid, Hawk picked up two of the bags and carried them to the truck. They went to a lumberyard and picked up some two-by-fours and nails. John nodded toward a rack of work gloves. "Pick yourself out a pair that fits," he said.

On the way to the lodge, John pried into Hawk's background. "You running from something or someone?"

"No, sir," Hawk said. "I want to learn the outfitting business. I'm good in the outdoors. I figured I could get an easier start in the winter when there's not so many people around."

"What about school?"

"My dad was okay with me leaving. He's made a good living working hard. He figured I had enough school for what I want to do."

At a road sign for the lodge, John pulled off the highway onto a dirt road that snaked through the woods. At the end of the road was a large log structure and some parking to one side. There were outbuildings in the back. Hawk could see the lake through the trees. John drove around behind the lodge, where they unloaded the supplies. "Get your pack," he said. "I'll show you where to stay." He took Hawk to a cabin behind the lodge. "This is the crew cabin, the bunkhouse. You can sleep here. Right now, you're the only one. Your roommate, Larry, will be here in a few days. He works on an ore freighter, and they're about to quit for the winter. He comes here then to work. Good hunter, fisherman. You can learn a lot from Larry. There's some wood by the stove there. If you want heat, light her up. You got to keep the wood supplied yourself. You take your meals in the kitchen. Millie, she's my wife, is the cook. If she needs anything, you get it for her. We're about to have lunch. Then I'll put you to work and see what you can do."

The kitchen was located at the back of the lodge. A stocky, solid woman was at the stove, pulling bread from the oven as John and Hawk came in. "Wipe your feet," she said without looking up. "I just swept."

"This here's Charles," John said. "He wants a job."

Millie wiped her hands on her apron and extended one to shake with Hawk. "Nice to meet you," she said. "Sit down and have some lunch."

After the meal, John took Hawk for a tour of the lodge and the surrounding grounds. They walked down to the lake where John showed him the boathouse. Another building held two trailers carrying Ski-Doos. "After hunting season," John said, "we get lots of folks from downstate who come up to ride through the woods. It's good business." Beside one of the outbuildings, he had dumped a pile of cut-up logs ready for splitting. He handed Hawk an ax and a splitting maul. "I want this all split and stacked. Fill up the bin beside the lodge first, put some by the bunkhouse, and stack the rest under this woodshed here. There's a wheelbarrow you can use to move it around."

Hawk put on his gloves and started in, putting a log up on the chopping block. He picked up the maul.

"You can stay a couple of nights," John said. "We'll see how you do. Then we'll talk about whether we want to hire you."

"Fair enough," Hawk said as he took the first swing through the log. "How small you want the pieces?"

CHAPTER SEVENTY-SIX

By six o'clock, Hawk had split all the wood and had begun stacking. John came around. "Wash up," he said. "Dinner's on. You can finish this later."

At the table, Millie served fried chicken, dumplings, gravy, and a big salad.

"You're a good cook, Mrs. Colton," Hawk said.

"Thanks. Name's Millie," she said. "Mrs. Colton was my mother-in-law, who died ten years ago. If you got any laundry needing done, just put it on the back porch there by the door."

"You got a driver's license?" John asked.

"No, but I know how to drive—learned on a stick shift."

"Well, at least you can drive around camp, although nobody much cares around here if you got a license, especially in the wintertime."

"I know a little bit about engines. I worked for a motorcycle dealer for a while."

"That'll come in handy during snowmobile season," Millie said.

After dinner, Hawk went back to the woodpile, working by the outdoor lights off the lodge. By nine, he had stacked all of the wood. He put the tools in the shed and went to the bunkhouse. The room was stone cold and had no lights. Hawk got out his flashlight and found a kerosene lantern. It was fueled. A box of matches sat on the shelf. He lit the lantern, then built a fire in the stove. The room warmed up while he got his gear out. He put the sleeping bag on top of the bed, stoked the fire, turned out the lantern, and went to bed.

Hawk woke the next morning to pounding on the door. "Breakfast in fifteen minutes," John called. Hawk roused, went to the bathroom, and splashed water on his face. The cabin was cold again. He dressed quickly and was glad to arrive in the warm kitchen.

"You did real good with the wood," John said. "I think we can work something out." He explained the terms of employment: free room and board, cash payment every two weeks. "Don't pay no social security. You want that, you'll have to pay it yourself." He looked across the table at Millie. "One other thing. If we give you this chance, you got to stick it out. I don't want to be looking for workers midwinter. The hunters will be coming in here next week, and we're going to be busy for the season."

"I think I'll need to get some warmer clothes," Hawk said, "along with some winter boots. Anyplace where I can get that stuff?"

"There's a Carhartt store in town," John said. "We'll go in today after chores. I'll advance the money, take it out of your pay. We'll get what you need. It won't be fancy, but it's good working gear."

"I appreciate you taking a chance on me," Hawk said. "I'll do my best for you."

CHAPTER SEVENTY-SEVEN

By the time George got to Silver Bay, the trail had gone cold. The town was closing down for winter hours, leaving open a few essential stores, gas stations, and bars. At the Shell station, George showed a picture of Hawk to the clerk. She paused as if she might know something, then shook her head and turned to fix some stock behind the cash register. "Sorry, I can't help you," she said. "There's always tourists coming in here. I just don't pay attention to them. You might try up at Grand Marais. That's a kind of watering hole for folks passing through." She looked out the window and saw Bear sitting beside George's truck. "That your dog?"

"Belongs to the kid," he said. "I'm trying to put them back together again."

"Well mannered. What's his breed?"

"Just a mutt," George said, "but Charles trained him. The dog would do anything for him." George headed for the door. "Thanks for your time."

"Why don't you leave me your phone number in case the kid shows up?"

"I'll stop back," George said. "I don't have a place to stay yet. I need to find a motel."

"There's some tourist cabins up the road. Not too expensive, and they'd be okay with the dog. Lots of hunters stay there. They've still got some rooms for let."

George drove up the road and found Lighthouse Cove Tourist Cabins. "We rent by the week," the owner said. "A hundred forty in cash, in advance."

"I've got a dog," George said.

"Okay, as long as you keep him off the bed."

George paid the cash and got the room key. It was a ten-by-twelve room with a small bath and a black-and-white TV. "All the comforts of home," George said to Bear.

After settling in, George fed and watered Bear and took him for a walk. He brought a blanket from the truck and put it on the floor. "Lie down there, Bear," he said. "I'll be back soon."

George drove back to town to the Pickerel Grill, a bar that he'd seen going through the main drag. He went in and got a table by the window. The waitress came over. "Hi," she said, "Welcome to the Pickerel. Here for dinner?" George looked around. "Yeah. It's pretty quiet in here."

"It's midweek, not much action. Can I get you a drink to start?"

"A beer," George said. "Maybe some coffee later." She handed him a menu.

"Any specials?"

"The chicken."

"Okay with me," he said. "I'm new to town, looking for a job," George said. "Maybe with an outfitter. Know of anyone hiring?"

"There are several lodges in the area," she said. "You might just have to drive around, explore a bit. There's plenty of work if you don't mind spending the winter. Sometimes the owners come in here, so you might hear of an opening."

George ate his meal and left a good tip. On the way out, he saw her by the cash register, cashing out a customer. “Good food, Sally,” he said. “Maybe I'll see you again.”

“I hope so.”

George and Bear made the rounds of the town the next day, but came up empty. Back at the grill the next night, Sally was there again. After she brought his food, she nodded back behind her toward the bar. “The guy at the end is John Colton,” she said. “He owns one of the lodges. He might know of something open.”

After he finished his meal, George walked up to the bar and sat down beside John. “Say,” he said. “I'm new here, looking for work. Any of the lodges hiring?”

John studied his beer, then swiveled to meet George. “You're about a week late. I just hired someone, but I'm sure there's others around looking. Check the local weekly. And lots of folks just post on the bulletin boards around.” John looked at George's fatigue jacket. “Vet?”

George nodded. “Nam. Got out about a year ago.”

“I'll keep my ear to the ground. If I hear something, I'll leave a message at the bar here.”

“The guy you just hired, from around here?”

“Why you wanna know?”

“No reason. It's just that I'm from out of town. Wondered if locals would hire me.”

Colton laughed. “In the wintertime, around here, we're glad to hire anyone who's standing up and breathing, as long as he can put in a day's work.”

“Well, just wondered.”

“Like you, this guy just showed up unannounced. Nice kid, though. Mexican, hard worker. He's a keeper.”

“Kid?”

“Yeah, about sixteen. Why?”

"No reason, I just thought kids would be in school, that's all."

"After sixteen, no one cares. Especially up here."

"Well, thanks," George said. "I'd appreciate knowing if you hear anything."

That night, George called Mel. "Just checking in," he said. "I'm in Silver Bay, but no one claims to know anything. One guy told me he recently hired a young man, called him a 'nice kid.' Thinks he's Mexican. I'll try to check that further without spooking anyone."

He then called Christine. "We've got nothing at this end," Christine said. "Darles made contact with the sheriff there, at least to alert him, but I get the feeling that there's not a lot of interest on the part of the police in driving around looking for a runaway."

"These folks are pretty independent and closemouthed. No one's going to rat out anybody. Hawk can stay hidden if he wants to."

For the next few days, George continued to canvas the businesses that were open, describing Hawk, showing his picture. One store manager said, "Seen one Indian, you've seen 'em all. They all look the same to me." At the end of the week, George had found a cabin off Highway 1 that he could rent for the winter. He and Bear moved in and settled down. George stopped daily at the Shell station and, after he found the rental, he left his phone number with the clerk. George went through his inventory of photographic equipment and mounted his long lens. "Bear, it's time we did some recon."

CHAPTER SEVENTY-EIGHT

George and Bear drove to Ely to look for an outfitting shop. At the store, George bought some basic camo—reversible with a white side he could use in snow. For equipment, George settled on a Coleman Peak1 stove, a large can of fuel, a Sigg set of pots, an ax, a portable saw, and a one-man tent. He also purchased snowshoes and ski poles. He saw some leather booties made for dogs. "Mushers use those," the shopkeeper said. "Keep the dogs' feet from freezing." George tried them on Bear and bought a set. He also bought a sled he could pull behind to carry his camera equipment and the survival gear.

After he cashed out with the clerk at the outfitter's, George stowed the gear in the truck. "Come on, Bear," he said. "Let's walk around town." They started down the street. The town, at the edge of the wilderness area, was oriented mostly for tourists, hunters, and fishermen. Some places were already closed for the season. A green Minnesota Forest Service truck was parked in front of one of the open spots, Mabel's Café.

"You stay outside here, Bear," George said as he went in the door. The place was empty except at the counter where the forest ranger sat. George took a stool a couple down from the ranger. An older woman in a long dress with a white apron came over and set a porcelain mug down in front of George. "Coffee?"

George nodded. "Yes, ma'am."

"That your dog out there?"

"Yep," George said. "Name's Bear."

"Well," she said. "Bear's welcome to come inside, long as he stays over by the window, out of the food line."

George smiled, walked to the door, held it open for him. "Come on in, Bear." George directed him to a spot under the front window. "Lie down there, boy. Stay."

"Good ol' Mabel," the ranger said. "Always a soft spot for critters." He looked over at her as she brought George a menu and silverware. "Maybe I'll send over one of my kids, see if she'll take him in and straighten him out."

"If he can wash dishes," Mabel said, "I'd give him a run for his money."

"It'd be good for him to learn."

"A woman that likes kids and dogs," George said, "can't be all bad."

Mabel drew a pencil out of the pile of white hair she'd pulled into a bun. "What'll it be?"

George put in his order: eggs over easy, bacon, hash browns.

Mabel turned to the grill behind her, cracked two eggs, and moved the potatoes and bacon onto the warm side of the grill. "Whole wheat or white?" she asked over her shoulder.

"Whole wheat," George said. "Dry, please."

George turned to the ranger. "I'm George Wheeler," he said as he stuck out his hand.

They shook. "Eric Knutsen. I'm over at the Kawishiwi Ranger Station."

"What do you guys do in the winter?"

"It's a little slower, but it'll pick up with the start of hunting season. During January and February, we also work on the wolf project."

"What's that about?"

"Minnesota has the last pack of healthy wolves in North America. Some guys downstate are studying them, trying to get them on the endangered list. Get them under protection."

"I'm from Oklahoma," George said. "The ranchers there were always complaining about wolves getting to their stock. The boys I know were pretty much hell bent on killing them all."

"They're important to the ecosystem," Eric said. "They can be a problem where their territory is encroached on. Grazing stock make easy pickings. Up here, they keep the balance, weed out the weaklings."

Mabel set the food down in front of George. She took a piece of bacon over to Bear. "Wolves are beautiful animals," she said. "Smart, too. Ol' Bear here's probably got some wolf in him from some past generation." She walked back to the counter. "I love to hear them howl at night."

"How do you track them?" George asked.

"By plane, mostly, and during the winter, because the leaves are off the trees, they show up well in snow. We've captured some and then released them with radio collars on so we can monitor individuals as well as the packs. The batteries only last about six to nine months, so every year we have to catch new ones to collar."

Eric looked at George's fatigue jacket. "Where'd you serve?"

"I was a Ranger—spent almost a year in Vietnam. I love the outdoors, so I'm trying to find a job that will let me work outside. Heard about the Boundary Waters. Thought I'd come up here and look for work, but it looks like I'm a bit late. I'm also learning photography. So while I'm looking for work, I thought maybe Bear and I'd go out and try to take some pictures in the wild."

"Actually," Eric said, "we're putting our winter crews together now. You could get an interview. The station's up on Kawishiwi Lake. Week from today, the boss will be there. I'll arrange an interview for you. You got any ID?"

"Got my discharge papers, driver's license."

"Good enough." Eric drained his coffee cup, got up, and slapped a five-dollar bill on the counter. "Got to run. Thanks, Mabel. Keep the change." He stopped to pet Bear. "Hope to see you next week, George." Eric left the restaurant, got in his truck, and drove off.

"Nice guy," George said.

"Yep. He grew up around here. Knows the woods like the back of his hand. Has his dream job."

"I should have asked where the station's located."

Mabel went to the cash register, pulled a map from under the counter. "Here's the lake," she said. "Take 61 up to this county road and drive back a few miles. You'll run into it."

Some guys came through the door then and took up a table in the corner. Mabel left the map for George to look at. She took coffee and mugs to the table and poured it around. "Howdy, fellows," she said.

One of them gave her a pat on the butt. "How's my beautiful Mabel?" he said.

"Same as always, standing up, working for slugs like you."

The others laughed.

"I'm gonna marry you someday," he said.

"If shootin' bull printed money," she said, "you'd be wealthy. Then maybe I *would* marry you." She turned to the others. "You all want the usual?" They nodded. "Coming up."

When she got back behind the counter, George had folded the map back up, put his money on top of his tab. "Thanks."

"You come back," she said. "I lost one of my boys in that war. I'd like to ask you about it."

"Army?"

Mabel's eye's misted just for a second. She wiped them with a towel and shook her head. "Navy."

George tipped his hat. "It's a long story," he said. "Ugly, too. But you pick a night when you're closed. I'll take you to dinner and tell you anything you want to know."

"How about next Tuesday? I don't serve dinner, so I close at four. I'll meet you across the street, over at the Voyageur, say five o'clock?"

"Deal," George said.

She reached behind, pulled off another piece of bacon, and laid it on a napkin. "For Bear," she said and turned to the grill to begin cooking.

CHAPTER SEVENTY-NINE

Back at the house, George sorted things and then called Christine. "If I find Hawk, and he's getting along fine, doing a good job for a hunting lodge, I'm wondering if he could stay here working for the winter."

"He's almost sixteen now," Christine said. "Under Oklahoma law he can quit school if he wants to, but once his dad finds out where he is, he might demand that he come home."

"What if we don't tell him?"

"Can't do that, George. If we know where he is, his dad has a right to know."

"All right, I understand. If and when I find him, I'll let you know. It'll be up to you to sell the old man on leaving him here. At this point, he's moved enough, and it'd be good for him to have some success. Bear is my ace in the hole. If I find Hawk, Bear will be the key to keeping him cool."

"Don't go rogue on me, George. By the way, I talked with Gina and filled her in on the details. She wants to write to Hawk when we get an address for him."

"I'll keep you informed. But I'm not about to force something on the kid. According to the lodge owner, Hawk's doing well. It's a good situation for him. Of course, I've got to verify that as well. I'll get some pictures, send them to Kodak for processing, and use your address for the return. That way you'll get the photos first after they're processed. It's okay if you want to share them with Hawk's dad. He may be willing to let Hawk stay if he sees that he's safe and sound."

The next morning, George took Bear and some gear and drove to a forest entry point. He filled out the ranger forms for a day permit, and they hiked in. Snow had fallen overnight so there was a three- to four-inch layer, which made dragging the sled easy. George strapped on the snowshoes. He stumbled a bit getting used to walking with them, but with the ski poles he started to get the hang of it. They walked for about an hour away from the parking lot, then stopped for a break. George laid the white tarp on the ground and stretched out on part of it.

"Bear," he said. "Come here, boy. Lie down there." Bear lay next to him, then George folded the rest of the tarp over them. He practiced shooting pictures with his camera. After an hour or so, they moved on to a new site, getting Bear used to the routine. George had lots of snacks to reward Bear for obeying. By late afternoon, they were back at the truck, headed home. When they got back to the cabin, George built a fire in the stove and put Bear's blanket close to it. Then he practiced his yoga exercises.

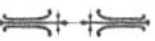

Out on Highway 1, George found the sign for Colton Lodge. He marked the road on his map, then drove beyond it looking for a place off the road where they could get entry to the woods. They pulled off into a highway rest area. He spread the map out and took some compass bearings. He and Bear set off, working their way back toward the lodge. When the buildings came into view, they hunkered down. George looked at the terrain to see how they could approach without being seen. There was little ground cover—persons walking in the woods would be easily visible. Not a good situation for surveillance. George spotted a small rise running toward the lake. They worked their way over there and hunkered down on the tarp. George played with the telephoto, looking for open views, deciding on the best place for observing.

As evening approached, George and Bear went back to the truck and drove home. He stoked the fire, fed Bear, and put an aluminum tray with a TV dinner into the oven. "We'll be up early tomorrow, Bear. Get a good night's sleep."

CHAPTER EIGHTY

Colton Lodge was starting to come alive with hunters arriving. As the activity increased, George could observe more but still hadn't seen Hawk. Colton was there with another guy George didn't recognize. Pickups were filling the parking lot. One afternoon, when George was about to pack it in for the day, a young man walked out of one of the buildings, heading down toward the lake. George lost him for a bit in the trees but had his telephoto ready when the youth came back toward the lodge. He went inside a barn and began hauling gear toward a van parked near the barn. George edged himself into position and began shooting photos. "Got you," he whispered. That night, he put the film in a Kodak mailer to drop off at the local post office the next day. He then called Mel.

"I saw him today," he said. "I've sent Christine some photos so that she can inform his dad. Now I have to figure out a way to connect with him without causing him to panic and take off again."

"Maybe you can talk to the owner of the lodge when Charles is not around."

"I'll work on that. I've got time on my side. He doesn't suspect that I know where he is, so he'll be relaxed."

"Keep me posted. How's the weather there?" she asked.

"Winter's coming. It's Minnesota. Frigid, crystal clear, beautiful."

"Take care, George," she said. "You're doing the right thing."

"I'm starting to like it here. Could be a new beginning for both of us."

"What about me?"

George laughed. "You're in the picture, too. You should see this area. It's amazing."

"And I believe you said cold?"

"Only outside."

The next Tuesday, George went to the Voyageur Bar and Grill. He took a table near the back corner, where he could see the door, and ordered a cup of coffee. A few minutes later, Mabel walked in. George waved her over to his table.

"I saw you arrive," she said. "I was sitting in my car, waiting to be sure you'd show. I didn't want to come in here by myself."

The waitress came over. "Hi, Mabel. What can I get you to drink?"

"Coffee's good," she said. "I'm too old for anything stronger." She raised her hand toward George. "This here's my friend George. He's up visiting from Oklahoma, wanted to see some of the northland."

"Pleased to meet you, George."

"She's making me buy dinner," George said, "so make sure I get the check."

"That's Mabel's way," the waitress said. "They's lots of old bachelors around here looking for someone to cook and clean up after them. She's about the only eligible one around, so she can at least get a free meal once in a while."

"I guess there's no harm in trying," George said. "A man needs a good woman."

"All right, you two," Mabel said. "Quit jawin' about my love life. What's on special tonight?"

After the orders were in, George asked, "What's your son's name?"

"Lars," she said. "He was my youngest of four. Two boys, two girls. The girls are married. My first boy was too old for the draft when the war came. Lars was the trailer, came along a bit later. He was a good kid—smart, good-looking. Had everything going for him."

"How old was he?"

"Twenty. He was working nights, attending community college in Duluth. Recruiter told him he could earn money for full-time college, so he signed up for the navy. Became a medic. Thought he wanted to be a doctor."

The food came, and they talked around things through dinner. The waitress brought coffee. George moved his elbows off the table to let the waitress clear the dishes.

"Worst day of my life," Mabel said, "when that yellow sedan pulled up. It was a Sunday. Café was closed. When I saw the officer get out, I knew what had happened before he even got to the door."

"That has to be awful," George said. "When it happens in combat, when you're there, it's horrible. But at least it's in context. Everyone in battle knows it can happen. But when you're at home with no idea of what's going on a continent away, the shock has to be terrible."

Mabel nodded. She dabbed at her eyes with her napkin.

"How'd he get in-country?"

"I thought he'd be offshore, out of harm's way, but he was assigned to a marine unit. He ended up somewhere in the northern part of the country. He wasn't there more than ninety days before he was killed."

"That's the worst time," George said. "When someone's new, not yet experienced. That's when the mistakes are made."

"Lars got a Bronze Star. They said he was killed by a mortar while trying to take care of a wounded marine." She looked away from George, off into the tavern, watching folks in conversation. "That would be Lars," she said. "He'd do what he had to do, not thinking about himself."

"One of my best friends was gunned down that way. We were in the same Ranger unit, pinned down, had some guys cut off. He ran to them through intense fire and brought them back. He was hit while carrying a wounded guy back to safety."

"I'm sorry," she said. "I'm sorry for all the kids lost in that war."

"I can tell that Lars was like my friend. Out of the chaos—the noise and smoke, like the fires of hell—there are some extraordinary men who rise up and take action, doing things no ordinary person could ever achieve. I'm sure that's the way it was for your son. I'll never forget how it happened with my friend."

"I never did get why we were there in the first place," Mabel said. "I heard all about the domino theory, the communist threats, that stuff, but I didn't see what it had to do with us. Our country should have stayed out of it."

"Worse yet," George said. "Once we got into it, the politicians took over. Tried to run the war from Washington. It's now a mess. The sooner we get out of there, the better."

George paid the bill, but they sat at the table, talking for another hour. Finally, Mabel brought it to a close. "I've got to get home," she said. "My day starts early."

They got up and left the restaurant together. Outside, she gave George a hug. "Thanks," she said. "You're the first one who would talk to me about the war. I guess everyone's been afraid to discuss it with me. You've helped a lot."

"You can't replace your son," he said. "But you should be proud of him. It's the government that screwed up." George hugged her back. "I'm glad we could get together."

CHAPTER EIGHTY-ONE

The following night, George was back at the Pickerel Grill for dinner, sitting at his favorite table in the back corner. There was a light crowd. A game of pool was going in another corner, two men playing a match while others looked on.

Hawk and another man came in, one George had seen at the lodge during his surveillance. Sally gave them a table not far from the pool table. Hawk didn't see George and sat down, his back to him. A big blond-haired guy in a plaid wool shirt finished off the game. He grabbed the money off the bumper and then noticed Hawk. He studied him a minute as if he recognized him. Hawk looked over, and when he saw who it was, looked quickly back at the menu in front of him.

The man drained his beer, set it roughly down on an empty table, then walked over to Hawk's table.

"Hello, faggot," he said.

"Hello, Olie."

"I see you've got a new boyfriend."

Larry looked up at Olie. "Can I help you with something? Maybe change your diapers?" Larry nodded over his shoulder. "The changing room is back behind the bar."

"Shut up," Olie said. "This pretty boy owes me something, bein' I gave him a ride up here from Duluth. It's time he paid up." He grabbed Hawk by the shirt collar and arm and pulled him out of his chair. "We're goin' out to the truck," Olie said, "where this little queer can do his thing."

Larry slid his chair back to get up. Olie kicked it over, sending Larry sprawling backward. Olie started dragging Hawk toward the door. When he got around the next table, George was there.

"Let him go," George said. When Hawk heard the voice, he turned his head, realized it was George. Olie tightened his grip.

"Get out of my way numbskull, or you'll end up on the floor too."

Olie tried to move toward the door, but George maneuvered to block him.

"I said, let him go."

Larry got to his feet and went to the cue rack, pulling down a cue. He walked back toward Olie.

Hawk, still squirming in Olie's grasp, shoved his hand into Olie's face, twisted around and brought his knee up into Olie's groin. Olie gasped and released Hawk. George stepped in and slugged Olie, knocking him backward to the floor. Olie lay there, one hand on his crotch, the other rubbing his chin.

"C'mon, get up," George said, "we're not done yet."

Olie got up slowly and reached for his left back pocket. Someone said, "Watch out, he's got a shiv."

"Hawk," Larry said. He tossed Hawk the pool cue.

Olie pulled the knife out, the blade flashing into a locked position.

"That's right," Olie said. "And most people don't know I'm left-handed. They get surprised."

George faced Olie squarely and waived him forward. "That's not your only defect, you big piece a shit."

Olie started toward George, holding the blade low. As Olie lunged with the knife, Hawk jabbed the butt end of the cue stick into Olie's chest. Olie flinched. In that split second of distraction, George parried the knife thrust, and in one fluid motion, landed one more punch, twisted Olie's arm inside and backward, then slammed his elbow sharply down on Olie's extended arm. Olie's elbow cracked. The knife fell to the floor. Olie dropped to his knees, doubled up in pain.

"What the…" Olie said. "You broke my arm."

Another man started forward, but Larry stepped in front of him. The man hesitated.

"I think it's over," Larry said. "We all good here, fellows?"

The man raised his hands and backed off.

George raised Olie to his feet, took him by the collar and belt. "Let's go for a walk," George said, as he frog-marched Olie toward the exit.

Hawk went ahead to open the door.

Olie, paralyzed with pain, hobbled along, George push-pulling him.

Outside, Hawk pointed to an old gray panel truck parked near the door.

"That's his truck," Hawk said. George marched Olie over to the driver's side.

"This your truck?" George said.

Olie didn't answer.

"I said"—George rammed his head into the driver's door—"Is this your truck?"

Olie grunted.

"Good," George said. He rammed Olie's head into the door again. "Get in it. Lucky for you, the shift's on the right side. That's your good arm. Your other arm's bent in a funny angle, but you can drive yourself to the hospital. You should see a doctor." He shoved Olie backward, causing him to fall down. George stood over him.

"Here's a word of advice, scumbag. You get your arm fixed. Then you find a new watering hole, 'cause if I see you around this young man again, you'll be in a world of hurt."

Olie spit red in the gravel but said nothing.

Back inside, George picked up the knife, closed it, and handed it to the bartender. "Give this to the sheriff next time he comes in." George then pulled out a wad of cash from his pocket and peeled off a hundred dollars. "Drinks around," he said, "Sorry for disturbing the peace."

Hawk was still wide-eyed. "Where'd you come from?" Hawk asked.

"Corner table."

"When did you get here?" Hawk asked.

"I've actually been in town about two weeks." George clasped Hawk on the shoulder. "You should be in Ranger training. You led me a merry chase of escape and evasion. I've looked all over hell's half acre for you."

"How'd you find me?"

"Doesn't matter. The main thing is, I did. You look great."

"This is Larry," Hawk said. "He and I work together at Colton's Wilderness Lodge."

"Pleased to meet you," Larry said. "You've got good timing."

George pulled a chair over from another table. "Would you guys mind if I joined you? I'm eating by myself." They all sat down together.

Sally came by. "Would you like your meal brought over?"

"That'd be great," George said. "Thanks."

"How's Bear?" Hawk asked.

"He's good. I've got him covered."

Hawk turned to Larry. "Thanks for the cue stick," he said. "That was a good idea."

Larry tipped his hat. "Learned a few things runnin' with the ore boats."

"Who was that guy, anyway?" George asked.

"His name's Olie. I was hitchhiking. He offered me a ride up here from Duluth. Then, along the way, he tried to make me go down on him to pay for the ride. I managed to get away from him, but he left me out in the middle of nowhere."

Sally was back at the table with George's food and a fresh napkin and silverware.

"Thanks, fellows," she said. "That guy's a bully, always pushing people around. Likes to fight."

"He's not that good at it," George said.

"Just big and mean. I've watched him growing up around here. I've been waiting awhile for someone to put him in his place."

"What's for dessert?" George said.

"We've got apple pie à la mode or hot fudge sundaes."

George looked at Hawk and Larry. "Whatever they want, I'm having."

They finished dinner with conversation about the lodge and Hawk's work. George picked up the check. After dinner, on the way out, George said. "Hawk, I forgot to tell you. Holdress was sentenced. The judge gave him two five-year terms to run consecutively, so he got the max. Apparently, he didn't have a good pre-sentence report."

"Good," Hawk said. "He deserves every bit of that. When does he get out?"

"That's up to the parole system, but it won't be for awhile." George clasped Hawk on the shoulder.

"I'll come by tomorrow morning," he said. "We need to talk about Oklahoma."

CHAPTER EIGHTY-TWO

The next morning, George put Bear in the truck and drove to the lodge. He stopped at the edge of the parking lot. As they got out of the truck, George saw Hawk walking up from the storage buildings. "Bear," George said. "Do you see who it is? It's Hawk. Go to him, Bear. Go on, go."

Bear started walking toward Hawk. Then he barked and broke into a run. Hawk was caught off guard, seeing the dog running toward him. "Bear? Come here, boy." Bear jumped up, and they fell down together in the snow, Bear licking him, Hawk hugging him and ruffling his fur.

By the time Hawk looked up, he saw George standing in front of him. George took Hawk's hand, pulled him to his feet.

Hawk took a step backward. "George, thanks for coming up here and for what you did last night, but I'm not going back to Oklahoma."

"So, you think I drove a thousand miles over the last two weeks just to have a bar fight? You had my phone number. Why didn't you just call and save me the trouble?"

"You knew I hated it there."

"I didn't know that. I know some bad stuff happened, but that's no reason to give up on your family."

"What family? What's left of it now?"

"Your dad, Three Songs, your community. They're all your family. And what about Gina? Is she a throwaway too?"

"You don't understand everything that's happened to me."

George kicked a stone, sent it skittering across the parking lot. He walked a few steps away, looking off toward the woods, his hands in his pockets. He turned back to face Hawk.

"You know, you're starting to piss me off. Maybe I should leave you here and head back to Oklahoma. Hang out with some adults for a change."

"That's what you'd really like, isn't it? Get back to living on your own. Well, go ahead. I'm not changing my mind."

"Hawk, we've been through hell together. First Horse, then your mom, all kinds of stuff in between. You've got no right to say I don't understand."

Hawk knelt down to pet Bear, refusing eye contact with George.

"I'm sorry I made you come all this way, but I like it here. I'm staying."

John Colton and Larry came around the corner of the lodge. "Charles," he said. "You got a visitor?"

George extended his hand. "I'm George Wheeler."

"I remember you. We met at the bar."

"I'm Charles's guardian. I've been looking for him. His dad wants him to come home."

"Where's home?"

"Oklahoma."

Colton looked at Charles. "So you're not from a farm downstate?"

Hawk shook his head. "I'm from Oklahoma. I came up here to get away from there."

John swore under his breath. "Well," John said, looking at Hawk. "What do you want to do? You gonna go home?"

"I want to stay here."

John turned to George. "You got any kind of court order that says he has to go?"

"No, just his dad's concern."

"I ain't no lawyer, but he's sixteen now. He came here on his own. I don't see why he has to go back without some kind of legal order. I could understand why his dad wants him home, but he's done nothing wrong, and I don't see how forcing him to leave does anybody any good. Besides, we're just starting our season, and I don't have time to find another employee." He nodded to the other man. "Larry, here, is my only other worker. We operate with a small crew."

"John's right," Larry said. "The kid's good. He can be on my crew anytime. We really need him here."

John bent down to pet Bear. "That's my dog, Bear," Hawk said. "I raised him from a pup. Could he stay with me?"

"Don't make no never mind to me. Course, Millie probably won't want him around the kitchen, so he'll have to stay with you in the bunkhouse and keep out of the way."

"He's well trained," Hawk said. "I'll keep him under control."

"Give me just a minute," George said. He walked to his truck and came back carrying the deer-hide pouch. "I believe this is yours," George said.

Hawk pulled the tomahawk out and showed it to Larry and John.

"Horse gave it to you," Hawk said to George.

"Yeah, but it belongs with you."

John took the tomahawk in his hand. "So you're Indian?"

"Cherokee," Hawk said. "I'm sorry I lied to you about my background. I was worried that you wouldn't hire me if you thought I was an Indian."

George turned to John. "Here's what I suggest. I have to call Charles's dad. Tell him I found him. Then I'll go back to Oklahoma and talk to him. I can't make any promises. It's his dad's call. For now, though, let's agree that Charles can stay here, working with you. I'll be back after the holidays. I've talked to a forest ranger over at Kawishiwi, and he's hired me for the winter to work with him on the wolf project. Then when your season's done, Charles can make his decision."

"That'd be okay with me," John said.

George looked at Hawk. "Are you good with that?"

"Yeah, I guess."

"All right, then. I'll stop by tomorrow morning. Then I'm headed back to Oklahoma." George started toward his truck. "Hawk," he said. "I talked to Gina before I came up here. She's worried about you. Write her a letter tonight that I can take back with me."

George called Christine that evening. "I talked with Hawk today. He's fine, working hard. His boss likes him, wants him to stay. Hawk is adamant that he's not coming back to Oklahoma. I'll be leaving here tomorrow, and I'll talk to Albert when I get back there. Bear can stay with Hawk at the bunkhouse where he's working. So Hawk's good for now. He just doesn't want to come home."

"Thanks, George. I'll let his dad know and tell him you'll see him next week."

The next morning, George stopped by the lodge to say goodbye to Hawk. Hawk came out of the bunkhouse carrying a large envelope with the lodge logo on the front. "For Gina," he said. "Thanks for everything. Say hello to my dad. Tell him I'm okay." George took the envelope, gave Hawk a hug, and bent down to pet Bear.

"Have a nice Christmas," George said. "I'll see you in a few weeks. In the meantime, call your dad and tell him yourself."

CHAPTER EIGHTY-THREE

Millie asked Hawk to bring some wood into the kitchen along with some kindling. The room was heated by a small potbelly stove that sat in the corner beside the pantry. Hawk brought in the wood and stacked it neatly in the rack there. Then he filled the kindling box. He opened the stove door and stoked the fire a bit. Millie was sitting at the kitchen table, reading. The kitchen was warm and homey with the smell of cookies baking.

"What are you reading?" Hawk asked.

Millie turned the cover of the book toward him. "It's a history of the transcontinental railroad. Very interesting. Do you read much?"

"Not really," Hawk said. "I read some in high school, assigned stuff mostly, boring. I don't have any books at this point."

Millie got up. "Wait here a second," she said. She left the room and in a few minutes came back with a book and handed it to Hawk. "You might like this," she said.

Hawk leafed through it. "*The Adventures of Huckleberry Finn*?" he said. "What's it about?"

"Read it and find out," Millie said. "I think you'll like it."

"Okay," Hawk said. "I'll try it."

"Charles," she said. "I know there are no electric lights in the bunkhouse, so you're welcome to come here to the kitchen and read. No one will bother you. You might even find the supply of cookies to be useful in your studies."

Hawk grinned. "I think I will. Thanks."

"When you get done with that," she said, "I want you to read some stories by Jack London. Those are more modern, but they deal with adventures in the wilderness, mostly Alaska. Good stuff."

Hawk set the book on the pantry shelf. "If it's okay," he said, "I'll leave the book here and come back this evening to start it."

Later that evening, Hawk sat in the kitchen reading. There was a large platter of cookies in the center of the table and an empty glass with a note. "Milk in the fridge."

When he finished for the night, Hawk found a pencil. He turned the note over, drew a sketch of the diving hawk, talons open. Below it, he wrote "thanks" and slipped the note under the plate.

When Millie came into the kitchen the next morning, she saw the empty plate with Hawk's drawing. The book was on the pantry shelf with a scrap of paper marking a spot about a fourth of the way into the story.

As the men came in for breakfast, she showed the note to Hawk. "You draw this?" she asked. Hawk nodded. Larry took the paper from Millie. "That's great," he said. "I'd like to see more."

"Just so the work's done," John said.

Millie shot him a look. "Pancakes this morning. Anyone want a fried egg beside?"

"Larry," John said, "I want you to take the lodgers out today and show them the deer stands we've put up. Bow season starts tomorrow, so today's a good day for them to get their bearings. The weather's still decent. You can get in on most of the logging trails with the trucks. Some will have to drive their own vehicles and follow you in."

Larry looked over at Hawk. "Mind if I take Charles? Be good for him to see the procedure. Plus, he can carry some of the gear."

"Things are in good shape here," John said. "So yeah, if he wants to go. I'll be in town getting supplies."

"I do," Hawk said. "I'd like to go."

"Better leave Bear here," Larry said. "He might get a scent and take off running after a deer. We don't want that messing up the hunting."

As the men ate, the lodgers began to drift in. John looked over at Hawk. "Finish up," he said. "You can help Millie get the hunters served. Larry and I'll be there in a few minutes to explain the day's activity."

Hawk finished, put his dishes by the sink, washed his hands, and went into the dining room behind Millie. "Grab your coffee over at the urn, there by the wall," Millie said. "We'll bring the refills to you." She rattled off the choices for breakfast, taking notes of their orders. Hawk poured glasses of water, set out butter, syrup, jelly, and ketchup for home fries, and went back to the kitchen to await instructions.

After breakfast, the men loaded up in trucks and followed Hawk and Larry to the hunting sites.

"Charles, you ever done any hunting?" Larry asked.

Hawk nodded. "Used a bow. I've done some trapping with snares and deadfalls. Small animals mostly. I've helped gut a deer and butcher it, but I've never shot one myself."

"I'll talk to John later," he said. "If he's okay with it, you can go out tomorrow and sit in a stand with me, watch how things go. I also have a compound bow you can practice with."

"That would be great."

"Gets cold out there, so you'll have to dress warm."

At dinner, the hunters selected their stands by drawing numbers out of a coffee can. "We're up early tomorrow," Larry said. "Before daybreak. We'll want to be in the stands as the sun starts coming up. Breakfast will be ready by five. And we'll have to walk from the timber road. Don't want truck noise scaring the deer off."

CHAPTER EIGHTY-FOUR

When he got back to Oklahoma, George took Mel to visit Gina. "Hawk's really doing well there," George said. "I think the wilderness agrees with him. He's working hard and learning a lot."

Gina opened the envelope and brought out several sketches. She looked them over one by one before passing them to her parents.

"His work gets better and better," Mel said.

"Stunning," Fred said. "We could get them framed, put them over the fireplace mantel." Gina looked inside the envelope again and found a note stuck inside. It read: "Merry Christmas, Gina. I miss you." It was signed with the hawk embossing. Gina leaned into her mom's shoulder.

"When can he come home?" Gina asked.

"That's up in the air," George said. "He wants to stay there, and his boss needs him for the rest of the winter season, so he'll be there through February. I'll be talking to his dad, who may insist that he come home, but as a practical matter that would be very difficult to accomplish if Hawk doesn't want to leave."

"So he won't be home for Christmas?"

"No." George paused. "One thing you should know. Hawk has had a difficult time over the past few months, and he's now found some peace there living and working with the nice couple who own the lodge. So it won't be easy to get him to move back. He's in his element there. He loves the wilderness."

"Can I write to him?" Gina asked.

"Yes, of course. You can use the address on the envelope. I'm sure he'd love to hear from you. You might send him a picture as well."

"Mom," Gina said. "Remember when you promised to teach me how to knit?"

Sarah nodded.

"Can I get something done in time for Christmas?"

CHAPTER EIGHTY-FIVE

After the close of the hunting season, Larry left to visit his sister's family in Duluth for the holidays. John took Hawk and Bear out into the woods and found a small, well-shaped hemlock. They cut down the tree and carried it back to the truck. They set it up in the Coltons' living quarters at one end of the lodge, and Millie made some popcorn. She and Hawk strung the popcorn with cranberries while John hung the lights. "We'll give this to the birds after Christmas," she said. She brought out a box of old ornaments, and they hung them together. Then they stood back, admiring. "That's about half-nice," Millie said.

"After Christmas," John said, "the snowmobilers will start coming in, so we've got a few days to get things tuned up—get the lodge ready." He turned to Hawk. "You said you've done a bit of engine work on motorcycles?"

Hawk nodded.

"We'd better get started, then. I'll see you out in the barn."

As Hawk walked back to the shed, he saw a dark shape pass through the woods near the dock; heard the sounds of the animal passing through the underbrush. He ran down a trail away from the dock, heading for the sound. At the edge of a clearing, he saw it then, a large black bear nosing into the snow. He wondered why it wasn't already hibernating, or was there another reason it was near.

"Stalking Bear?" Hawk called. "It's me, Hawk."

The bear lifted its head, snorted, and disappeared into the woods.

CHAPTER EIGHTY-SIX

After visiting Gina, George and Mel stopped at the Italian restaurant for dinner. After their meal, George took a detour on the way home and drove out to the edge of the city. "I want to show you something," he said. George found a place to park off the highway at the edge of a wide expanse of undeveloped land. He took a blanket from behind the seat, and they sat on the hood of the truck with the blanket wrapped around them, looking at the sky. It was a clear but moonless night. The sky was filled with brilliant stars.

"Honestly, George," Mel said. "I've never seen anything like this. It's extraordinary. I see why you love the outdoors."

"It's even more spectacular in true wilderness spots."

They sat quietly watching the sky.

"I wonder if Hawk will ever come home," George said.

"I think he will. He's young, and everything is new and interesting. But he still has a strong connection to his family and his tribe."

"I think I caused all this. Maybe I should have just left him at home with his dad."

"Don't look back, George. You did what you could. Some terrible things have happened to him, but he's smart and resilient. He'll get past the bad stuff."

"The Coltons are good folks. They've already helped him a lot."

"And Hawk believes in you," she said. "He may not be able to express his feelings now, but he knows there's one person in the world who truly cares about him, the guy who tracked him halfway across the country to find him. That's what you mean to him."

When the night air had chilled them, they got up, folded the blanket, and drove back to Mel's apartment.

"George," Mel said. "My roommates are here, and I've got an early start tomorrow. I need some sleep. Can we spend next weekend at your place?"

"We can decorate my Christmas tree."

"You bought a tree?"

"No, but I will if you'll go with me."

"Do you have any decorations?"

"I've got some dirty socks we can hang on it."

"It's a deal." She pulled him to her. "I'll bring some pantyhose to hang on the fireplace—that way Santa will fill two stockings for me."

"Don't get greedy."

She kissed him good night. "I'm glad you found Hawk."

"I'd like you to come to Minnesota with me. There's a town there at the edge of the wilderness you need to visit. It's the perfect spot for an artist and a wannabe Indian."

Mel was still leaning into him. "Mmm," she said. "That's a lot to consider." She kissed him again. "Maybe."

CHAPTER EIGHTY-SEVEN

After breakfast on Christmas morning, John and Hawk worked in the barn, tuning up the Ski-Doos, getting their equipment ready. By early afternoon, Millie had a big turkey cooked and was finishing the side dishes.

"Dinner's almost ready," Millie said as the men walked in to the kitchen. "We'll eat out in the main lodge, but let's go into our living room first. I think Santa stopped by."

There were small presents all around. George had sent Hawk a sturdy wool shirt and enclosed some drawing supplies from Mel. Hawk gave the Coltons some pencil sketches of the lodge, each sketch highlighted with a bit of color.

"These are beautiful," Millie said. "I can't wait to get them framed and hung."

Millie gave Hawk a collection of Jack London's short stories. At the end, she brought out a package from Gina. Hawk rattled it a bit before opening it, trying to guess the contents. Inside, he found a decorative can of cookies and hard candies with a note from Patti and Traci. "To Hawk, our wandering friend, Merry Christmas."

Hawk then opened a soft package and unfolded the scarf inside. It was hand knit in big loops of reds and oranges. There were two photos also enclosed: a studio picture of Gina's family and one taken of Gina at the mall with Tommy and Santa. A note said, "Hawk, stay warm. Wear this so I can find you. Love, Gina."

Embarrassed, Hawk stuffed the note in his shirt pocket but put the scarf around his neck. He could smell a hint of perfume in the wool. He held part of the scarf against his face while trying to act casual.

"Wow," Millie said, "I bet you'll sleep in that. I can see I'll have trouble getting that off you just to wash it."

"Hey, Charles," John said, breaking the mood. "Send those cookies over here."

After dinner, Hawk helped Millie with the dishes. They worked silently together for a time.

"Millie, this is the best Christmas I've ever had," Hawk said.

Millie dropped her tea towel on the counter and wrapped her arms around him. "Charles," she said, "it's the best Christmas we've ever had. We're glad you found us here."

Millie picked up the towel and began to dry dishes again. "Charles, that was a special thing your friend did."

"What do you mean?"

"I don't know why you left home or how you got here, but when someone takes off to hide out, their folks sometimes just say 'good riddance.' But that's not what George did. He broke his neck to track you down. Friends like that are hard to find."

"I don't want to leave here. There's nothing back there for me."

"There might be more there than you think."

"I don't know. Everything bad piled up at once. I just wanted to get away from it all."

"Charles, over a lifetime, everyone has their share of bad. You're young, got your whole life ahead of you. Maybe your future will be with us, but don't turn your back on your family."

Hawk still had the scarf around his neck, and Millie took one end and held it up.

"I don't know the young lady who made this, but she must be special, too."

Hawk looked away toward the window over the sink, wiped an eye with the back of his hand.

"I don't know what to do."

"John and I never had kids, so I'm not good with advice, but my hearing's okay. I'll be glad to listen whenever you want to talk about it."

Smiling, Hawk held the scarf up against his face.

"Give it some time," Millie said. "You'll come up with the right answer."

ACKNOWLEDGMENTS

I am truly grateful to all of the people who have contributed their comments and careful edits to my manuscript. They include Marcy Campbell, Carole Norton, Anne and Ken Graham, Toby Emerson, Roberta Looney, Sara Patton, Tony and Maryanna Biggio, Dave and Carol Briggs, Adam and Vikki Briggs, Bob and Pat Herbold, Bob and Joan Wallace, Sarah Brown, Amanda Vacharat, and Beth Mulcahy.

Special thanks to the following veterans:

Major Walter H. Kearney, US Army, who served in Vietnam from June 1969 until June 1970. Dr. Kearney was first assigned as the medical officer for the First Brigade of the Fifth Infantry (5th Mech) stationed in Quang Tri Province, then later assigned as a surgeon to the Ninety-First Evacuation Hospital located in Chu Lai. Dr. Kearney was awarded a Bronze Star for his service in Vietnam.

Captain Charles E. Brown Jr., USMCR, who served in Vietnam from November 1969 to November 1970. He was stationed in Da Nang where he served as chief trial counsel for the First Marine Division. Captain Brown was awarded the Navy Commendation Medal with Combat V for his service.

Captain Frank "Gus" Biggio, USMC, who served as a civil affairs officer with the First Battalion, Fifth Marine Regiment in Helmand Province, Afghanistan, from April to December 2009.

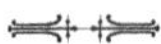

Thanks to Brandon Emerson for the cover design and to Shanon Emerson for her marketing advice and assistance.

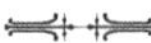

Thanks to the following editors for their exceptional and timely assistance:

Cole Gustavson and Margaret Wright of Kevin Anderson & Associates. Mr. Gustavson is a managing editor with the firm with over fifteen years of professional writing and editing experience. Margaret Wright has been a professional writer and editor for the past thirteen years.

Victoria Wright, my editor at CreateSpace.

Thanks to David Wiesenberg of the Wooster Book Company for his patience and advice in getting this book to print.

REFERENCES

I utilized many references in researching the background for this novel. The following list, while not exhaustive, represents some primary sources.

Arn, Edward C. *Arn's War: Memoirs of a World War II Infantryman, 1940–1946*. Akron, OH: University of Akron Press, 2006.

Bonds, Ray, ed. *The Vietnam War.* Crown Publishers, New York, NY, 1979.

Busbee, Patricia, and Trace A. DeMeyer. *Two Worlds: Lost Children of the Indian Adoption Projects.* Greenfield, MA: Blue Hand Books, 2012.

The Cherokee Word for Water. Produced by Mankiller Project, LLC. Kamama Films, 2013.

Devanter, Lynda Van, and Christopher Morgan. *Home before Morning: The True Story of an Army Nurse in Vietnam.* New York: Warner Books, 1983.

Garrett, J. T., and Michael Tlanusta Garrett. *The Cherokee Full Circle: A Practical Guide to Ceremonies and Traditions.* Rochester, VT: Bear & Company, 2002.

Garrett, J. T., and Michael Tlanusta Garrett. *Medicine of the Cherokee: The Way of Right Relationship.* Santa Fe, NM: Bear & Company, 1996.

Herr, Michael. *Dispatches.* New York: Knopf, 1977.

Jacobs, Margaret D. *A Generation Removed: The Fostering and Adoption of Indigenous Children in the Postwar World.* University of Nebraska Press, Lincoln, NE, 2014.

Mails, Thomas E. *Secret Native American Pathways: A Guide to Inner Peace.* Tulsa, OK: Council Oak Books, 1988.

Mech, L. David., and Luigi Boitani. *Wolves: Behavior, Ecology, and Conservation.* Chicago: University of Chicago Press, 2003.

Nez, Chester, and Judith Schiess. Avila. *Code Talker.* New York: Berkley Caliber, 2011.

Online Resources of the Cherokee Nation. http://www.cherokee.org/.

Sharpe, J., Ed., and Shirley Simmons. *The Cherokees, Past and Present: An Authentic Guide to the Cherokee People.* Cherokee, NC: Cherokee Publications, 1970.

Sheeler, Jim. *Final Salute: A Story of Unfinished Lives.* New York: Penguin Press, 2008.

Tripp, Nathaniel. *Father, Soldier, Son: Memoir of a Platoon Leader in Vietnam.* South Royalton, VT: Steerforth Press, 1996.

US Department of Agriculture, Forest Service. *Ecological Studies of the Timber Wolf in Northeastern Minnesota.* Edited by L. David Mech and L. D. Frenzel Jr., 1971.